M000014614

Readers love KC BURN

Cop Out

"I suggest you pick up *Cop Out*, grab a glass of red wine and indulge!"

—Guilty Indulgence Book Club

Banded Together

"Wow! This was a fantastic story that caught my attention early and then hogtied me to my e-book reader by the 50 percent mark so that I couldn't escape until I read to the end. I love, love, loved it."

—Hearts on Fire Reviews

"*Banded Together* is well written and a wonderfully engaging novel. Devlin's transition from a broken man into something more was deftly and elegantly handled."

—Joyfully Jay

Tea or Consequences

"If you want a book that will captivate you and have you thinking the whole way through, then this book is right up your street, it's a perfect little whodunnit."

—OptimuMM

"Murder, mystery, and mayhem. What's not to love?"

—Diverse Reader

By KC BURN

Banded Together
Grand Adventures (Dreamspinner Anthology)
One Pulse (Dreamspinner Anthology)
Pen Name – Doctor Chicken
Rainbow Blues
Set Ablaze
Tea or Consequences

FABRIC HEARTS
Tartan Candy
Plaid versus Paisley
Just Add Argyle

TORONTO TALES
Cop Out
Cover Up
Cast Off

Published by DREAMSPINNER PRESS
www.dreamspinnerpress.com

SET
ABLAZE
KC BURN

DREAMSPINNER
PRESS

Published by
DREAMSPINNER PRESS

5032 Capital Circle SW, Suite 2, PMB# 279,
Tallahassee, FL 32305-7886 USA
www.dreamspinnerpress.com

This is a work of fiction. Names, characters, places, and incidents either are the product of author imagination or are used fictitiously, and any resemblance to actual persons, living or dead, business establishments, events, or locales is entirely coincidental.

Set Ablaze
© 2018, 2019 KC Burn.

Cover Art
© 2018 Jennifer Vance.
JenniferVanceStudios@gmail.com
Cover content is for illustrative purposes only and any person depicted on the cover is a model.

All rights reserved. This book is licensed to the original purchaser only. Duplication or distribution via any means is illegal and a violation of international copyright law, subject to criminal prosecution and upon conviction, fines, and/or imprisonment. Any eBook format cannot be legally loaned or given to others. No part of this book may be reproduced or transmitted in any form or by any means, electronic or mechanical, including photocopying, recording, or by any information storage and retrieval system, without the written permission of the Publisher, except where permitted by law. To request permission and all other inquiries, contact Dreamspinner Press, 5032 Capital Circle SW, Suite 2, PMB# 279, Tallahassee, FL 32305-7886, USA, or www.dreamspinnerpress.com.

Mass Market Paperback ISBN: 978-1-64108-071-2
Trade Paperback ISBN: 978-1-64080-617-7
Digital ISBN: 978-1-64080-616-0
Library of Congress Control Number: 2017919627
Mass Market Paperback published April 2019
v. 1.0

Printed in the United States of America
∞
This paper meets the requirements of
ANSI/NISO Z39.48-1992 (Permanence of Paper).

For my hubby, who put up with a lot more than normal while I wrangled this book into shape.

Author's Note

WHEN I wrote this, I had no idea we were going to see the type of fires in California that we did this year—this fire season has been rather terrifying. I have a huge amount of respect for what these firefighters do to keep us safe. In my story, Hayden works for the Pasadena Fire Department, and they coincidentally had an open house at one of the stations where I was able to get some specific questions answered. I'm super thankful they were willing to answer my questions, and if there are any errors or deviations from reality, they're my errors.

Chapter 1

HAYDEN HURST toweled off, then wrapped the pristine white towel around his waist before he started shaving. He grinned at his foam-covered reflection. It had been far too long since he'd gone cruising for a hookup, and he was so damned ready to get his rocks off with another person. It was like the universe was giving him a blessing: his last shift at the firehouse had been uneventful, he'd come home and slept solidly for several hours, and he'd woken feeling rested but oh so fucking horny. Sure, it was a Tuesday evening, which wasn't the best night to find a hookup unless he went looking via app, but more importantly, he didn't have to be back on shift until 11:00 a.m. on Thursday. Which meant he could have a couple of drinks too.

He hummed as he scraped off stubble and shaving cream, then grabbed a smaller towel and wiped the final streaks away. Still humming, he hung both towels on a hook behind the bathroom door, then wandered naked into his bedroom.

Rummaging for the perfect pair of boxer briefs—or even a pair of skimpy Andrew Christians—that said he was ready to play, he froze when his phone rang.

No, no, no. He needed this. He needed some time where he could be himself. But he couldn't ignore the phone. They were heading into the dangerous Santa Ana fire season, which meant he could get called back into work.

Mentally preparing to gear up, he reached for the charger on his bedside table and let out a sigh of relief as he read the caller ID.

"Hey, Miguel, what's up?" They'd both left their small hometown in Northern California, and now Miguel was a Los Angeles firefighter while Hayden worked for a Pasadena firehouse, but their friendship dated back to kindergarten.

"You're off tonight, aren't you?"

Hayden's shoulders tightened. Not work, but this didn't bode well for his plans, and although Miguel was his best friend, he hated it when Hayden blew him off to go to a gay club. He couldn't convince his very straight friend to be his wingman. "Sure. What's up?"

"Let me treat you to dinner tonight. Maybe a few beers."

The invite itself wasn't unusual, but something in Miguel's tone made him wary.

"Yeah, I can do that." He could always hit a club or bar afterward. "Should I give the other guys a call, see who else is free?"

"No."

Hayden almost took a step back at Miguel's unexpected yet forceful response. "Uh, okay."

"Look, I have to talk to you about something. Meet you at Messhall? Seven-ish?"

"Fine." Messhall was about halfway between their places, and not too near where Hayden had planned to go, but better traffic was the other advantage of Tuesday night. He had time to stream another episode of *Supernatural* before he left. He could *not* seem to keep up with that show. It was like it proliferated supernaturally.

Hayden managed to squeeze in two episodes; then his Uber hit unexpected traffic, so Miguel was already seated on the patio when he arrived.

Miguel stared into the fire pit at the next table over, tapping his fingers agitatedly on his beer, and didn't even notice Hayden until he'd sat down.

"Hey."

Hayden nodded and grabbed a menu. Might as well order; he had plenty of time to figure out what was bugging Miguel. But he wanted to eat light. If he ate too much, he'd be too sluggish to want to hook up, and he didn't want to miss this opportunity.

As soon as they ordered, Hayden put on his most attentive pose, but he wasn't about to demand to know what was going on. Miguel didn't respond well to that sort of intrusive inquiry.

Miguel let out a gusty sigh. "Dude, I need a huge favor."

At least no one was sick or dead. "What?"

"You remember my baby brother? Jez?"

Sort of. It had been well over a decade since he'd seen Jez, who'd been a gangly kid when an eighteen-year-old Hayden moved to Los Angeles—or more specifically, his grandmother's house in Pasadena. Jez had been six years younger than him and Miguel, and suffered from a severe case of hero worship. It had been both amusing and irritating, especially when he'd started to wonder if Jez's attention was rooted in something else. Miguel had never mentioned if Jez was gay, but Hayden was glad he'd left Willow Ridge at eighteen, before anyone noticed anything amiss and started unsavory rumors. They'd have been true about Hayden, and he wouldn't have wanted to tar Jez with that brush, whether he was gay or not.

Miguel never talked about Jez much, and from the awkwardness Hayden had sensed the few times he'd gone back home with Miguel, there had been a definite falling-out between Jez and the rest of his family. All Hayden knew for sure was that he was some sort of actor and he lived in New York.

"He's moving to LA."

"Good for him." This was leading somewhere, and Hayden didn't know if he'd like where this conversation ended.

"Yeah. Job offer. A good one, or so he says." Miguel avoided making eye contact while he drained the last of his beer. "Anyway, he needs a place to crash. Until he finds an apartment. And… well… I'd have him stay with me, but…."

Hayden closed his eyes. "I suppose you could wedge an air mattress in beside your bed." In truth, Miguel's tiny apartment in Silver Lake didn't have a spare inch, and would barely hold Miguel and his set of free weights, never mind a second human. And the few times Hayden had been over there, he'd caught a whiff of mildew. He shuddered.

"Aw, man, don't make me do that. I'm in my prime. Living like I'm in a college dorm again would suck. It would only be for a couple of months. Maybe three, tops. And he'd pay rent. Or I would."

Hayden took a large bite of steak and chewed slowly, giving himself a few minutes to think. He rattled around the two-story Craftsman house his grandmother had willed to him, but a roommate? He swallowed, then followed up with a sip of beer. Then again, if Miguel had gotten a job with a Pasadena firehouse instead of Los Angeles, they might already be roommates.

"I swear he wouldn't be any trouble. And your place is big enough you might never even see him. Please, I'm begging."

Except for having to share the kitchen. But Hayden worked twenty-four-hour shifts, and he slept at odd hours. As long as Jez didn't make a ton of noise, it might not be too bad.

"Fine. But you owe me. When is he coming?"

Miguel's cheeks flushed a ruddy color. "Friday. Maybe Saturday."

"Friday? *This* Friday? What the fuck, Miguel?"

"I know, I know." Miguel held his hands up, palms out. "I didn't know, okay? He called me yesterday from Philly. Pittsburgh? Something east that started with *P*. He called from a fucking U-Haul. On his way."

"Without a plan?"

"I guess. But that shouldn't change anything, right? I mean, your place is always fucking pristine."

Maybe so, but that didn't mean it was ready for a long-term houseguest. Lodger? Roommate?

"You gotta help me out, Hayden. Bad enough he's driving across the fucking country all by himself. It's like forty hours."

That made Hayden feel better. Forty hours was a long drive, but if Jez wasn't showing up until Friday, that meant he was at least resting regularly.

"Why didn't you call me as soon as you heard from him?"

Miguel shrugged. "I don't know. It's a big thing to ask, and you were at work. I thought I'd have a better chance of you saying yes if I saw you in person."

Hayden suppressed a grimace. "It's fine. Don't worry about it. Jez can stay with me. Give him my cell and tell him to let me know when he expects to show up, and we'll figure something out with the key. I have a shift Thursday, but I'm off Friday, so that works out."

Miguel's shoulders slumped in obvious relief. Then he tucked into his meal like he hadn't eaten in days. Situation normal, in other words.

After they finished eating, Miguel picked up the check. "Want to go see a movie tonight?"

"Uh." Hayden still wanted to get laid, even though Miguel had thrown him off his stride. But a good orgasm or two would shut off the mental list-making he'd been doing all through dinner to prepare for Friday.

Miguel curled his lip. "Fuck. You weren't going out to a club, were you?" He squinted like he was trying to avoid imagining Hayden having sex. It wasn't like Hayden wanted to imagine Miguel in the sack either, so he didn't know why any discussion of him meeting up with guys always felt so awkward when Miguel hadn't ever seemed to mind he was gay.

"I had planned to, yes." Hayden hated this bit. Coming out to Miguel had been easy. Not like when he'd done the same with his parents. But *being* gay around Miguel, living an open life as a gay man, hadn't been easy. Had it been those years apart when Miguel had remained in Willow Ridge until he got a place in LA? Hayden didn't know, but he tried to avoid talking about guys or sex with Miguel. Or any of his friends.

"C'mon. Come to a movie with me. You can go clubbing anytime."

Sure he could, as long as he didn't tell Miguel, who was the worst cockblocker in history. Assuming Hayden managed the miraculous and found someone special, Miguel was going to have to learn to deal with this, but until that day came, Hayden did his best not to rock the boat.

"Fine. A movie." Then right home. Hayden now had laundry and cleaning to do, closets and cupboards to rearrange, and keys to duplicate. Miguel clapped him on the shoulder and led them out to his truck. At least Hayden could make Miguel drive him home instead of Ubering.

"WHEW. WHAT a fucking shift." Jordan slapped Hayden's back a trifle too hard, making him cough.

"Sorry, man, got a lungful of that smoke." A white lie. The wind had shifted and Hayden hadn't been prepared, still distracted by the prospect of the roommate due to arrive about an hour after his shift ended, and nearly ended up with a faceful of toxic smoke. That one moment of inattention had acted like a slap, getting him back in the game. But it sounded better than telling Jordan he'd smacked the breath out of him. Putting up with the resultant ribbing wasn't worth it.

Nevertheless, he was exhausted. Their shift had been hopping, mostly with medical emergencies. At least there hadn't been any wildfires in the area, but the last call out had been to a bad house fire, and it had been a battle to keep it from spreading.

"You need medical?" Jordan asked, concerned. "You should have said something on scene."

"No, no. I'm fine." Jordan surprised him sometimes. A lot of guys on their crew didn't like him, and in many ways Hayden could sympathize. Jordan had a lot of rough edges that seemed to get rougher over time, but he'd been Hayden's first friend in Pasadena. He hadn't been disgusted or angry about working with a gay man, and if his jokes skated the edge of politically correct, well, Hayden turned a blind eye. Ear? Anyway, they worked together well, and between them they'd developed a small group of guys who hung out regularly.

"Good, good. Coming to the pub after shift?"

"I don't know."

"We fucking deserve it after this shift. Vic will be there. Kevin's going too, right?" Jordan raised his voice, bringing Kevin into the conversation.

"Yeah, definitely." Kevin continued on into the locker room. Hayden needed to get in there too. Shower the stink of smoke out of his hair.

"See? And that loser Miguel would be there too, if it weren't for him getting stuck on a different crew from Vic."

Vic had befriended Miguel on the job, and several years ago, the four of them had formed the core of their group. A few months ago, though, Miguel had been switched to the C crew at his station, and now he had fewer days off in common with Vic. Secretly, Hayden suspected Miguel had been pleased by the change, considering Vic's increased bitterness after his second failed marriage.

"It sounds good."

"Then don't be a pansy, and come out with us."

Hayden rolled his eyes and glanced around, but no one appeared to have overheard. Hayden knew Jordan didn't mean anything by it, but he had to be more careful at work.

"So are you coming?"

"Yes, yes." Only because he'd worry less about his new roommate if he had something else to do while he waited for Jez to arrive. And he was starving. Getting off shift at 11:00 a.m. always meant he ate a huge lunch.

Jordan smiled at him and pounded his back again before retreating into the kitchen. Hayden sighed and headed for the showers.

HAYDEN SIGNALED the server for his check and pulled out his wallet in preparation. He'd already stayed too long, and if Jez had pushed it, Hayden might be late getting home.

"C'mon, buddy, stick around for another one or two." Jordan, a bit sloppy from the beers he'd downed at a rate of almost three to Hayden's one, slapped him on the back. At this rate, he'd have a hand-shaped bruise over his scapula.

"Sorry, man."

"Getting old there?" Vic chimed in. "We all know you're not obeying a little woman, like Kevin."

Kevin, who was usually the first to leave to go home to his wife, gave the table of firefighters the finger, and the others erupted in laughter. Hayden shrugged, quashing any niggles of discomfort. He was out at work, and it was mostly okay, even if his buddies acted like overgrown frat boys. Maybe it would be more of an issue if he couldn't pass for straight, but sure as shit he wasn't going to chastise them for words that didn't matter.

All of his friends were firefighters or cops, and he was the only gay one. Although they accepted him, things might be different if he managed to find a boyfriend, when they'd have to face the fact that Hayden might like it up the ass. Good thing Hayden had given up on that pipe dream. The occasional mocking insult didn't bother him all that much.

The check arrived with another beer, and Hayden glared at the table, all of whom looked guilty but unrepentant.

"Seriously, guys, I gotta go." He slipped a couple of bills under the damp receipt paper. "I'll be in no shape to drive. Did you forget I'm meeting my new roommate today?"

Kevin, the only other guy not the worse for drink, spoke up. "I forgot. Miguel's brother, right?"

Hayden nodded.

Vic gave an exaggerated leer. "That's right. The Broadway actor. Think he leans Hayden's way? Or do we need to warn him he's about to shack up with our resident butt pirate?"

Hayden forced a strained smile. "I don't think there's anything to worry about." Not that Hayden had ever asked, but he'd assumed Miguel would have mentioned if the kid was also gay when he'd begged Hayden to let Jez room with him.

"Oh ho. Maybe you will be pussy-whipped. Or dick-whipped. All those theater actors are queer as three-dollar bills."

The server, a lovely woman trying to break into acting, who'd been flirting with Vic since they'd arrived, scowled and slammed down the beer she'd been about to set in front of him.

Vic's eyes rounded as he stared up at her. "What?"

She didn't reply, but the ice in her demeanor could have frosted all their beer mugs. If Vic thought he was getting lucky tonight, he was soon going to find out otherwise.

"You don't need to worry about Jez. Or me. Nothing's going to change. This is only temporary until Jez finds his own place."

"Ha. If he's built anything like Miguel, he'd snap you like a twig if you even looked at him funny."

This conversational detour into his sex life made him cringe, especially in reference to Miguel's little brother. Definitely time to get going. "Don't drink too much. Jez said he didn't have a lot of stuff in the truck, but if it's more than I can handle, I'm calling you fuckers tomorrow for free labor."

After Hayden stood, Jordan didn't waste any time snatching up the untouched glass in front of Hayden's seat.

"I'm going to go too," Kevin said, throwing down some bills as he stood.

A few more jeers about Kevin's balls, or lack thereof, flew around the table, but Kevin shrugged it off as good-naturedly as ever, diverting attention from Hayden's new living arrangements. Hayden waited for Kevin, and together they headed for the entrance.

Out in the parking lot, Kevin spoke again. "You should bring Jez out sometime."

Hayden shrugged. "Maybe. I'm sure he's got his own friends." Like Hayden knew if he and Jez would get along. Hell, he'd barely remembered Miguel *had* a younger brother. Jez didn't even go home for holidays, at least not when Hayden had been back there.

"This isn't his hometown. That's seven hours north. And he hasn't lived in California in almost a decade. He might not know anyone here aside from his brother."

"Yeah, you're probably right." And too fucking thoughtful to put up with the rest of their lunkheaded friends. Maybe a wife did have a softening influence. Or maybe it was that characteristic that had ensured Kevin was the first one of their group to find a long-term partner. Either way, he made a good point, although Hayden hoped Jez would be so busy starting a new job and finding his own apartment that Hayden wouldn't get stuck being the token friend.

Hayden didn't have any idea how to be friends with someone whose life experiences were so different from his, and aside from the couple of cops who'd started out as emergency-scene acquaintances, Hayden hadn't socialized with anyone but firefighters, and sometimes their wives, for more than a decade.

HAYDEN DROVE along the wide tree-lined road toward home. Sometimes it was altogether too quiet, but he'd never been tempted to get a roommate. He often had the guys over during major sporting events for beer and snacks, and that had helped to combat the loneliness.

Maybe—just maybe—if Miguel had gotten a job in Pasadena, they could have roomed together. But Hayden wasn't comfortable sharing his private life with his other coworkers. Hayden understood Miguel's reason for asking for this favor, but that didn't make him any less wary.

Eh. How bad could it be? Miguel was his best friend. Jez needed a place to live, not a ready-made bestie, even if Hayden were in the market. Miguel could perform any required mentoring or basic friend services.

A small U-Haul cube van sat by the curb, parked askew with the wrong end toward the front door. Hayden pulled out his phone and grimaced. Shit. He had ignored a couple of calls from an unknown number. He should have known that was Jez.

He didn't like being late. He had already been a little unsettled by the teasing at the bar, and the truck loomed like a guilt trip.

Hayden parked his truck on the street behind the cube van and got out. A few boxes had already made it to the porch, but of Jez himself there was no sign. Presumably he was around somewhere outside. Hayden had the spare key in his pocket, and he never left his doors unlocked, so Jez wouldn't have been able to make himself at home. Miguel would have mentioned if Jez had taken up cat burglary in his spare time. Hayden frowned. This had all been set up last-minute.

Surely if Jez was running from legal troubles, Miguel would have at least warned him.

Yeah. Miguel wouldn't hide a bombshell like that from him.

He strode up the walk to his front door and found a guy stretched out on the couch on his porch, an arm draped across his face. His bright teal T-shirt had rucked up, revealing a strip of flat, toned brown belly. There was some sort of graphic on the T-shirt, but the guy's other arm obscured it.

Whether Jez—and this had better be Jez—looked like Miguel or not, he wasn't built the same as his brother. Jez lacked both Miguel's height and bulk, although he appeared to be as fit as Miguel, in a different way. Jez's black hair was fluffy or perhaps spiky, tipped with a vibrant red the likes of which never occurred in nature.

What sort of role had Jez landed that would require that hairstyle? Miguel had been vague, although he had been adamant Jez was moving to California for work. Whatever Miguel had or hadn't said, Hayden suspected a bit of desperation behind Jez's move. Acting was a hard business, and maybe Jez was trying a different coast in a bid to make it somewhere. It might have been more the dream of a job than actual employment that had brought him back across the country.

Without a mortgage, Hayden could afford to float Miguel's brother for months, rent-free if need be. If Miguel needed him to.

"Jez. Hey, Jez." Hayden didn't yell, but his gruff, impatient tone startled Jez awake and he swung upright immediately, blinking and looking slightly lost.

For all of a second or so. Long enough for dread to curl around Hayden's belly, sending despair through him as he stared at the hottie swan, former ugly duckling Jez. Breathtaking, even if Jez wasn't his normal type. Hell, he wasn't supposed to find Miguel's little brother attractive. But no matter how his brain screamed out in denial, the sudden dampness of his palms, the increase in heart rate and breathing, and a twitch in his groin told the truth.

Then Jez scowled and leaped to his feet with an unexpected grace. He was shorter and slighter than Hayden and almost at the opposite end of the spectrum from his brother. If Miguel got the mass, Jez got the looks. Not that Miguel was ugly, but wow.

Was Jez maybe a little too graceful? A little something? Then Hayden noticed the graphic on the tee. A unicorn with a rainbow mane, *shitting* rainbows. Fuckity fuck fuck. The last thing he needed was an effeminate gay guy rooming with him. When the guys met him, the teasing would be relentless, and Jez wasn't even his damned type.

"About time you got home. Can you let me inside already?" Jez snapped.

Hayden bit back a growl and stepped around a couple of scattered boxes to unlock the door. After pushing it open wide, Hayden turned around to find Jez standing right there, a large cardboard box in his arms.

"Let me help you with that." Hayden reached out to grab the box, but Jez swung it away with a yelp. "Did you hurt yourself? I can take that for you if it's heavy." He was careful to modulate his tone so he didn't freak Jez out again.

"No, it's fine. I can take this. I'm not weak, you know." If tones could literally be venomous, Hayden would be convulsing on the floor.

"Okay, okay." Hayden backed into the house, giving Jez enough room to pass through the doorway.

"Where should I put my stuff?" Jez's prickly voice didn't ease up much, but it became more conciliatory as he brushed past Hayden.

"Up the stairs, last door on the left. You want to do it all yourself, or am I allowed to touch the other boxes?"

Jez, already partway to the stairs, paused, his shoulders slumping.

Guilt swept through Hayden. Jez had driven by himself across the country in a matter of days to move to a city he'd never lived in, in a state he hadn't returned to—at least to Hayden's knowledge—for the better part of a decade. He had to be exhausted, and although he'd sniped first, Hayden should be apologizing for being late rather than sniping back. If his gran could hear him now, she'd be terribly disappointed.

"Sorry. This one's fragile. If you could please help with the others, I'd appreciate it." Jez didn't look back at Hayden, but he sounded sad.

Hayden took a deep breath, determined to start fresh. "No problem. We'll have your stuff unloaded in no time."

To give them both time to regroup, Hayden headed out to the truck to see if he'd been lying about how long things would take to unload or if he was going to have to call in the army of free labor, even if his prickly new roommate might object.

One glance was all it took. Jez didn't have a lot of stuff, and there didn't seem to be any furniture. Good thing Hayden's spare room had a bed.

JEZ BOUCHET gently placed his cardboard burden on the bed, then spun around, leaped for the door, and slammed it shut, panting like he'd just run a marathon.

Hell, this wasn't how he'd wanted to renew his acquaintance with Hayden. He'd been such a bitchy ass, but he'd been driving for fucking ever, and he didn't have just himself to think of anymore.

Jez cocked his head, listening for Hayden's approach. The stairs had creaked enough that no one would be sneaking by, ever, and Hayden was bigger and heavier than Jez. But the stairs were silent.

The lock on the door looked like a forceful jiggle would open it, but Jez flipped it anyway, then approached the precious box on the bed. Pressing the flaps back, he peered inside.

"Hey, baby. Just a little longer."

Mournful brown eyes looked up at him from a furry, wrinkly face of fawn-colored fur—a mute objection to being trapped in the pet carrier. His adorable pug pup made Jez want to scoop him right out and cuddle, but he didn't dare. Not yet.

"Don't worry. We'll find us a pet-friendly apartment faster than you can clean your dish." Which was fast. For a little bit of a thing, his pup could vacuum up food like nothing he'd seen. Jez didn't know Los Angeles at all and hadn't wanted to run the risk of accidentally committing to an apartment, sight unseen, only to discover it was in a shitty part of town where he'd have to worry about getting bashed, or that the apartment was in worse shape than online photos indicated.

Miguel had assured him Hayden didn't mind putting Jez up for a couple of months, but Jez hadn't told him about his puppy; Miguel's apartment was pet-free, and Jez was all too aware that Hayden didn't like dogs. At all.

Jez partially unzipped the duffel bag–style carrier and stuck his hand in the opening, letting his puggy baby, Fang, slather his hand in kisses.

"I know, I know," he whispered. "You've been so good, but I can't let you out yet." He could maybe give his baby a little more room to move, though.

Extracting his hand, he assessed the size of the closet. Much larger than the closet in his Brooklyn apartment. Jez shifted the cardboard box into the closet, grabbed a puppy pad from the pocket in the carrier, and spread it out inside the box, surrounding the carrier. Then he unzipped the rest of the flap, and Fang barreled out and jumped toward Jez on his stubby little pug legs.

"There's my big tough boy. Good Fang."

Fang's curly tail didn't just wag, his whole puppy butt wiggled.

"You be a good boy now. Not much longer." Next step would be sneaking in Fang's food and water bowls; then Fang would be fine until they got the rest of the truck unpacked. Afterward, Jez could claim exhaustion—which wouldn't be a lie—and retreat to his room, letting Fang out. He'd been such a good sweet baby on the drive from New York, although he'd also been in his carrier on the seat beside Jez and was able to see Jez the whole time. Jez had pushed through the last couple of hours, desperate to make it to Hayden's before the end of his shift so he could get Fang into his cardboard Trojan horse, but then Hayden hadn't come home right away. Jez had fallen asleep in the cool afternoon breeze on Hayden's porch, but as soon as he awoke, he'd freaked, worried about Fang. It could have been hot as Satan's nutsack if he'd moved in the summer.

Jez was also super lucky Fang hadn't developed a proper big dog bark. The only noises he made were a snuffle-grunt that might one day evolve into a bark, and quiet whimpers, neither of which should—hopefully—be loud enough to draw Hayden's attention through a closed door.

God. This was such a fucking mess. Jez's *life* was a fucking mess. The only silver lining, aside from Fang, was the unexpected job offer that allowed him to ditch the life he'd been building in New York without a backward glance and flee for the West Coast.

He only wished it had sunk in earlier, when Miguel had first described the incredibly small size of his apartment. Jez had been so sure he'd be able to crash at Miguel's place, but Miguel had gone and made arrangements with Hayden.

Then again, it was possible that Miguel was more interested in not letting Jez get in the way of him getting laid than he was worried about having nowhere for Jez to sleep.

Nah. His brother could be a dick, but that seemed more asshatted than normal. Besides, even if Jez had a place to sleep, he had a half-grown pug pup that would have to be hidden from the landlord, and he needed someplace to stash his stuff.

Jez was thankful for the sanctuary at Hayden's house. But that didn't change the fact he'd never be able to fully relax, never be able to breathe properly. Not until he got a place of his own.

As he shut the closet door, he took a glance around the guest room. For a house as old as this one was, the room was almost devoid of character. It did have a bed, at least. Initially he'd had no idea what to expect, but from what little he'd seen so far, Hayden had the bones of a great place. It was also large enough that he and Hayden wouldn't be on top of each other. His cheeks heated at the double entendre. Jez might have been only twelve the last time he'd seen Hayden, but he'd sure remembered him later, during his teenage years. And as much as he didn't want to like Hayden, it was a little embarrassing to recall how many times during his restless, hormonal puberty he'd imagined Hayden on top of him.

Then Jez grimaced. No TV. His own had broken shortly before he moved. Would Hayden let him watch the few shows he considered do-not-miss? Still, this was more luxury than he'd expected. Maybe more than he deserved.

The distinctive creak of the stairs alerted him that Hayden had finally run out of patience with Jez's temper tantrum. It had been uncalled for, and Jez probably owed Hayden an apology. However wary Hayden made him, Jez was exhausted and desperate for a place to crash and didn't want to make an enemy of Miguel's best friend. In a few days, after he'd recovered a bit, he'd start figuring out how to build a new life. Whether he needed legal assistance. Scope out his new workplace. He had another two weeks before the job started, which should be enough time for him to find a new place to live.

Hayden's footsteps drew closer, and Jez lunged for the door, unlocking and opening it in a single swift move.

Hayden grinned at him over another cardboard box, and Jez was finally forced to acknowledge the alterations in Hayden's appearance. Worry about Fang and grogginess from his interrupted nap had let him ignore Hayden's attractiveness earlier, but now it hit him like a blow. He'd half convinced himself that the Hayden he remembered from his preteen years had been a fantasy born of innumerable wet dreams. The Hayden who'd left their small town at eighteen—while a closeted twelve-year-old Jez mourned—was now obviously a man. The Hayden who stood before him had been fired by the kiln of adulthood into something infinitely sexier and more appealing, however impossible that was. Dark hair, mossy green eyes, skin susceptible to burning. And lickable all over, damn him.

Why couldn't good things happen to him? A Hayden with a beer belly or thinning hair might be easier to resist. Then again, that stupid, sexy, heartfelt smile would be Hayden's into his old age, and it was that smile that set Jez's heart thumping.

Hayden's expression didn't change, which meant Jez's thoughts hadn't shown in his expression. Thank fuck for small favors.

"Ready for some more boxes?"

Chapter 2

A FEW hours later, Jez surveyed his room. He needed to get the truck back, but before he did so, everything had to be set up for Fang. Afterward, he'd unpack a few essentials like toiletries and clothes and towels.

Food and water dishes in the closet—check. He'd have to rig something up to ensure Fang didn't manage to accidentally close the door, but that was a concern more for once he started working. Until then, he'd be around enough that Fang wouldn't starve to death.

Doggie bed tucked away in the corner, with dresser blocking the view from the door—check. Pet carrier on the top shelf in the closet, pushed all the way back—check. Puppy stairs... in the closet for now. He'd bring them out when he went to bed so stubby little pug legs could get up and down from the bed easily, but until Jez was on his own, Fang was going to have to forgo sleeping on the bed when Jez wasn't around. Emergency puppy pads laid out in the closet—check. The nail on the wall inside the closet made a perfect spot to hang a leash and poop bags.

If Hayden stumbled in, Jez's room didn't have any obvious and immediate clues that this space also housed a not-yet-full-grown pug. Not that there would be any reason for Hayden to enter Jez's private space, but he wasn't about to take any chances.

Jez rescued his sleepy pup from his carrier and gave him a snuggle. Fang licked his face, and Jez straightened the adorable plaid bow-tie collar he'd ordered a mere week before he'd been obliged to pull up stakes. He'd have to switch it out soon to the plain purple one, because Fang would try to chew at the bow tie, but the purple one was fun too.

At least he'd had Fang long enough to get him mostly trained and housebroken, but a glance at his watch told him he needed to smuggle Fang out to the backyard soon, although it could wait until he got back from returning the truck. He settled Fang on the doggie bed, then slipped out of the room, making sure to close the door firmly behind him. Unpacking the rest of the boxes could wait until later. Or not at all, depending on how soon he found a suitable apartment.

He wished he had a lock for the door, but hopefully he could trust Hayden to not be a giant dick.

Jez had almost made it to the front door before Hayden called his name and he froze, reaching for the handle.

"Yeah?" His heart rate picked up. Had Hayden discovered Fang? Surely not. Jez had been so careful.

"You want to take the truck back now?"

"Uh, yes. That was the plan."

"Let me grab my keys and I'll follow you."

"I thought you were going to have a shower." The temperature in Pasadena might be mild—a typical day in early October, or so he'd heard—but they'd worked hard and they were both sweaty messes. Well, Jez was. Somehow Hayden still managed to look merely disheveled and all kinds of delicious.

"That can wait."

This felt like a trick. Or perhaps his paranoia was getting the better of him. The whole reason he was here was because Miguel wasn't a dick, so it stood to reason his friends weren't either. Jez wasn't about to base any decisions on the character judgment of his horny twelve-year-old self. Even his twenty-five-year-old self was suspect in that regard, based on Jayson Bain, his last choice for a boyfriend and the poster boy for self-hating closet dwellers. But he was also basing his life and safety on the judgment of an older brother he hadn't laid eyes on in eight years. He wasn't sure if Hayden had figured out Jez was gay—not that he did much to hide it anymore.

He also wasn't sure if Hayden had held on to the hidebound conservatism that had dogged their tiny hometown or if he'd adopted the more liberal and open-minded attitude of LA. Once he'd figured out how shitty being openly gay in Willow Ridge would be, he'd wondered, just for a moment, if that was why Hayden had left so abruptly. Rumors abounded about Hayden being gay, but Jez had heard just as many about some chick in Sacramento he'd knocked up, then run from to avoid a shotgun wedding. Jez just had to trust that Miguel wouldn't drop him in a situation where his actual safety was in jeopardy. If they had being gay in common, surely Miguel would have mentioned it.

He hadn't quite known how to interpret the heated looks he'd gotten when Hayden first presented himself. He'd been groggy from his nap, but he'd thought Hayden had been checking him out and liking what he saw. But then all he'd seen was anger. Stupid to think it could be anything else.

Jez turned, and the sincerity on Hayden's face convinced him. "Sure. That would be great. Thanks."

THE THICK, awkward silence in Hayden's truck made the fifteen-minute drive time seem a lot longer. Or it might have been his paranoia and exhaustion talking. Jez didn't recall Hayden being chatty, so maybe silence was normal. It didn't help that Jez couldn't stop sneaking glances at Hayden's angular jawline, muscular arms, and strong hands as he deftly steered his truck through the residential Pasadena backstreets. If he thought Miguel would tell him for sure, he'd ask if Hayden was also gay. A few things his brother had said over the years had made Jez suspect that might be the case, but his first look at Hayden the man had convinced him his suppositions were wrong. Not that gay men couldn't be built like Hayden, but Jez wasn't that lucky. Even if Hayden was gay, undoubtedly he'd be a self-hating closet dweller.

Jez sighed. Then again, a garden-variety closeted jerk might be a step up from his last boyfriend. Either way, getting comfortable in Hayden's house wasn't likely, and Jez planned to be long gone before familiarity smoothed away any of his self-preservation instincts. A man who didn't like dogs wasn't to be trusted.

Hayden's place, like half of the houses on the street, had no driveway, so Hayden pulled to a stop in front of the house. Seemingly unconcerned by Jez's silence, he nevertheless paused after turning off the ignition. Jez froze in the midst of reaching for the handle and waited.

"I'm going to take a shower, but then I thought I'd order in some pizza. Any allergies or toppings you don't like?"

A muscle twitched in Jez's jaw even as his stomach grumbled in yearning. He didn't want to alienate his new roommate on the very first day, not if he could help it, but Jez was fucking exhausted. He needed a shower of his own and some cuddle time with Fang—after the pup did his business. On the other hand, Jez hadn't eaten since leaving Kingman, Arizona, over eight hours earlier, had no interest in trying to grocery shop, and hadn't had pizza in a long time. Maybe he deserved a bit of a treat.

"Thanks. That sounds good. Except. Um. I'm vegan."

A tiny grin lifted the corners of Hayden's mouth as he nodded. "Well, you picked a good city to move to. I'll find a place with vegan pizza that delivers."

Jez sucked in a deep breath. "Thanks, Hayden. For everything." Despite his fears, he was grateful Hayden had agreed to open up his home, and the offer of pizza was beyond what Jez expected.

"Any time, Jez, any time."

Hayden's voice rang with sincerity, but Jez had been fooled before. However, making nice was only wise, and Jez didn't want to live where he had to be wary of his roommate the whole time.

They got out of the truck and headed for the door. Hayden handed him a key on a ring with a red fire engine, making Jez grin.

"I almost forgot. Opens the front and back doors. I don't have a security system, but neither do I leave the doors unlocked. The area is pretty safe, but I'm friends with some cops who'd kick my ass if I didn't take basic precautions."

Jez cringed internally at the thought of Hayden's police friends. He hadn't had any great experiences with law enforcement back in New York, but he'd try not to paint Hayden's buddies with the same brush. "Thanks." Oooh. Hayden's shower would give Jez ample time to sneak Fang out for a pee break, and then Jez could dash back and grab the quickest shower he'd taken in his life.

"So, I'll meet you in the living room after showering?" Hayden asked. "We could watch a movie or something while we eat."

A little of Jez's elation disappeared. A movie was longer than he'd intended to spend downstairs before crashing, but he didn't want to blow Hayden off.

"Sounds good." Jez lingered, letting Hayden precede him up the stairs, giving him the added bonus of seeing Hayden's spectacular ass flex in his well-worn jeans. Yeah, this was going to be a challenging time for him, both mentally and... libidinously? Was that even a word? Whatever. He was going to be horny and wary until he was in his own place, as well as worried about Fang, and he foresaw a lot of tension in the coming days.

A police siren screamed in the distance, sending Jez's heart rate soaring. He paused on the stairs, taking deep breaths, hoping the sudden noise wasn't going to trigger an anxiety attack. That was the last thing he wanted to explain to Hayden.

A few minutes later, he was mostly back to normal. It seemed jumping at loud noises and panicking around too many people was his new normal. The bone-deep weariness didn't help, but if he went to sleep now, he'd be awake all night in an unfamiliar place, and that would be worse. If nothing else, at least his libido had returned to hibernation. Better for everyone if it stayed there.

HAYDEN ORDERED two pizzas because he wasn't sure he could handle eating the meatless, cheeseless atrocity he'd ordered for Jez. Hayden ate healthy with lots of vegetables—he couldn't afford to get chubby or he'd be less effective as a firefighter. But full-on vegan seemed overly difficult and unnecessary.

He settled down in front of the television to wait for Jez to finish with his overlong shower. Good thing the water heater was in decent shape, but taking long showers was something most Californians had gotten out of the habit of after the recent lengthy drought. The past winter had seen enough precipitation to make things less dire, but the reprieve might only be temporary. Maybe he'd mention it in passing, although he didn't want to seem like he was scolding Jez. So far Jez wasn't anything like he'd expected, and he'd noticed an odd twitchiness, like Jez was poised for flight, that made Hayden slightly uncomfortable. He didn't want Miguel's brother *afraid* of him. That wouldn't be right.

His unexpected—and unwelcome—attraction to Jez had triggered an intense curiosity. He hadn't intended to offer pizza, but unless either of them saw fit to purchase a television for a bedroom, they were going to be spending some time together in the living room. Not that Hayden spent all his off-shift days binge-watching TV. Not all his days. But that was a favorite way for him to unwind. When he and Miguel had days off together, they'd go hiking or camping or even drive down into Mexico. Drink too much with the guys. Watch football or baseball, sometimes even hit the games live. Clubbing when he was desperate for dick. Couldn't be that different from what Jez did for fun, right?

But Hayden couldn't get that unicorn shirt, the likes of which Hayden wouldn't be caught dead in, off his mind. Did that mean they were too different to get along?

Idly flipping through the channels, Hayden waited. He hadn't expected the pizza to arrive before Jez was finished showering, but Jez was cutting it close. He stopped on a baseball game, a repeat of one of the recent postseason ones. He didn't follow either team, but it would kill the time. And maybe he was wrong about his assumptions. Jez could surprise him. Maybe the dude was wild about baseball.

Hayden checked the time again. Should he do a health check, make sure Jez was okay? How long was too long? What if he burst into the bathroom only to discover Jez rubbing one out in a leisurely fashion?

Unexpected waves of heat swept down Hayden's entire body, and he shifted with discomfort. The last thing he wanted was a mental image of Jez slick with water, eyes half-closed as he stroked his hard dick.

A small groan escaped Hayden's throat as he adjusted himself. He'd never before had any predilections toward masochism, but what else could this be? He needed to get laid. Not tonight, though, because he'd determined that tonight would be getting to know his new roomie—platonically.

The odd clanging of his old pipes signaled Jez had turned off the water, and Hayden breathed a sigh of relief. The sooner Jez showed up, fully dressed, the sooner Hayden could stop thinking about his lean, naked, wet body.

Dammit!

Hayden shoved himself off the couch and stalked into the kitchen to grab a couple of beers to go with the pizza, as well as some paper towels. Holding the two beers, he did a quick mental calculation. Yep, Jez was old enough to drink, and hopefully the cold beer would help cool down his libido. Stupid dicks. Sometimes there was just no reasoning with them.

He'd no sooner put down the beers and slumped back onto the sofa when the doorbell rang, and he sprang back up to answer it.

With pizzas in hand, he stood in the entryway, unsure if he should turn the oven on to keep Jez's pizza hot. His own stomach was about ready to scarf down anything—up to and including vegan pizza, which smelled every bit as good as his own. If Jez didn't show up soon, his instincts for politeness were going to fail and he was going to dig in.

The floorboards in the upstairs hall creaked, the sound of a person approaching the staircase. Hayden grinned—decision made. He took both pizzas into the living room and dropped them on the coffee table.

The stairs creaked like Jez was either treading tentatively or trying to be silent, but this old house was never truly silent. And if Hayden had never had any luck sneaking past Gran, Jez didn't have a prayer. Jez didn't have Hayden's motivation to hook up without spelling things out for his gran. She'd been understanding and supportive in a way his parents hadn't been, but that didn't mean Hayden had felt comfortable sailing past her room saying, "I'm going out trolling for cock, back in a few hours!"

An uncomfortable sensation swept through him. Would Jez bring back dates? Hayden couldn't say no, but he wasn't sure how he felt about sharing living space with someone who had a sex life. If Gran had had a sex life while she was still alive, she'd been super stealth about it—for which Hayden's psyche would be forever thankful—but he'd never lived with a roommate. It wasn't the same as bunking with another guy during his training or napping at the firehouse.

Would he be able to... *hear* things? Would he be able to hear Jez have sex? The reverse wouldn't be true, because Hayden never brought hookups home.

Hayden had definitely not thought things through, because thinking about Jez's sex sounds wasn't doing anything to cool him off from the shower montage.

With a full-on shiver, Hayden forced all inappropriate thoughts away just as Jez showed up.

"Doing okay?"

"Yeah, sure. That's a good shower."

"The water pressure is good for an old place." Hayden refrained from rolling his eyes. Why on earth was he talking to Jez about fucking water pressure?

Jez nodded, clearly wondering the same thing.

"Pizza's here."

Jez cracked a smile. "I see that."

Hayden's cheeks heated. More stating the obvious. Next he'd be telling Jez the sky was blue and water was wet. Still, he grinned in response. "I also got you a beer."

That got him a nose crinkle. "Sorry, I don't drink beer."

Didn't drink beer? "Really?"

Jez shrugged. "Too many calories for not enough enjoyment. The pizza's enough of an indulgence for today. I can grab myself a water." With the same sinuous grace he'd demonstrated all day, Jez padded into the kitchen. Hayden allowed himself the briefest glance at the rounded ass stretching a pair of well-worn jeans before he made himself comfortable on the sofa, with both bottles of beer on his side of the coffee table.

He should have known better. He'd hooked up with enough wannabe actors and models to know they were all super picky about food. Hayden ate healthy, both on his own and at the station—pizza was an indulgence for him too—but he wasn't sure he could give up beer. If nothing else, it made things simpler when he was hanging out with the guys. He'd have to take Jez grocery shopping tomorrow, because even though Hayden didn't eat like a frat boy on a budget, he still ate meat and cheese and seafood. There wasn't enough in the house to feed Jez for any length of time, and he'd never purchased any of the pseudoproteins a vegan might need.

Jez returned with a glass of water, and he sat down carefully at the other end of the sofa. Hayden wanted to blurt a question out into the awkward silence, about whether Jez minded if Hayden was eating meat, but he wasn't about to give up meat in his own damned house.

"Thanks for ordering the pizza. I hope it wasn't too much trouble."

"No trouble at all." Especially since the pizza place the firehouse ordered from had vegetarian and vegan options. A couple of the guys did make the occasional vegetarian meal or order meatless pizza without having to field too many complaints. But he didn't think he could maintain his muscle mass and protein intake on a strictly plant-based diet. When Jez flipped up the lid of his pizza box, the "cheese" didn't look quite right. Cashew-based products couldn't simulate the gooey, melty goodness of mozzarella.

Settling back on the couch, Hayden flipped the TV to another baseball game, but Jez's nose wrinkle made him sigh inwardly.

"Not a sports fan?" His question didn't make Jez relax any, as though he suspected Hayden of passing judgment. It would prove a bit of a challenge for them to share the TV, although Hayden did have a DVR that would get more of a workout than it currently did.

Jez shrugged. "Not much. I don't mind watching the occasional hockey game, but mostly no."

Hayden couldn't contain his shock. "Hockey? For a native Californian? Why hockey?" It was a sport, sure, but half the fun of the sports he watched was the personal experience in playing the game either during school or in the semiregular baseball games composed of teams made up primarily of emergency-services personnel. Hayden had never been on ice skates in his life, and he knew damned well ice-skating hadn't been part of Jez's formative years.

"I did spend eight years in New York. They do love hockey in the North. I also dated, briefly, a player in the minors for a team feeding into the NHL. I grew to appreciate it."

Hayden blinked. There it was. Out in the open. What Miguel never said once, in plain speaking. Jez was definitely gay. Or bi. Gay men in professional sports existed, although the ones anyone knew about were scarce, but no women played for the NHL. Hayden might not know much about hockey, but he knew that. Not that Hayden hadn't had his suspicions about Jez long before he showed up on Hayden's doorstep wearing that rainbow unicorn shirt. After all, they'd both left Willow Ridge as soon as humanly possible. The difference was that Hayden had returned home at least three times since he'd moved away, but as far as he knew, Jez hadn't ever gone back.

"You dated a professional hockey player? What happened?" Hayden blurted out the question before he could stop himself, although he normally resisted asking intrusive personal questions in the hopes of never having to answer similar questions himself.

Jez faced Hayden for the first time since he came downstairs, eyebrow raised in surprise, either at Hayden's intrusive curiosity or the fact that Hayden hadn't questioned the fact Jez had dated a man.

"He wasn't out." Hayden heard the disappointment in Jez's voice, clear as day. Was Jez one of those guys who thought every gay man should be out, as a matter of principle? Or was he saddened that the relationship hadn't worked?

"That's it?"

"No. Not exactly. But it might not have ended the way it did if he hadn't got called up to the NHL."

"Oh. Sorry." Hayden returned his attention to his pizza, not sure if either of them wanted to continue pursuing this topic.

They both ate in silence for a few minutes before Jez sighed, but this time it was a good sound. "This is awesome."

Hayden nodded, swallowing hastily so he could respond. "I've never had a vegan pizza from there." Or anywhere, ever. Hopefully never. "But I like their regular pizza, so I was hoping it would be okay."

"It is. Better than okay. Thank you."

The slight tension dissipated as they ate, but they were still watching a baseball game. "How about a movie? What do you like to watch?" He didn't imagine any overlap in their tastes there either, but after years of living with his gran, he could watch just about anything and find a way to enjoy it.

Jez shrugged again. "I never had a lot of time for movies. But I like comedies. And action."

Hayden let out a relieved breath. He had been a little concerned Jez's favorite films would be subtitled art-house films or depressing tragic dramas, which were his least favorite. Hell, Hayden didn't even mind a good rom-com or those heartwarming Christmas made-for-TV ones, although he'd never admit that to his buddies.

A quick search of his streaming service revealed *Sahara*, which they'd both seen and liked. Low-impact viewing—didn't require a lot of attention or brain power, but still engaging and amusing.

Jez ate a couple of slices before declaring himself full. He waited until Hayden had finished half his pizza before taking both boxes into the kitchen and putting them away in the fridge. When he returned to the living room, he hesitated, like he wasn't sure he was going to sit down again, but eventually he slid back into his place at the other end of the couch.

WHY DID Hayden have to pick one of Jez's favorite movies? The damn thing was like Kryptonite. It didn't matter when it was on, Jez had to watch it. Jez had even bought it on DVD during those incredibly lean times when he'd first moved away from home and couldn't afford anything but the most bare-bones data plan for his phone. Not that he had a DVD player, but his laptop played DVDs just fine, and so many times when he'd been depressed about a difficult class, teacher, classmate, the pain he'd been in, or his lack of progress on Broadway, this had been one of a dozen or so DVDs that he'd turn to. And if it showed up on TV? Well, he'd just watch it then too. At this point he almost had the entire script memorized.

He'd never have expected to find any sort of commonality with Hayden, never mind this early. It gave him a bit of hope that living here wouldn't be entirely heinous.

The normality of it all, like Jez was sitting on the couch with a date or a boyfriend, gave him some comfort. He kept sneaking glances at Hayden's jawline and strong, muscular form, like he'd done in the car. If Jez could build a man from scratch, he'd look a hell of a lot like Hayden. And running into burning buildings to save people? So sexy. At least, in men other than his brother.

In fact, this might be the best date he'd been on in a long time. If only he didn't have secrets he didn't want Hayden to learn. If only Hayden would confirm—one way or the other—if he was gay or bi. If only Hayden could see Jez as an attractive man and not the annoying brother of his best friend. If Jez were wishing for unattainable things, though, he'd wish that he hadn't had to give up his life in New York without any notice. But if wishes were fishes, they'd all be knee-deep in stinking fish carcasses.

Unfortunately Jez didn't think he had it in him to stay awake for the whole movie. Lethargy had crept into his bones and made his eyes burn with the effort of keeping them open. He didn't want to appear rude, though. Hayden truly was doing him a favor.

Hayden cleared his throat and Jez tensed.

"So how come you go by Jez now? I know Miguel didn't pronounce it with an *h* sound, but either way, Jez Perez? Does the rhyming name help you get parts in plays or whatever you've been doing in Broadway?"

Goddamn Miguel. No, that wasn't fair. Miguel was the only one of his family who'd ever given a damn, and Miguel had never told the family they were still in contact—which was probably wise—but neither had he ever wanted to talk about anything that might touch on or be related to Jez's sexual orientation. Not that his fucking job had anything to do with the fact that he liked cock, but Miguel had it all wrapped up together in his mind and never wanted to crack the seal on the reality of Jez's existence.

Somehow, though, when Jez had called Miguel, begging for help, and Miguel had taken control, saying he'd squared things away with Hayden, Miguel hadn't bothered to tell Hayden much more than he'd have told the family, which was nothing. How could Miguel think that wise? After all, Hayden *could* be a bullying homophobe. Miguel wouldn't recognize a homophobe if he tripped over one.

"For the most part, unless people hear my name, they get all squirrelly about someone named Jesús. There wasn't one white teacher in school who didn't trip up over the pronunciation at least once, and often more than once. It was like they're constitutionally incapable of understanding it's a fucking name, and a fairly popular one in the Latino community. I was taking a stage name, and what I did was just take the anglicized first syllable of my first name and pair it with the last letter of my last name." Like he wanted to be saddled with Perez for the rest of his stinking life. He didn't want his career, and the new life he'd fought so hard for, to be linked in any way with the family that had disowned him.

He'd been lulled into a sense of relaxation by Hayden's laid-back attitude and the almost dreamlike normalcy of things since he'd woken up on Hayden's porch. But all of that was gone now.

Hayden grunted. "Huh. Interesting. So you go by another last name, then?"

Jez barely avoided rolling his eyes. Seriously, what *had* Miguel told Hayden? Or maybe Hayden was just one of those guys who only pretended to listen. "Yes. Bouchet."

"That's French, isn't it? What made you pick that?"

What, just because his heritage was Latino, he shouldn't pick a fucking French name? Aside from Miguel, Jez would just as soon pretend his family didn't exist. Being disowned did that to a person, but he had a feeling Hayden didn't know about the past strife in the Perez family. As soon as he could afford it, he'd changed his name officially.

Instead of venting his bitterness, which Hayden didn't deserve, Jez shrugged. "Dunno. Came across it somewhere and it just called to me." It was more or less the truth. In a crappy motel room many years ago, when he'd been forever banned from the family home, he'd been desperate for any sort of distraction that would keep him from thinking. The motel's television had been on its last legs, and he'd watched movie after movie through eyes grainy and sore from crying. He didn't recall the movie—any of them—that he'd watched, but he'd seen the name Bouchet in the credits, and it had called to him. Like it belonged to him. So he took it and made it his, a use name that suited him far better than his birth name ever had. Jesús Perez died in that dingy hotel room, and Jez Bouchet was born.

"Jez Bouchet." Hayden sounded almost like he was savoring Jez's name as thoughtfully as someone taste-testing wines. Jez was man enough to admit it sent a little shiver racing down his spine, hearing his chosen name in Hayden's mellow baritone. "I like it. I predict you'll have great success."

Jez lifted an eyebrow. "Uh, thanks?" Some might argue he'd already had some modest successes, but he wasn't going to brag about it. Given Miguel's apparent circumspection, Hayden might not even know exactly what Jez did for a living, never mind what roles he'd performed. Didn't matter. Not like he needed Hayden's condescension. Besides, he had a puppy upstairs who might well be upset at yet another change of venue, and crashing for about twelve hours, or as long as Fang let him sleep, sounded like heaven, despite his love of *Sahara*. Walking on eggshells around Hayden wasn't easy when he was tired. All it did was tire him out quicker.

"I think I'm going to head up to bed. It's been a long day."

A flash of disappointment—perhaps—crossed Hayden's face, but it was gone in the blink of an eye. "Sure. I'll see you tomorrow. For a bit, anyway. I'm on again. For future reference, shifts are eleven to eleven, and my schedule is on the fridge."

"Thanks for the pizza." Shit. That reminded him. He had literally nothing to eat in this house besides half a pizza.

Hayden seemed to almost read his mind, though. "I can take you out to the grocery store tomorrow, but help yourself to whatever food I've got here."

"Appreciate that. Although I'll see what I can do about getting a car or figuring out the public transit."

Hayden shrugged. "No worries."

A fucking car. Yet another thing on his list. Jez couldn't fool himself, though. He'd be better off driving to work, despite the traffic, than trying to rely on public transit or Uber. It had been a long fucking time since he'd driven. The days he'd spent fighting with that shitty bucket of bolts masquerading as a rental moving truck didn't count as driving. He hadn't ever owned a car before because it hadn't been necessary in New York, but he had to accept that he wasn't in New York any longer and he might never return.

At least he had a warm, snuggly puppy to cuddle up to. He hadn't been sure about getting Fang, but if not for that half-grown pug, Jez would have lost his fucking shit all over the place a thousand times over.

As he headed upstairs, he took one last glance at Hayden and sighed. He missed having a man to cuddle with, and fuck senseless, but even if he could classify Hayden as an old friend, far too many things about him made Jez nervous, not the least of which was how he'd react to a dog hidden in his room.

Chapter 3

SLOPPY PUPPY kisses in his ear brought Jez to wakefulness.

"Ugh. That's just gross." Jez attempted to scold his fat, warm puppy, but Fang licked up his nose in response. Jez sputtered and wiped at his face. "Seriously, just yuck."

Fang's little butt didn't stop wiggling, though. Probably because Jez couldn't inject any real censure or disgust into his tone. Fang was too fucking cute; Jez hadn't gotten truly angry at him once in the four months since he'd found himself owned by the furry fawn bundle.

Fang let out one of his gruff little barks that didn't sound like an actual bark, and Jez noted how bright his room was. He scrabbled for his phone, plucking it off the charger. Fuck. He'd slept until after noon. Jez was more of a morning person and only slept late after a night of drinking. Which, given the empty calories in booze, did not happen all that often. Gaining weight in his profession would cut down significantly on the jobs he got, although he might have a tiny bit of wiggle room with this new job. Since it was a television show with hiatuses, he might be able to relax his diet and exercise schedule periodically.

Jez stretched, and the gentle ache in his muscles reminded him it had been over a week since he'd exercised properly. Between the frantic packing, doing his best to finalize his life in New York, then the draining, debilitating, and fatiguing drive along the hypotenuse of the country, he hadn't had the time for anything not strictly required to keep body and soul and puppy together.

But he was starting to feel the lack and would have to see where and how he could remedy that. Failing anything else, he could jog around Hayden's neighborhood. Through the haze of his exhaustion, he'd noticed an abundance of green and extra-wide residential roads as he guided the rental truck through Hayden's area of Pasadena.

Fang grunted and pawed at him, and Jez sat up and glanced over at Fang's puppy pad. Damn. He must have missed Fang trying to wake him during the night, based on the almost-dried yellow spot. First things first. Get puppy to a patch of green before his buggy little eyeballs turned yellow. Or before he had an accident in Hayden's house, off the puppy pads, because that wouldn't endear either of them to their temporary landlord/host.

Jez sleeping in so late meant Hayden would be at work, which meant he could safely stick Fang out in the backyard. Not on his own and not off leash until Jez had a chance to scope things out. If the backyard didn't work or didn't have any privacy fencing, he might have to avoid neighbors seeing Fang as well. Hayden didn't seem like the sort who got chummy with his neighbors, bonding over barbecues and lawn mowers, but one never knew. Jez couldn't risk any of them asking Hayden about the new dog.

Jez got up and dressed in the first T-shirt and shorts that he pulled out of his duffel, an awesome benefit of living in southern California. October in New York would be much chillier. He scooped Fang into his arms and loped downstairs, noting how each step creaked. That was going to be difficult to explain, when he had to go for "air" twice or three times a day. Maybe he was going to have to fake a smoking habit.

When Fang had taken care of business out back—which was both private and well fenced—Jez kept him on the leash while they explored their new living quarters.

He'd seen some of the house the previous night, although he hadn't paid it much attention. The bones were great, but it was stark as fuck. Spartan only strived to be as bleak and austere as the walls in Hayden's place. From the outside, the house was typical rustic Craftsman, but the interior had been whitewashed. The only things saving it from looking like some sort of institution were the battered brown leather chairs and matching couch in the living room, the dark wood furniture in the dining room, and the hardwood floors. Even the kitchen had all-white furniture on gorgeous terra-cotta tiles. If Hayden was responsible for the atrocious paint job, how much did that burnished warm sienna irk him?

Hayden hadn't said any rooms were restricted or private, so Jez wandered through the kitchen, Fang's nails clicking against the tile as he followed along. Jez loved the layout of an old house. It didn't have that manufactured cookie-cutter layout that newer houses seemed to have. This place had a surprise around every corner, whether it was a tiny nook, a whole other room, or a fireplace. Although he suspected firefighter Hayden didn't use the fireplace.

Jez opened the door off the kitchen to find another stark room that Hayden had claimed as a home gym. In the far corner sat a desk and a filing cabinet, but Jez assumed they didn't get much use. Aside from paying bills and doing taxes, he didn't know why Hayden would bother with an office portion. It didn't take more than a glance at Hayden's impressive body for Jez to know the gym part of the room was far more important.

Biting his lip, he tried desperately not to picture Hayden working the weights, skin slick with sweat, muscles pumped, veins prominent on his corded forearms. Blood flowed south, and Jez's cock thickened.

No, for fuck's sake, no. No lusting over the alpha male who might or might not be gay. Who probably wasn't gay and might not appreciate fueling the sexual fantasies of his best friend's younger brother.

Developing a crush on yet another unsuitable man would be the height of folly, and if Jez screwed up here, his options for refuge would become severely limited.

Jez backed out of the room, shutting the door with a decisive bang. His cock needed to get the message pronto—Hayden was off-limits.

Another door, beyond which he'd expected to find the garage, opened onto a laundry room. He laughed. No more laundromat, at least while he was here. Laundromats sucked, and he'd heard LA apartments with en suite laundry were notably scarce and a real luxury.

On the opposite side of the house, running along half of the side yard, was a... Jez didn't know what it was. Covered porch? Sunroom? Something like that, and yet it wasn't exposed to the elements. But this room had an entire wall of windows that went from ceiling to three-quarters of the way to the floor. Hayden clearly didn't take advantage of the gorgeous, light, airy atmosphere, given it contained nothing more than a white wicker love seat and matching coffee table. Nobody sane would sit on cushionless wicker for any length of time. Unlike much of the rest of the main floor, this had a plush sort of Berber carpet in a pale sand color. Jez snorted. Had Hayden looked for snow-white carpet? He must have realized at some point that even if he'd managed to hermetically seal the house, white carpet was a bad fucking idea.

Nevertheless, this room would be ideal for Jez to exercise. Hell, it was nicer than the studio he'd rehearsed in most of his career. In fact, just thinking about putting himself through his stretches in this room, the lush greenery visible through the windows, sunlight streaming in, soothed him like he'd popped an antianxiety tablet. Without all the muzzy-headed side effects.

Fucking hell. He wanted this room and was already anticipating the regret he'd feel when he found a new apartment. Even more than he'd regret no longer having a laundry room. His new job had studio space where he could stretch and rehearse, but Jez had no delusions about being able to afford an apartment with room enough to exercise in. He was going to have to find a gym as well, hopefully close to this mythical apartment he needed to find.

A prioritized list might help. First, find a car, because that would make it easier to check out apartments and to take Fang to a park on the days when Hayden didn't work.

Just like that, most of his tension returned. He picked up Fang, buried his face in the warm fur, and just breathed.

Determined to stave off another bout of despondency, Jez went back upstairs. Since the downstairs was large, there were several rooms on the second floor. He resolutely avoided Hayden's room. Sitting on the couch last night beside a freshly showered Hayden had wreaked havoc on his olfactory senses. He could only imagine a whole room where the scents of Hayden—and ones more intimate than bodywash— permeated everything. Devastating. Especially for a man dead set on not falling in lust.

One of the doors led to another guest room every bit as stark as the one Jez resided in, one door deceptively led to a shallow linen closet, and another opened into a stairwell that appeared to lead to the attic. The last room, though, interested him plenty.

Its walls had also been painted white—Jez could not believe the institutional color scheme had been original to the house—but it was stacked with cardboard boxes. And not the haphazard jumble of different-sized boxes Jez had scrounged from his local markets and liquor stores. No, these were the type that had been purchased from a moving company and were all identical in size and stacked precisely against one wall.

Desperate to know what was in those boxes, Jez shifted a couple. They weren't as heavy as he expected, but none of them appeared to be labeled. Curious. For someone who enjoyed a very regimented living style, neatly packed cardboard boxes with no labels seemed wildly out of character.

No way could he justify snooping, though. Not if he expected the same courtesy from Hayden. And he couldn't think of any subtle way to ask.

An angry grumble from his stomach interrupted his musing, reminding him he'd slept past both breakfast and lunch. Hopefully he could find something in Hayden's kitchen to eat, since grocery shopping would have to wait until tomorrow when Hayden was off again. Jez had no delusions about his ability to buy a car in an afternoon, even if he could afford to walk right into a showroom and buy something new off the lot. Which he couldn't.

Exploring the attic was tempting but would have to wait for another day. He needed to investigate the pantry and then review car-shopping venues and consumer reports. He tucked Fang away in his room— no sense letting him get used to having the run of the house—then sprinted back down to the kitchen.

The house echoed a bit, had an odd sense of emptiness that it hadn't had the day before. Hayden left his mark on a space, which maybe wasn't hard in this wintry white backdrop. But Jez hadn't expected to miss that presence, even as Hayden's absence allowed

Jez to relax, as much as he could. Relaxing hadn't come easy in the past weeks, even before he'd decided moving away—fleeing—was the smartest thing he could do. It would be a long time before he felt safe, if he ever could. For now, he had pills to create a reasonable facsimile of calm, but if the change of location didn't help, he'd have to add finding a therapist to his ever-growing mental to-do list.

Jez sighed. Hayden made him nervous but also strangely made him feel safe. The dichotomy made him wonder if he was losing his fucking mind, for real this time. Hayden should have unnerved him, period. But he suspected spending the night alone in this creaky house would rattle him even more. Last night he'd slept deeply and for a long time, and he didn't think he could attribute that to the nearly three-thousand-mile displacement from where his life had imploded.

CURLED UP on Hayden's amazingly comfortable leather couch, Jez watched another movie as he ate popcorn and shared a bit with Fang, who cuddled up beside him. What Hayden didn't know wouldn't hurt him. With Fang's super short hair, he didn't shed much, and Hayden was working a twenty-four-hour shift. No need to keep his baby locked up when it was just Jez rattling around this big place.

He leaned forward, listening closely to the dialogue. The couple was in bed, confessing their love for each other, but their voices were quieter than the previous scene. He had picked up the remote to raise the volume when a loud bang propelled him to his feet. Fang let out a woof as Jez whirled around, glancing from the window to the door. Clutching the remote in suddenly chilled fingers, he tried to ignore his racing heart.

It took him a fraction of a second to figure out he'd heard a car door slam, and another twenty minutes of staring fixedly at the television for the adrenaline to drain away. The last time he'd been in such a large house, he'd lived at home, and with his parents and siblings, he'd almost never been home alone.

Sudden bursts of sound, like a car driving by with loud music or the occasional siren, startled him. The walls of his New York apartment had had paper-thin walls, but even though he'd been living on his own, the tight quarters and knowing other people were mere feet away comforted him. Hayden's place felt a lot more isolated, and if Jez thought about it too hard, he could imagine himself in a horror movie.

Just thinking about horror movies had him up again, closing the blinds. Felt a bit like someone might be watching him, even though that was ridiculous. He was scaring himself a bit.

But being too scared to sleep would be a humiliation Jez didn't need, whether or not Hayden or his brother ever learned the truth. Instead, he wrapped his favorite fleece throw around himself—Hayden would have an apoplexy at the riot of color—and concentrated on the romance.

At least he'd been able to cobble together something to eat. The pizza had been good, but not two days in a row. Hayden wasn't a complete caveman when it came to food. He obviously cooked—it wasn't easy to keep in such good shape living on takeout and ready-made food—but meat, cheese, and eggs figured heavily into it. But Jez had found enough vegetables and seasonings to whip together a decent stir-fry, and the can of baked beans he'd found at the back of the cupboard were vegetarian, so he'd eaten those as well to get a bit of protein. Probably Hayden had bought the vegetarian version by mistake, but it worked in Jez's favor.

He wouldn't starve, and maybe Hayden would still be willing to take him grocery shopping tomorrow. Buying a car was going to take more effort than he'd thought—there were just so damned many, and all the features and prices and consumer reports made him feel like he was back in school. He loved to read when he wasn't dancing, but he read novels, not research. Figuring out what kind of car to buy when it had been years since he'd even driven one? That kind of reading made his head spin.

Given the size of Hayden's truck, he didn't think he'd get appropriate advice from his new roomie. Maneuvering the rental truck had put him off driving anything large. Small, sweet, reliable, and inexpensive. Those were the four keywords, and yet somehow it wasn't as simple as he'd thought it would be.

His phone rang, and Jez glanced at the screen. Miguel. If it were anyone else, he'd let it roll to voicemail.

"Hi, Miguel." Jez paused the movie as he answered.

"Hey, baby bro."

Jez rolled his eyes. His big brother bent over backward to sound like a dude bro, and it irritated the fuck out of Jez. Maybe because he'd been picked on and harassed by so many of them. "What's up?"

"Just checking to see how you're settling in. Hayden's okay, right?"

Jez didn't even know what that last question meant. "Sure. He's okay. Everything's good." He and Miguel might not have visited with each other the whole time Jez lived in New York, but they spoke on the phone on a regular basis. Nothing too deep, but it was a connection, and Jez was grateful to have his brother in his life. Miguel worried about him, even if he never wanted to hear about Jez's dating life.

"I'm heading out to a couple of clubs tonight with some friends. Did you want to come with me? I know Hayden's on shift today."

Miguel deserved a cookie. He made the offer without sounding like he'd rather get his wisdom teeth extracted without anesthesia, even though Jez knew damn well Miguel didn't want him to say yes. And he was 60 or 70 percent sure Miguel would even include him in conversations and such when he could. However, it was Saturday night, Miguel wouldn't be setting foot in a gay club, and Jez had no real inclination to hang around a bunch of testosterone-poisoned straight men while Miguel and his friends did their best to sleep with the female population of Los Angeles.

"Thanks, M, but I'm still beat from that long drive. Maybe next time." Jez wasn't an actor for nothing, because he didn't sound like he'd agree round about the same time Satan next went ice-skating.

"Sure. Sure. Need anything?"

Jez sighed. "I don't know. Think you could take me to look at some cars this week?"

Miguel made a noncommittal sound in his throat. "Mm-hmm. Maybe. I've got four days off starting Wednesday, but I'm heading up to Big Bear Lake with some of the guys to camp. I'll be spending most of my day off Monday running errands for that. Can it wait until next week?"

"Yeah. Sure. No rush." Filming didn't start until the first week in November, although he had to attend some earlier preproduction meetings. Who knew? Maybe Jez would figure out on his own what kind of car he should get before then and the problem would be solved.

"Is Hayden going camping with you?"

"Nah. We've got plans to trade out for a long weekend cold-weather camping after Thanksgiving sometime, but he's not going this time."

Jez wasn't sure if he should be pleased and relieved, but he was, even though Hayden's four-off started Tuesday—according to the calendar attached to the fridge—and Jez wasn't sure how he'd smuggle Fang out to do his business while Hayden was hanging around. Then again, maybe Hayden had enough of a social life that he'd be gone for most of it anyway.

Given the heated looks Hayden had maybe directed toward Jez, would he still date women? Was he bisexual? Closeted? A tiny spot of blackness curdled in his belly. Man or woman, he didn't think he was at all interested in being around when Hayden brought a sexual partner back to the house.

Not a problem to discuss with his brother. Anything related to Jez's sex life or career made Miguel uncomfortable enough to talk over Jez or change the subject.

As if Jez planned to tell his big brother about the first time he came from a prostate massage or got rimmed. Those weren't details for family, even if Miguel hadn't had a pathological fear of TMI.

"Have a good time camping." Jez wanted to be upset that Miguel hadn't dropped everything to help him, but it had all been so last-minute, so it wasn't fair to blame Miguel. After all, he had made sure Jez had a safe place to stay.

"Thanks, man."

Jez rolled his eyes again. "Did you want to maybe have dinner sometime? Maybe after your trip?"

"Sure, sure. We can go when Hayden and I have a day off together. The three of us could go. It would be fun."

The three of them? Was Miguel worried about being seen with him? Or was he just worried about awkward silence?

"Sounds like fun." That still left Jez on his own far too much. Dammit. He was going to have to find some friends. Most of his friends in New York… well, they hadn't had his back when he needed them, and he'd left them behind as surely as he'd done everything else. Which left him with Fang. Who was great, but a little light on verbal repartee and absolute shit at giving advice.

"Gotta go," Miguel said. With the unmistakable sound of a dude bro herd becoming audible in the background, Jez wasn't surprised.

"Have fun tonight."

Miguel laughed into the phone before the call cut off. Yes, that was the sound of a man intending to get laid. Jez was a tiny bit jealous, because it had been so long, and breaking his dry spell required suitable prospects. He had none. Not until he figured out where the good clubs were—some way other than wandering aimlessly through West Hollywood—and if he could get there without having a panic attack.

Also, he needed to regain some of his energy, both mental and physical. His recent relationship with Jayson had almost convinced him psychic vampires were real. Jayson had drained him dry, and only adrenaline had kept Jez running all the way to Los Angeles. Now the adrenaline had worn off and Jez had zero reserves.

If he went out, he'd want to have fun as well as get off. No chance of that if the clubs here were anything like the clubs he frequented back in New York. The crush of guys, the sweat, the heat levels, the pulse of a bass beat that throbbed deep in the gut... these were all things he usually liked. With his recent anxiety, though, he'd last a good thirty or forty seconds before he ran out screaming. Not exactly cock-raising material, for anyone involved.

"You still love me, don't you, Fang?" Fang wiggled his butt and corkscrew tail before climbing up Jez to lick at his chin, making Jez laugh. "Good boy."

For now, all the excitement he needed was happening on-screen. If he was desperate to get off, he had porn, lube, and a private shower. An embarrassment of options. And if he was tempted to roll around in Hayden's sheets while he stroked one off, that was a secret he didn't need to share with anyone. Not even Fang.

AGAIN WITH the super long showers. Hayden would really have to say something. The drought might be temporarily over, but that didn't mean squandering water was a good idea. It just wasn't as plentiful as it was on the East Coast.

He checked his watch. If they didn't get going soon, the grocery store would be jammed with the

postchurch crowd shopping for Sunday supper and
the hungover brunchgoers who'd realized they'd be
eating takeout all week if they didn't do something,
and Hayden hated getting caught up in that. Sometimes he got groceries delivered, but most times he
went shopping either just before or just after a shift
on a weekday. That kept him from getting homicid-
al. No one seemed to have a plan, just meandering,
carts wobbling back and forth along the aisles. Was
it so hard to push a cart as you'd drive down a street?
Sticking to the right? And the number of people who
didn't seem to have lists or know if they had more
than fifteen items or even know where they'd put their
fucking wallet grew exponentially on the weekend.

As a rule, he never went shopping on Sunday unless he could go before his shift, not after. The moment
he walked out of the station at eleven was already too
fucking late for groceries, never mind coming back
to pick up Jez only to find him still in the shower. He
also hadn't been thrilled to find Jez's dishes from the
previous night still in the sink when he'd come home.
Washing the dishes hadn't taken long, but he'd still
expected Jez to be done before he was. Nope.

The time kept ticking, and Hayden desperately wanted to call off this errand and crash for a few
hours, but that wasn't fair to Jez. Hayden's pantry was
not suited to a vegan diet, and he didn't want Jez to
starve. But neither did he want to spend any more time
in a grocery store than he had to.

Screw it.

Hayden bounded up the stairs and paused outside
the door of the guest bathroom. What if this wasn't a

simple case of luxuriating under the hot water? What if Jez was jerking off?

Now, like the day Jez had moved in, Hayden couldn't stop thinking about Jez in the shower. Those thoughts had consumed far too many of his waking hours at the station as well, truth be told, contributing to his pissy mood today. Developing any sort of attraction to Miguel's brother was bad news in itself, but Jez.... What would he do with Jez? Jez who was obviously gay. Who seemed to hit most of the stereotypes right on the head. Whose fine, round, tight ass swayed ever so perfectly when he walked—bordering on sashaying—even when he was carrying cardboard boxes. Hayden had arranged most of moving day so that he was behind Jez, imagining kneading that ass, licking it, biting it, and fucking it for days on end.

It was one thing to fuck a guy like that at a club. His friends wouldn't be around to make crude comments, so no risk of making either of them uncomfortable. No risk of even having to introduce them—hookups didn't get introduced to friends. But it seemed likely, given Jez's relationship to Miguel and being situated in Hayden's guest room, that Jez would end up getting invited to activities with the guys. He wouldn't fit in, and it would be even worse if anyone thought they were involved.

Hayden shuddered. Miguel would kill him for lusting after Jez, and the guys would either hate him or mock him. He didn't care for either option, but neither could he forget that smooth brown strip of skin—the very first part of adult Jez he'd spied. Wondering if it would be as smooth against his tongue as it looked had kept him half-aroused and fully irate since Friday afternoon.

He straightened his back. His willpower was strong. Strong enough to withstand a lean scrap of sexiness. He was in control of his destiny—and his fucking cock—and he was going to ignore his desire. Exhibiting control was something he did almost every day. When facing down a blaze, when the exhilaration of adrenaline warred with its fear aspects and sometimes it was a battle to remain calm rather than to plunge wildly forward or run as fast as he could in the other direction. Resisting one slender actor should be a fucking breeze in comparison.

Then the door opened in a swirl of condensation, Jez standing right there, wide-eyed, smelling like warm sugar, and most devastating of all, wearing nothing but a towel around his hips. Hayden bit back a groan as his willpower melted away, as the fates laughed wickedly. Hayden hadn't ever met anyone who hit all his buttons like this. Had he been mistaken about his "usual" type? An odd fluttering took place in his gut as his mind blanked. He leaned in and lifted his hands.

"Uh. Hi. Is something wrong?"

Hayden's ears heated. He'd been so lost in his impossible thoughts he hadn't heard the water turn off. Hopefully Jez wouldn't realize how close Hayden had come to grabbing him and kissing him.

"No. Yes." His cheeks joined the party, and Hayden inwardly cursed skin that flushed red under all sorts of emotional circumstances, including utter embarrassment. "I mean, it's better to get to the store before it gets busy. Sunday afternoons can be bad. And also… you might not recall, but California is prone to droughts?"

Whoa. Way to not waffle. And his sarcasm was off the charts. Hayden wished he could go back downstairs and forget this ridiculous conversation had ever happened.

"Oh. Shit. Sorry. I guess I ought to take shorter showers."

Hayden shrugged like it didn't matter to him. Like it hadn't propelled him upstairs, intent on letting Jez know the score. Like he hadn't been distracted by the thought of opening up that fucking towel and sucking on what lay beneath. Because he was starting to suspect his irritation over long showers had roots in his inability to feel settled since Jez had shown up on his doorstep. His annoyance over the dirty dishes was founded on a hatred of dirty dishes and was completely rational, but perhaps Hayden could give Jez a free pass. If it continued, Hayden would be sure to say something.

Jez cleared his throat, and Hayden dragged his gaze up from Jez's delectable chest to meet his eyes, a muscle involuntarily ticking in his temple, a physical manifestation of his growing annoyance—with himself.

Jez was waiting, and Hayden pulled on his memory. Right. They'd been having a conversation, however stilted. "Shorter showers. Yes. Just do your best. We're not on water rations or anything, but there are still regulations to adhere to about watering the lawn and things."

Watering the lawn? He was a fucking idiot. It wasn't going to matter what opinion Hayden's cock

had on the matter, Jez wasn't going to want anything
to do with him if he didn't get his shit together.

Jez nodded. "So if we're going to get going, I
have to, uh, go get dressed."

Which was when Hayden realized he'd blocked
Jez in the bathroom. While he leered. Yeah, that
wasn't going to win him any prizes in the best-room-
mate competition.

"Right. Sorry." Hayden stepped aside and Jez
gave him a funny little grin, like Hayden was being
weird and cute at the same time. Both the fluttering
in his gut and his dread for the future increased astro-
nomically. "I'll, uh, meet you downstairs."

Hayden stormed back downstairs and flung himself onto the couch, stabbing at the TV remote aggres-
sively, hoping to find something that would take his
mind off the last ten excruciating minutes.

What the ever-loving fuck was wrong with him?
Guys didn't get under his skin this way. Could it be
nothing more than forbidden fruit?

Almost before Hayden had regained his equilib-
rium, Jez padded down the stairs. No rainbow uni-
corns on his shirt, but it was some sort of dark pinkish
color that Hayden wouldn't ever think to wear, and
tight enough to strain Hayden's sensibilities. This
time Hayden wasn't going to trail after Jez, because
those painted-on jeans weren't going to help his barely leashed libido.

"Ready?" Hayden's voice had dropped an octave,
and he cleared his throat. Grocery shopping, not sex.
Not sex. No godforsaken sex. Ever. Not with this man.

"Yes. Thanks for doing this. Hopefully it won't
take me too long to get my own car."

Hayden grabbed a few reusable cloth bags from the hall closet. An odd little gasp made him twist around.

"Something wrong?"

Jez smiled, but it lacked a bit of sparkle. "No. Just realized reusable bags need to go on my list. I'm pretty sure I forgot to pack mine."

Great. Hayden couldn't get his mind out of his pants—or out of Jez's pants—and Jez was getting weirdly emotional over grocery bags. Quite the fucking pair. He led them outside into the noonday sun, and his stomach growled. Yet another good reason for his irritation, and a damn fine reason not to go grocery shopping at this time. He'd end up with a cart full of ice cream and Oreos.

"Holy fuck, it's hot out."

Hayden chuckled. "Yeah, we don't get cooler weather as early as we did in Willow Ridge. And even though it's only October, it could be snowing in New York right now. We're just lucky the day you moved in was quite mild, because otherwise that could have been fucking miserable."

Jez laughed, the first time Hayden had heard him do so since the days back in Willow Ridge when Jez was a kid. And it turned the fluttering—which he thought he'd finally gotten under control—up to eleven. Un-fucking-acceptable.

Hayden pressed his lips together, jaw so tight it was almost petrified, and drove them to the store in silence broken only by Jez fiddling with the satellite stations on his radio.

When they parked—all of about seven minutes after getting in Hayden's truck, and too damned far from the doors—Hayden breathed a sigh of relief and bounded out of the truck. Perhaps they should have talked. As it was, nothing had distracted him from Jez's sugary-sweet smell, which reminded him of oatmeal and apple pie and chai tea. Bodywash? Cologne? Aftershave? He had no idea, but the product had to be full of voodoo and black magic.

What had he done to deserve this? Clearly he'd fucked up big-time in a past life and karma was laughing her ass off at his predicament. If only Jez seemed equally affected, Hayden might not feel so damned idiotic, but Hayden hadn't caught one salacious glance. Not one.

And if he was honest, it stung his ego.

After walking through the automatic doors, he sucked in a big breath. The grocery store always smelled like a weird combination of earthy vegetation, spoiled milk, and bleach. It was enough to drive the scent of Jez out of his nostrils.

"I got a cart. We might as well share it," Jez said from behind. Hayden nodded reluctantly. There went his brilliant idea of telling Jez he'd meet him at the register in like twenty minutes. Or half an hour.

Jez smiled at him, and Hayden just couldn't bring himself to suggest it. The guy knew no one here; Hayden could at least shop with him.

Hayden whipped out his phone. "I start in produce and work to the other side of the store. Where's your list?"

"Oh good. I like to start in produce too. But I don't have a list. I like to see what fruits and vegetables look interesting; then I sort of build from there. On the fly."

Hayden stared, hoping he'd heard wrong. Grocery shopping *on the fly*. On a *Sunday afternoon*. Forget karma; he must have died and gone to hell.

An hour later, waiting in an absurdly long line for the cash register, Hayden was forced to conclude two very regrettable things. First, Jez was the sort of shopper who sent Hayden off on curse-laden rants—in his mind, of course. Second, Jez was pretty enough and entertaining enough that Hayden hadn't minded spending more than double his usual time in the supermarket. And there was even a third thing. His pantry and fridge were soon going to be filled with a number of items Hayden wouldn't have ever thought to eat, much less purchase.

It had been both charming and terrifyingly domestic, especially when he'd had the almost unavoidable involuntary reflex to guide Jez with a hand at his lower back. Each time it happened, Hayden had managed to catch himself before he touched, but he didn't know what was wrong with him. He'd never had a boyfriend, so he didn't know what it was about Jez that prompted all these feelings and actions he associated with people who had significant others.

Then again, he'd also never gone grocery shopping with anyone except his mom, when he was a kid. By the time he moved in with his gran, she'd already started to decline, and Hayden had done all the shopping himself. There was a distinct appeal in having company for the task, even if it meant it took twice as long.

After an eon or two, they made it back to the car. Jez was smiling, so he hadn't hated their outing, and for that alone Hayden was willing to maybe even take him shopping again.

"Did you want me to cook dinner for us both tonight?"

"Oh, don't worry about me. I'm going to crash for a bit when we get home. I'll figure out something for dinner when I get up." Like one of the fat, juicy steaks he'd picked up. With broccoli and asparagus so it wasn't too tremendously bad for him.

"Are you sure? I promise vegan food isn't all tofu and kale."

Hayden snorted. "I'm supposed to believe that, am I, when I saw you put both of those exact things in the cart."

That got him another laugh. "Okay. Sometimes it's tofu and kale. But I wouldn't subject you to that. And I don't have any recipes combining them that I like. You're safe. Don't let that be the reason you won't eat what I cook."

If he was honest, it was a bit of the problem. He didn't see anything in Jez's portion of the groceries that would be filling enough for him, even if it tasted fantastic. But he hadn't been lying when he'd claimed he was tired.

"I really am beat. We had a couple of fires we were fighting during the night. There wasn't any real downtime and I'm in serious need of a nap." Which didn't sound too manly, but it was the fucking truth. At the moment, staying awake was almost painful. His Jez-interrupted sleep hadn't helped either.

"Oh. Of course. You should have said something. I could have gone shopping by myself."

Hayden didn't bother asking how he would have gotten there, because he didn't want to admit he wouldn't have loaned Jez his truck. Not until they knew each other better and not until he'd witnessed how he drove something aside from a poorly balanced, shit-for-suspension rented moving truck. Because he hadn't done spectacularly with the cube van, and Hayden had a serious love for his truck.

"Happy to do it." More or less. "And I needed groceries anyway." Truth. "But the night is catching up with me more suddenly than I expected."

Jez nodded, seemingly placated. An enormous yawn cracked Hayden's jaw and made his eyes water. Definitely not the day for experimenting with food. He couldn't be objective.

"I'm going to try to find a car this week."

Jez's defeated tone almost had Hayden reaching across to pat him on the knee. Hayden didn't need any concrete proof to know touching Jez in any way would only make this impossible infatuation worse. Instead, he addressed the issue verbally. "What's so bad about that?"

Jez shrugged. "Not bad, I suppose. I just don't know much about cars, and I'm not sure what I should get. The options are almost endless and sort of overwhelming."

"Huh. I never had that problem. I've been driving pickups since I learned how to drive, and this one"— Hayden patted his baby's dashboard—"I wanted her right away. There weren't any other options."

Jez rolled his eyes, making Hayden laugh. "That's no help. I don't suppose you know anything about regular cars anyway?"

"Nope. Sorry. Can't help you." A couple of the guys at the station had recently bought cars with wives or girlfriends, and they might have some insight, but Hayden didn't want to ask. What would they make of that sort of question? He was already worried about ending up at an event with both Jez and the guys, because he wasn't sure he'd be able to hide his attraction. Asking for car recommendations sounded like Hayden had taken a too-personal interest in Jez, didn't it?

"No worries. I'll figure something out. Quickly, I hope."

Hayden hoped he did too. He sniffed discreetly, getting another taboo whiff of Jez's sweet and spicy scent, which hadn't faded. What good was spoiled milk if it didn't douse such a delectable smell?

They were almost home before Jez spoke again. "I was wondering if I could use the sunroom. For exercising. It doesn't look like you use it much."

"No, I don't. If I want sun, I go out onto the patio." Hayden paused. "I guess that might be hard with your allergies, right?"

Jez gaped at him and Hayden laughed. "Dude. I barely recognized you when you showed up, but I do remember Miguel's kid brother who spent half the year sneezing and trailing tissues."

Jez might be blushing, but he was definitely squirming, and, uncharitably, it pleased Hayden that he wasn't the only one who'd been embarrassed today. "I'm on medication now. It's a lot better."

Still, Hayden remembered how miserable Jez had been, especially when his sisters had started getting flowers from boys. Roses seemed to be okay, but just about anything else was impossible.

"Look, my gran spent a lot of time building up the plants in the yard. I don't have a green thumb at all and have done my best to keep it neat and tidy, but if there are any plants out there that are especially bad, let me know and we'll get them out."

He'd managed to surprise Jez again. "Hopefully I'll find an apartment before that becomes necessary, but thanks for the offer. That means a lot."

Fucking hell. That was a stupid offer to have made. Jez was only here temporarily—he was not an actual roommate. Things could get uncomfortable if Jez were here longer.

Hayden cleared his throat. "I also have a bunch of weights and some gym equipment in my office. You're welcome to use them." Preferably when Hayden wasn't at home. He enjoyed the sight of a big muscular man working out, but watching the less muscular but no less fit Jez work out would make him lose his damn mind.

"Oh. Thanks. I might take you up on that, but I really liked the vibe of the sunroom."

Vibe. Who was this guy? If it weren't for Miguel's assurances and some similarities around their eyes and mouths, he didn't know how anyone would figure out the two were related. The other siblings, from what he recalled, had a lot more in common with Miguel than Jez. But then, they'd all stayed close to home, Miguel going the farthest afield to Los Angeles.

Nevertheless, he wasn't about to deny Jez's request to use the sunroom. The place was far too large for just him anyway. It was going to be nice—in an incredibly torturous way—to have some temporary company.

"Sure. Do what you want. We can move the furniture to the patio or garage if you want it out of the way."

Jez bounced a bit in his seat like Hayden had done him some spectacular favor. "That would be perfect. Thank you. That cross-country drive was long, and I've been missing my workouts."

Hayden was not going to think about it. He had a bed calling his name, and he was going to sleep and not dream of any sort of workout Jez might engage in.

"If you're into running at all, we could go together sometimes." Where the fuck had that come from? Hayden wanted to smack himself. He was afraid to see what Jez would consider appropriate running gear.

"Thanks. I tend to prefer a treadmill, but until I figure out where I'm going to be living, I don't want to join a gym."

Those words came with a confusing mix of feelings Hayden was too exhausted to decipher, and he didn't want to know what it all meant anyway. Ignorance was bliss.

Once they got home, Hayden lingered downstairs only long enough to put away his groceries. Given that it had been years since he'd shared a kitchen, he'd expected a lot of getting in each other's way and bumping into counters and doors, but Jez moved around him gracefully, almost effortlessly. Before he could let that influence him any, Hayden escaped upstairs.

He settled under the sheets, without enough energy to deal with the half chub he'd been sporting almost nonstop since Jez had opened the door to the bathroom that morning. Jez was trying to be quiet, and while Jez disturbed Hayden on a deeply personal level, he liked knowing someone else was in the house. He'd been lonely.

Having a boyfriend, a partner, or a husband would help, but he didn't foresee that ever being an option. Maybe after Jez moved out he'd have to consider the roommate idea more seriously.

The distinctive creaking floors traced Jez's path to the sunroom, and it pleased Hayden that one of his gran's favorite rooms would get some use. There just wasn't enough of his life to fill up the house.

Chapter 4

HAYDEN WOKE from a hot and heavy dream that involved Jez's lithe form below him, naked and hard. He didn't know what had roused him, but he hadn't wanted to wake up. A quick glance at his door confirmed it was shut. Shutting it while Jez lived with him seemed wise, but it was a habit he'd lost after Gran had died, and it might take some effort to pick up again.

Slipping his hand beneath the covers, he dredged up the vivid dream and began to stroke himself. He closed his eyes against the sunlight and let his imagination have free rein in a way he hadn't since he first realized he wanted to lick Jez from head to toe.

Would Jez be smooth all over? Hayden hadn't ever slept with a woman and wasn't usually interested in smooth, but he could get addicted to soft skin over Jez's hard muscles. He imagined rubbing his five-o'clock shadow down Jez's incredible chest. Things got a little fuzzier when he got to Jez's groin. Was Jez's cock long and thin? Short and fat? Cut or not? More importantly, Hayden wanted to inhale that sweet, spicy scent with his mouth wrapped around Jez's cock—whatever its dimensions—and have his nose buried in Jez's pubes.

Unless… Hayden gasped and tugged hard and fast, precum easing his movements. There'd been that time Hayden had gone to a strip club—something he rarely did because it felt weird going by himself. One of the guys, built much like Jez although not as beautiful, had been completely hairless, shocking Hayden with a sudden surge of arousal. What if Jez was waxed bare? Hayden imagined sucking Jez's hairless balls into his mouth and groaned as he spurted into his fist.

Hayden held on to his softening cock as his heart rate returned to normal. He breathed deeply, letting postorgasm lassitude bleed through him, relaxing him in a way he hadn't been since Jez arrived. Next time he saw Jez—which might be in a few minutes—he'd have to be careful not to think about rubbing it out to a fantasy of a naked, panting, sweaty Jez. If he went the roommate route, he'd have to get one he wasn't attracted to.

A muffled, whimpery sort of bark made him sit up. Neither of his neighbors had dogs, and a bark had definitely woken him—he remembered now, because it hadn't blended in with the delectable sex sounds Dream Jez had been making. Hayden listened carefully, but he didn't hear anything else. Now that he was fully awake, his stomach chimed in with a loud growl. Holy shit, he was fucking starving. Grabbing his phone, he checked the display. No fucking wonder. Normally after a shift he napped for a couple of hours, then woke up and went about his day until going to sleep at a reasonable hour of the night like a normal person, but after shopping, he'd crashed hard and slept right through until morning.

The stickiness of cooling cum propelled him out of bed and into his en suite bathroom. He showered and dressed as quickly as he could with his stomach demanding food. Steak and eggs this morning, since he hadn't managed to wake up to make steak for dinner.

As soon as he opened the door, he was almost certain Jez wasn't around. Sure, his bedroom door was shut, but Hayden had spent too long alone in this house not to sense when another person was present. Strangely, though, despite Jez's absence, the house didn't feel as empty as it had for the past few years.

The creak as he put weight on the top stair was so familiar that the only reason Hayden even noticed it was that another muffled bark immediately followed. Had it come from behind him?

Hayden turned around and slowly walked along the hall, ears on high alert. One noisy floorboard, right outside Jez's door, drowned out what he thought might have been another bark. He hadn't seen a TV in Jez's belongings, but he'd also been at work all day Saturday. Jez could have gone somewhere and bought one, maybe left it on?

Something told Hayden he was grasping at straws. Generally the most obvious answer was the right one.

"Jez?" Hayden knocked. "Jez, are you in there?" But Hayden knew the answer. Except there was a noise. A scratching sound on the other side of the door, near his feet.

Fuck it. He'd apologize later. He opened the door.

A tiny brown dog leaped out, butt wiggling so hard it was almost curled into a circle. Big eyes stared pleadingly up at him, surrounded by all those sad little wrinkles and a squashed-in black nose. Hayden melted into a puddle right there in the hallway.

"Hello there." Hayden sat cross-legged on the floor, careful not to squish this apparent second, secret roommate, and found himself with a lapful of puppy. Pugs were small to begin with, but Hayden didn't think it was full-grown yet. A quick glance confirmed it was a boy puppy, and then he was completely occupied with not drowning in tiny puppy kisses.

"Aren't you a good boy?" Hayden hadn't forgotten about his own dog and the baby talk that went along with it when no one could hear you. He still missed Scout to this day and had entertained the idea of getting another dog after his gran had passed, but his hours made it impossible. It would require a boyfriend—or a roommate—who was home at more regular hours for that to happen.

How had he missed a dog carrier the day Jez moved in? He hadn't seen any boxes labeled as dog paraphernalia, and he'd been nosy enough to read every label. He had no idea why neither Jez nor Miguel had mentioned a dog. Although he was a little pissed about the secrecy of it all, he wasn't unhappy about the presence of a dog in his house.

Hayden loved on that tiny pug, losing track of time, until the pup calmed and settled in his lap.

Hayden took advantage of the lull to inspect the tag dangling from the collar.

"Fang?" Hayden let out a laugh and smoothed a finger over the New York phone number that he now knew belonged to Jez. "You, my friend, have an impossible task in front of you, trying to grow into that name. What was your daddy thinking?" He gently lifted Fang's lip and promptly got another kiss for his trouble. He wasn't sure Fang even owned teeth that would live up to that namesake—his personality was so sunny people would have to smile around him, like Hayden had done since he'd opened the door.

"Your daddy is a big mean daddy, isn't he, leaving you in his bedroom all the time." Maybe the little mite wasn't housebroken? Hayden sniffed, but the only thing he could smell was a faint remnant of Jez's enticing scent. No piss or shit at all. Fang had been barking, but it hadn't been because he needed to pee.

"How's your breakfast situation?" Hayden's stomach was not happy about delaying breakfast, but Jez wasn't here and this little baby had wanted something, either food or loving or both. And Hayden was more than happy to indulge him. He stood, carefully nestling Fang in the crook of his arm, and stepped into Jez's private space. Yet another thing he'd probably have to apologize for, if it weren't for the giant yet tiny secret in his arms. Hayden laughed again. His gran had devoured romance novels, and while Hayden hadn't ever read any of them, the secret baby had been a common theme. His gran would have been as amused as he was that Hayden now had evidence of his very own secret baby.

A white pad edged in blue lay on the floor near Fang's small doggie bed, presumably for accidents, but still pristine. Jez's floor and bed were covered with a disconcerting riot of clothes that had apparently exploded. They were draped over piles of boxes, some of which were open and mostly full. A suitcase lay on the dresser, spilling its contents like a clothing lava flow from Mount Disaster. Hayden grimaced. How could Jez stand it? More importantly, how was it even possible to create such a disaster in just a few days? He couldn't tell Jez to clean up his room, but he sure as hell wanted to.

He dropped a kiss on Fang's warm head and continued to poke around, searching for Fang's food and water. But he found nothing. Frowning, he opened the closet door, and Fang wriggled in his arms, eager to get down.

"There you go, boy." Fang dove face-first into a bowl filled with dry food. "Poor baby."

Surely Jez wouldn't have shut the closet door knowing Fang's food and water were inside? That didn't jibe at all with the sensitive boy he'd known, nor even with the prickly man he was learning about, although he still wasn't sure what to make of the secret baby. Then he noticed a wooden ruler lying on the floor inside the closet, tiny teeth marks marring it at either end. Jez must have used it to prop open the closet door, but hadn't realized Fang might mistake it for a chew toy. *Oh, silly baby*. He'd have to make sure Jez got Fang some proper doggie chews. Wood splinters weren't good for dogs. If Fang had gotten trapped inside the closet, well, he'd have been well-fed and watered, but Hayden would never have heard him, and that would have been a fucking shame.

He pushed the closet door wide open. Now that the secret was out, maybe he could convince Jez to put Fang's dishes in the kitchen, where spills would be easier to clean up.

With more light shining in the closet—also filled with a jumble of clothes hanging somewhat haphazardly—Hayden spotted a dog carrier on the shelf, back in a shadowed corner.

Nope. He definitely hadn't seen that on moving day. How the fuck had Jez managed to be so sneaky?

Hunger satiated for the moment, Fang turned and looked up at him, tongue out, wrinkly little jowls lifted in a puppy smile. Hayden's stomach chose that moment to inform him that something else required food. Now.

"Wanna keep me company while I make breakfast?"

Fang wiggled his butt in the affirmative and followed Hayden out of the room like he owned the place. Until they came to the stairs. Hayden made it halfway down before he heard a whimper and turned to see Fang pacing at the top of the stairs.

Hayden shook his head. He was so stupid. Not only was each riser almost as tall as Fang, he had to have been living in an apartment with Jez. It was possible he'd never had to use stairs before. If Hayden had been his owner, he'd have scooped the dog into his arms and carried him down the stairs to avoid any accidents in a common area.

Hayden was too hungry to try to teach Fang how to deal with stairs right now. He went back up, grabbed Fang, and carried him to the kitchen. Maybe after lunch he'd take him out back, see what Fang knew about fetching. The few steps from his patio down to the grass would be good for practicing going up and down stairs.

He'd need treats. Maybe a bit of cheese would do, since he didn't know where Jez kept doggie treats and didn't want to go rummaging in Jez's drawers to find them. Although he had to admit to being insatiably curious about what he could learn about Jez from going through his personal stuff, that was the domain of a total creeper.

Maybe he could even take Fang over to the local pet store and pick out a few things. He'd never been, but as he understood things, pets were welcome to go inside. Then again, maybe he could just putter around, get some laundry done, and relax in the yard, enjoying the company of a dog.

JEZ BLEW out a breath as he exited the Uber.

"Thanks, man."

The driver nodded and drove away.

Car shopping was going to be even more of a pain in the ass than he'd anticipated.

He'd gotten up early and done some yoga in the sunroom, trying to be as quiet as he could to avoid disturbing Hayden. Faint shadows under those mossy green eyes had attested to his exhaustion. Jez had eaten dinner by himself. Knowing Hayden was in the house was an unfamiliar sensation, but not unwelcome.

He was also sure Hayden had been giving him heated looks. Their trip to the grocery store had been laden with sexual tension and innuendo. If someone at a club had flirted with Jez like that, it might have led to orgasms. The past few weeks in New York had been so stressful, he'd wondered if he'd ever have an erection again. To have his libido stirred to life by a man who was so wrong for him troubled him. Not like Jayson had been wrong for him, because Hayden was a good guy. Jez's inability to find a suitable man spoke to some deep-seated flaw in Jez's character. It had to. Why was it the big, athletic, and bicurious or closeted men were the ones who rang his bell? However attractive, none of them would *stay* and be open. He'd have thought Jayson's bad apple would have killed the attraction to men like Hayden for an eternity.

He needed to find a damned librarian or a violinist to date.

Jez pushed his key in the lock and stumbled inside. He definitely wasn't going to be looking for a used-car salesman. They were the worst. Pushy as fuck and so full of bullshit their ears should have been sprouting potatoes. No, he didn't know anything about cars and should have done more research before heading out to the nearest used-car place, but he'd hoped to find someone who'd help him. Jez considered himself primarily a dancer and singer, an actor second, but after spending most of his adult life in the theater and around actors, he'd found it easy to spot someone being as phony as a three-dollar bill.

His time in the clubs had also taught him to identify the reek of desperation, and after hours of battling the bullshit trying to get a feel for a car that would suit him, he left feeling like he'd let someone pay him to indulge in a fetish he wasn't comfortable with: disillusioned and slightly dirty. Arriving in an Uber hadn't helped matters any. They probably thought he was as desperate as they were.

Without regard for the noisy floorboards, since Hayden should have left for work long ago, Jez ran up the stairs. Then he rocked to a stop at the top. His door was open.

"Fang?" Jez could barely get the word out. Surely he hadn't left his door open when he'd left this morning. He just couldn't have. "Fang?" But no puppy came to greet him with a waggly butt and corkscrew tail.

Just in case, Jez dove to the floor to check under the bed, but still no Fang.

Fear clawed at his throat. Where was his dog? Had Hayden found Fang?

He searched the entire house, even calling up into the attic and opening Hayden's bedroom door. But there was no sign of his dog.

Impending tears burned his eyes and stung his nose. How could he have been so stupid? Jez ran outside, back and front, calling for Fang, the bright sunny day an affront to his panic.

Had Hayden found Fang? Or had Fang escaped? He'd been wearing a collar with Jez's mobile number, but that didn't mean he hadn't ended up in the pound. Were there coyotes around here? He'd heard horror stories about small dogs and coyotes.

Sweaty and disheveled, he fell onto the couch, sniffling. With trembling fingers, he pulled up a list of nearby animal shelters on his phone, hoping with all his heart that one of them had Fang and that he wasn't hurt. If he didn't have any success there, he'd call Miguel, see if his brother could help him search.

The front door opened and he heard Hayden speak. "Who's a good boy? You look so handsome with that bandana." The door banged shut.

But it was the gruff little bark that sent Jez shooting to his feet and tearing into the front hall.

"Fang!" He fell to his knees and Fang greeted him as enthusiastically as ever, little puppy tongue swiping away the tears he just couldn't keep from falling. He sniffled into Fang's neck, dimly aware that yes, there was a new bandana over Fang's sweet little purple collar.

Then he took in a great shuddery breath and glared up at Hayden. "I thought he was gone. I came home and he was gone. I've… I've been looking everywhere." Jez couldn't bring himself to let Fang go and kept hugging him.

Hayden dropped to his knees in front of Jez. "I am so sorry, Jez. I should have told you I was taking him out. I left a note on the fridge, but you wouldn't have had any reason to look there. I should have made it more obvious. We just went and did a little shopping at the pet store." Hayden reached out and cupped Jez's face with a large hand before rubbing at his jaw with a callused thumb. They stayed like that long minutes until Jez's tears dried up and Jez put Fang on the floor. He immediately waddled his little puppy butt toward the kitchen like he had a blueprint of the house.

Jez hiccupped a little. Hayden groaned and got to his feet before helping Jez up. Kneeling on a hard floor wasn't ever comfortable, and Jez had only done it when he was drunk enough not to feel it. His knees got enough abuse dancing.

"You okay?" Hayden hadn't let go of Jez's arm, his grip warm and comforting. But this didn't make sense at all.

"I don't understand." Why would Hayden take Fang shopping? Judging by the bag he'd dropped by the door, the bandana wasn't the only new thing Fang had scored. Deep down, Jez had been so afraid that *Hayden* had taken Fang to an animal shelter.

"Why didn't you tell me about Fang? I don't understand *that* at all."

"You don't like dogs." Obviously. Why else would Jez keep it a secret?

"I love dogs."

Jez frowned, the movement pulling at his swollen eyelids, and he sniffed. Hayden frowned right back, but he didn't seem angry. Just as confused as Jez felt.

"C'mon. Get a glass of water in the kitchen. I'll meet you in there in a second."

Jez obeyed, glancing around for Fang, but it seemed he'd moved his little puppy butt elsewhere. The pounding anxiety had receded, leaving Jez drained. Some water was a good idea.

Hayden strode in as he finished filling the glass. "I don't have any tissues, so I just grabbed the toilet paper from the downstairs bathroom."

That was going to change if Jez had anything to say about it. With his allergies, he wasn't about to rely on toilet paper. But he took it gratefully and blew his nose.

"Why do you think I don't like dogs? I was devastated when my parents had to put down Scout. If it wasn't for the fact I spend twenty-four-hour shifts at work, I'd have a dog of my own right now."

Jez shook his head angrily. "No. I heard you talking to your friends about… Scout. You hated him. Said he was old and smelly and that you weren't going to miss him." The hero worship had abated somewhat after that incident, just a couple of years before Hayden left home. Jez had always wanted a dog, but his parents didn't believe in having pets, and not only had he been in awe of his older brother's best friend, he'd been insanely jealous of the dog Hayden had just for himself, since he had no siblings and never needed to share with them or wear hand-me-downs.

Hayden sucked in a breath like Jez had slapped him or something. "Fuck. I'd almost forgotten about that. That… did not reflect well on me at all. I was devastated. But I was also embarrassed about crying. About how sad I was. So I blustered and lied and said I didn't care to hide the pain. I wasn't sure the guys believed me, so I'm sort of surprised you did. But I guess you were really young then. I was sixteen, so you'd have been about ten or so?"

Jez nodded. He might have missed a subtle nuance like that in the innocence of his youth. It wasn't until a couple of years later, when he started realizing how much he deviated from his family's expectations and how hurtful people could be even when they didn't outright use insults or fists, that he started seeing the lies. Acting had given him an edge in reading nuances now, and the way Hayden was staring at him made him think thoughts that were far from innocent.

He took a tiny step closer, and Hayden didn't flinch or drop his gaze.

"I'm so sorry you felt you needed to hide Fang. I think he's adorable."

Jez quirked his mouth into a smile. "Yeah, I figured that out, even if I wondered for a moment if you'd been replaced by an alien." The bag of puppy spoils didn't lie.

Hayden shifted his feet, putting them closer together. "I guess Miguel thinks I hate dogs too, since he never mentioned Fang either."

Jez flushed slightly, skin already sensitive from crying burning a little hotter. "He doesn't know."

Hayden lifted an eyebrow. "You didn't tell your brother you got a dog? How long have you had Fang?"

"About four months. He's seven months old now, and he's on the smaller end of the spectrum, so he seems a little younger."

"Four months and you never told Miguel?"

Shit. Hayden wasn't going to let that go. He shrugged. "I don't know. Miguel and I don't talk all that often, and it's usually just a quick check-in, not like... a conversation. You know?"

Now Hayden stared at him like Jez was the alien pod person. Seriously, how did Hayden not realize Miguel might be the only family Jez acknowledged and who acknowledged him back, but they weren't close? Hell, Jez hadn't even seen Miguel in person since he left home at seventeen. Miguel probably hadn't changed much, but it had still been eight years. He wasn't sure either of them could pick the other out of a lineup at this point. Maybe Miguel didn't realize his refusal to discuss anything that could be considered too gay, like Jez's love life or his career, prevented them from being as close as Jez would like.

"I guess," Hayden said slowly. Then again, Hayden and Miguel were still close. Close enough for

Miguel to ask for a favor of such magnitude that only desperation drove Jez to ask Miguel for help. "Hopefully you guys can reconnect now that you'll be living in the same city."

Jez nodded, although he wasn't at all sure about it. Miguel hadn't been in a hurry to meet up with him. "So you're really okay with Fang being here?"

He'd been so damned afraid. Each mile closer to LA he'd fretted, planning how he was going to keep Fang hidden, and now one of his biggest worries had been destroyed with a few words.

"Of course. If he's housebroken, you don't have to leave him in your room. Even if he isn't housebroken, the kitchen might be a nicer spot to confine him."

Oh, he had Hayden's number now. Jez lowered his voice. "You just want a chance to spoil him."

Hayden grinned and shifted. "You figured out my secret plan. You could feed him in the kitchen too."

"Can I?" Somehow they ended up standing close enough that Hayden's body heat radiated against Jez like flames licking over his skin.

"Yes." Hayden's voice deepened, and he leaned in.

There was no mistaking that look, that move, and like he'd been waiting his whole life for it, Jez tilted his head in invitation—an invitation Hayden took without any further hesitation.

At first Hayden's lips were soft, placing exploratory nibbles along the seam of Jez's mouth. Then Hayden wrapped his arms around Jez's waist, and Jez sighed into the kiss, opening to Hayden's tongue, a choreography that flowed as naturally as anything Jez had ever experienced.

Jez slid his arms around Hayden's shoulders, pressing them together, and Hayden groaned into his mouth. An iron bar of need pressed against Jez's stomach, matching his own erection, and Hayden moved his hands from Jez's waist to his ass, gripping and kneading.

Hayden's tongue swept inside, and Jez met it as they devoured each other's mouths, the heat of the kiss rising fast and furious, hot enough to rival the sun.

Jez moaned and pushed himself closer, although he wasn't sure that was possible without being naked.

As though reading his mind, Hayden slipped one hand underneath Jez's shirt while the other continued to massage his ass in a rhythm so reminiscent of fucking that Jez couldn't help but move his hips in time, not quite ready to start dry humping but so close the distinction almost wasn't worth making.

Without breaking contact, Hayden moved his lips down Jez's chin to his neck, stubble rasping against his skin, sending goose bumps down his nape. Jez sucked in a few heaving breaths, but Hayden seemed determined that Jez forget how to breathe, and bit gently at the spot where neck met shoulder, one of Jez's favorite spots.

The breathy moan he let out told Hayden all he needed to know, and he attacked that same spot with a sensual precision that made Jez's head spin and his cock leak precum into his briefs.

It hadn't been this good in so damned long. Maybe hadn't been this good ever.

Something hit his leg, but Jez ignored it to focus on Hayden's hot mouth and sharp teeth, a tiny part of him hoping Hayden was leaving a mark.

Then something bounced off his leg again, accompanied by a sharp bark. Fang.

The noise pierced Hayden's sensual haze as well and, almost drugged, they pulled back and stared down at the little dog who wanted attention.

The lust, like champagne in his blood, faded enough for Jez to realize what he was doing and who he was doing it with. Oddly in sync again, they broke apart, unable to look each other in the eye and still sporting uncomfortable erections.

Just because Hayden had surprised him with his love of dogs didn't mean Jez should throw himself at him.

Hayden cleared his throat nervously. "Uh. Sorry about that. I was, uh, out of line."

Jez readjusted his pants instead of rolling his eyes. Like that had been all on Hayden. "Me too. That was, uh...." Awesome but too fast? They didn't know each other very well, and hookups were all well and good, but not when you lived with them. Besides, his experience with Jayson had made him a lot more wary of getting involved—even in just a quickie—until he got to know the man better. Friend of his brother's or not, he did not know Hayden all that well.

"God. Don't... don't tell your brother about that, okay?"

Just like that, the rest of his arousal faded. Hayden might love dogs, but that didn't erase the other reasons Jez shouldn't get involved with him, and Jez would do well to remember that.

"Don't worry. He's the last person I'd tell." Jez strove to keep the ice out of his tone, but judging by Hayden's grimace, he hadn't been successful.

"Does Fang need to go out or something?" Hayden still wouldn't meet his gaze, which was fine and fucking dandy. "I took him out in the yard a couple of hours ago and he peed then."

"He should be fine. Probably just wants to play." How weird. Fang might be the only way to maintain some semblance of normalcy between them. He almost said they should thank Fang for preventing them from making a bigger mistake than kissing, but he stopped himself. No one wanted to hear they were a mistake, however much they might agree, and if Hayden tried to say anything like that, Jez would be tempted to punch him in the mouth.

"I'm going to make lunch. Have you eaten?"

"Yeah, I got something while I was out with Fang. I didn't know when you'd be home."

Not like eating meals together was their thing. One time did not make a thing. But that reminded him. "What are you doing home, even? I thought you were at work."

Hayden turned to rummage in the fridge, pulling out a beer, while Jez started putting together a hummus sandwich. His fingers still trembled a bit, given the seesaw of emotional upheavals over the past hour. It would be a while before he settled down.

"Yeah, I traded off with one of the guys in C crew. His kid has a recital or something, so we swapped shifts. I'll be working Wednesday instead. I didn't bother marking up the calendar because we just arranged it a couple of days ago, but I'll try to be better about that."

Jez bit his lip against saying not to bother, that he wasn't going to be here long enough, but it was almost painful to keep repeating that, because he was strangely comfortable here. Probably that would all change once filming started and he got to know more people. Moved into West Hollywood. Mingled with his people. But for now, he didn't want to think about moving out, and it didn't seem like Hayden did either. And that better not be because he was hoping to get a convenient bed warmer and cocksucker, because that ship wasn't ever going to sail.

"Did you have an audition or something today?"

Jez wrinkled his nose. An audition? Why would he audition for anything when he had a job lined up, contract signed and sealed? Eh, there'd be other times to clue Hayden in on his work and career if Hayden demonstrated any real interest. "No, I was looking for a used car."

"Oh yeah? How did that go?"

He gripped the knife handle tighter. "Not so great. I felt a bit like chum in a pool full of sharks."

Hayden laughed. "Yeah, I can see that. When I bought my truck, I knew exactly what I wanted, what upgrades I'd be happy with and which ones I wasn't going to pay for no matter what. Even that was a bit of a struggle, getting them to listen to me. Without knowing what you wanted, they probably hoped to convince you to take the first shitbucket you came across, or the most expensive car on the lot."

"Or both, at different times." Jez twisted his lips. It had been annoying as fuck.

"Or both. Not surprising. Wish I had some advice to give you."

"Well, I did test-drive about half-a-dozen cars and came to the conclusion they couldn't pay me to drive them, so there's that. Process of elimination."

"Sure, sure. With that technique you'll have a car by January 2030 or thereabouts."

Jez laughed ruefully. "Truth." The dog and the car smoothed out some of the awkwardness between them, for which Jez was thankful. He didn't want to deal with any more conflict, from any source. "Watch a movie with me?" He couldn't face adult responsibilities more taxing than doing his laundry for the rest of the day.

"Sounds good."

Fortunately or unfortunately, Fang acted as a chaperone through three movies until they went to bed. Separately. Jez could own to a tiny bit of disappointment over that, even while conceding it was for the best. For both of them.

HAYDEN WAS so fucking happy to be home. As the weather got drier and windier, with hot Santa Ana winds blowing, work got tenser as the danger of fires, especially wildfires, increased.

Just being away from work wasn't the only reason he liked coming home these days. Jez had dropped into his life not long ago, but Hayden enjoyed coming home to a friendly face and a wiggly pup. He could even overlook, mostly, Jez's tendency to leave books and jackets lying around wherever he last finished with them.

Fang greeted him when he opened the door, curling into a C shape as he wagged his tail.

"Hey, boy. Your daddy home?"

Hayden couldn't remember if Jez was supposed to be at home today or not, but he couldn't hear the television.

"C'mon, Fang. We'll grab a quick snack, then head up to bed." Fang's treats now had a place in Hayden's cupboards.

In the kitchen, he stared down at the dirty dishes in the sink, gripping the counter tightly to keep from swearing.

Could he smell mold? Or was that just what tofu scramble remnants smelled like? It had to be too soon for mold to grow. Did tofu even get moldy?

With a shiver of disgust, he rinsed the dishes in hot water and loaded the dishwasher. He hesitated a few minutes, then started the dishwasher. Normally he was conscientious about not running the dishwasher until it was full so he didn't waste water, but that paled next to his worry that there might have been mold on those dishes.

Once the comforting whir of the dishwasher started up, Hayden cleaned the sink and was able to relax.

"What the fuck?" Jez roared into the kitchen, hair dripping, towel wrapped around lean hips.

Fucking hell. It wasn't easy to hold on to his anger in the face of Jez's water-streaked skin.

"You're home."

"Yeah. I was taking a shower; then the water got freezing. I didn't know what was going on down here."

"Dishes." Hayden gritted his teeth, holding back the rest of what he wanted to say. Hayden didn't want to scare Jez out of his house. Rocking the boat meant changes, and while Jez had been an unexpected addition to his life, the boat was on an even keel and he wanted it to stay that way.

"You could have left them. I was going to do them after my shower."

Left them. Hayden wanted to run upstairs and have a shower of his own. "No. Dirty dishes in the sink…. I can't relax or eat knowing they're there. I hate it."

"Hate?" Jez's eyebrows lifted. "That's a strong word."

"Please, please, either wash them or put them in the dishwasher as soon as you're done." See him ask nicely? He could do this roommate thing.

"Okay. I'll do better."

Hayden would just have to accept that at face value.

"Are you okay?" Jez stepped close and peered at him. The scent of Jez's soap wafted up to Hayden's nostrils, and he bit back a groan.

"Just tired. Nothing bad happened, but the shift seemed long."

Jez suddenly seemed to realize he was dripping on the kitchen floor, and his ears went red. "Oh shit. Sorry. Let me finish getting dressed and I'll wipe this up."

"Don't worry about it. I'll get it." Then he'd grab a quick sandwich before face-planting on his bed. Probably end up dreaming about Jez, but there were worse things to dream about.

JEZ SCRUBBED the sink until it shone. Hopefully that would appease Hayden. Not that he was even around to care. He'd left for his shift earlier this morning, while Jez had been doing yoga, but Jez hadn't forgotten his scolding yesterday. It had been a weird fucking moment. Within a few moments, Hayden displayed anger, lust, disgust, and exhaustion, like a whirlwind of emotion that ended up draining him. Jez thought Hayden was overreacting about the dishes, but

Jez liked living here and didn't want to piss Hayden off. Especially before he started working for real.

His first preproduction meeting was in three hours, and his stomach had been filled with mutant butterflies since he woke up. He wasn't at the point of discussing that sort of fear with Hayden, even if he'd had time before heading into work, and Jez had no friends he could call. His friends back in New York had sided with his ex, and Jez would never forgive them for that. But that left him terrifyingly bereft.

Cleaning until he had to leave was insane, but he couldn't concentrate on books or movies or yoga. He grabbed his phone and dialed the only other number in there that mattered.

"Hey, M. Want to grab lunch or a coffee?" Not that he'd be able to choke down food or coffee, but a cup of tea and company would be welcome.

"Hi, Jez. Uh. When would you want to do that?"

Jez gritted his teeth at Miguel's hesitant tone. It had been easier getting Miguel to talk to him when he'd been on the other side of the continent. "Today." He paused as he considered telling Miguel he wanted company because he was nervous about his first day.

"Oh. Today. Sorry. I can't."

"You can't? Surely you have to eat lunch."

"Yeah, yeah, but I'm meeting someone."

Jez barely kept in his snort. Either he had a woman coming over for "lunch" or he was still avoiding Jez. A bit too coincidental that Miguel was meeting someone, but Jez couldn't force him to go anywhere. Might be nice if plans with Jez didn't fall last in Miguel's priorities. "Right. Another time."

"Absolutely."

Jez disconnected the call, wishing they still had clunky phones like they did in old movies. Those looked damn satisfying to thunk down in a rage.

Guess he'd clean some more. At least Hayden would be happy with him.

Chapter 5

THE PAST two weeks had been better than Jez could have anticipated, aside from his inability to meet up with his brother. He had a few preproduction meetings and managed to not only leave them with more confidence that this job was perfect for him but also meet one of the set dressers and a makeup artist. They were friends and had asked him out for drinks. He hadn't sensed either of them angling for dates or sex either, which was a fucking relief. Paul and Tyson were good-looking, but they weren't his type, and right now he needed friends more than he needed sex.

He hadn't brought Paul or Tyson back to his place because he hadn't wanted to run the risk of Hayden becoming interested in either of them. Maybe that made him a shallow, selfish person, especially since he'd decided he and Hayden were a bad idea. That didn't change the fact that the air was thick with unresolved sexual tension, and Jez's cock, with the renewed vigor of a teenager, demanded satisfaction often enough he was almost chafed. Neither of them ever spoke about The Kiss, and most frequently, he imagined what would have happened if they hadn't been interrupted.

The Kiss might have created new tension, but Fang had broken some of the walls between Jez and Hayden. Some of them. Hayden grumbled under his breath about how messy things were and if Jez left the dishes in the sink too long. Jez had done his best to live like Hayden wanted, but he was getting desperate to Jackson Pollock up the stark white walls in a wild fit of coloristic expression. Decorating a temporary residence would be far too presumptuous. But Hayden didn't care about Fang's scattered toys and chews. Hell, Hayden provided half of his doggie booty, including yet another set of puppy steps so Fang could get up on Hayden's bed. They'd also started leaving their bedroom doors open all the way during the day and partially during the night to allow Fang options. The sexual tension might have grown exponentially, but they were nonetheless settling into a comfortable roommate situation. And if the open door gave Jez the occasional glimpse of naked torso while Hayden changed? Well, he deserved a bit of a reward, didn't he?

Fantasies aside, he'd been doing his best to start his life again. Tyson and Paul had given him enough advice that he'd been able to settle on a used Prius; shown him some of WeHo's hot spots, although the crowds still set off his anxiety; and were intent on helping him find a decent apartment. That was going somewhat slower, since part of him didn't want to leave. He was comfortable at Hayden's place. Fang adored Hayden and Hayden adored Fang right back. There was a yard. And that sunroom had become a perfect workout area and practice studio. He wasn't going to find an apartment that met even a quarter of the amenities he had at Hayden's, and it wouldn't have the perk of sometimes seeing Hayden after his workout in thin cotton clothes that got sweaty, translucent, and clung in the best way.

He hadn't told either of his new friends about The Kiss. Or the problems he'd had with Jayson. He wasn't ready to trust a friend any more than he was ready to trust a man. Hayden managed to squeak under his radar a bit because Jez had technically known him his entire life, yet even Hayden didn't get carte blanche in the trust department. Nor did Miguel.

When Jez had left this morning, Fang had been curled up on Hayden's bed. Yet another thing that didn't trigger Hayden's almost obsessive cleaning compulsion. Fang didn't shed much, but what little he did didn't bother Hayden at all. Fortunately Jez's allergies were confined to pollinating plants.

Hayden had gone to Vegas with some friends for his four days off, and he should be returning today. Jez had never been, but now that he was living just a few hours away, he'd have to check it out. It had been weird, saying goodbye to Hayden as he drove off. As far as Jez knew, Hayden hadn't gotten laid since he'd moved in almost three weeks ago, and selfishly, Jez wanted to keep it that way. The last thing he wanted to do was witness Hayden bringing someone home. But it wasn't any easier to imagine Hayden going away and getting laid in another state.

Jez met Paul and Tyson for brunch in Echo Park, wandered along Sunset Boulevard checking out some of the shops, then hit the grocery store on the way home. Hayden hadn't told him when he'd be home, but Jez had texted him anyway, asking if he should pick up any groceries for him. Hayden hadn't answered, and Jez tried not to obsess about why not. It was getting close to dinnertime, but for all he knew, Hayden was out of range of cell towers, or in a venue too loud to hear the chime of an incoming text. Hayden hadn't given him a more specific return time than "sometime on Sunday."

Finding parking on the street near Hayden's was more challenging than normal, even for a weekend. Someone must be having a party or something.

He slung the bag of groceries over his shoulder and headed up the walk. The atypical raucous laughter of several men indicated a party. Jez didn't know the neighbors well enough to get invited, even if Hayden had been. Still, Jez wanted to get caught up on *Dancing with the Stars*, one of several shows he'd taken to watching on the sly when Hayden was working. They had a number of shows and movies in common, but Jez hadn't bothered asking if Hayden liked any of the softer things Jez liked. Instinctually, he suspected Hayden would not consider them manly enough. A man who'd been an excellent football player in high school—not that Jez had any way to judge football skills—and was now a well-respected firefighter who owned his own home, should be proud, and yet, the opinion of others weighed heavily on Hayden.

Jez didn't understand it. He'd hidden so much of himself growing up that it had become unbearable. When he'd admitted his truth to his family, they'd been far from accepting, and rather than stifle himself any further, he'd left. Hayden... well, Hayden still confused him.

He opened the door and a wave of sound buffeted over him. Apparently Hayden was having the party. Jez pressed his lips together and slipped into the kitchen to put away his groceries, trying to ignore the sweat that slicked his palms and his breathing edging into hyperventilation territory.

Fang didn't come to greet him like usual, and after he was done, he went up to his room, hoping Hayden hadn't been careless with their—no, *his*—puppy with all those people over. But he wanted to cover his bases before he threw another uncalled-for emotional fit.

Okay, so maybe Jez wasn't completely heedless of other people's opinions.

Jez's bedroom door was closed, and he slipped inside to find Fang asleep on his bed. Fang was getting totally spoiled; Jez didn't think he'd seen Fang sleeping in the dog bed since The Kiss. Not that The Kiss had anything to do with Fang's actions, but it was, coincidentally, the same day Hayden had discovered that the cutest and least damaging skeleton hiding in Jez's closet was a fat pug puppy.

Good. At least Hayden had thought about Fang's well-being. That didn't stop a niggle of annoyance that Hayden hadn't mentioned this gathering to Jez. Not that Hayden needed his permission to have friends over, but it would have been nice to have a warning. It would have been even nicer to have gotten an invitation to join them, or a text letting him know Hayden was at home with people. Or even a reply to his text about the fucking groceries.

Jez paced a bit, trying to breathe slowly and calm down. He didn't enjoy being at the mercy of his emotions. They ended up embarrassing him more often than not. Hayden didn't owe him anything, and hell, Miguel might even be down there. Maybe Hayden thought it would be okay if Jez's brother was there?

More likely Hayden hadn't thought about him. After all, he'd been living on his own for years; hadn't roomed with anyone besides his grandmother, where he was more caretaker than roommate; and during one of their movie nights, Hayden had admitted to never having had a relationship. Hell, he'd never even brought a man home. At the time, Jez had sort of envied Hayden that lack of baggage. In practical terms, though, it meant that maybe Hayden wasn't aware of some simple courtesies.

This was the sort of minor transgression Jez could fix after the party broke up. Just a simple request that Hayden give him a heads-up, and that should be the end of it. Jez was a little more sensitive these days. His anxiety manifested as a severe dislike of crowds, and the size of the crowd didn't much matter if he came upon it unexpectedly. And a surprise group of people in the place he called home qualified as unexpected.

Meeting Hayden and Miguel's friends while angry and anxious wouldn't allow him to make a good impression. He took one of his antianxiety meds, hoping he'd be able to find a new therapist before they ran out.

He flopped back on the bed and waited. No way was he making an entrance into a room full of strangers until his meds had taken effect.

The sounds of laughter drifted up from the first floor, as irritating as a wool sweater against bare skin. He wished it didn't seem like Hayden and Miguel wanted to keep him away from their friends, not that either of them were under any obligation to include him. He focused on breathing and trying to flush out negative thoughts.

Finally the soothing lassitude of his meds took effect, the jangly tension bleeding out of his muscles. He could do this. He'd gone to New York not knowing anyone. For years he'd been the guy who'd never met a stranger. Then he'd started dating Jayson, and, well… thinking about Jayson was only going to ruin his current calm.

Jez swung himself off the bed and changed his clothes, freshened up a bit. Procrastinated. Checked his phone, although he didn't have any social media to use as a time waster. He'd deleted everything prior to leaving New York and wasn't ready to set up any new profiles.

He sucked in a deep breath, kissed his sleeping puppy, and slipped out of the room. Might as well get it over with.

JEZ STOOD unseen outside the doorway to the living room, hesitating. But he wasn't a coward by nature. If he were, he'd never have had the courage to see his dreams. He hated that a man who'd professed to love him made him second-guess himself.

Fuck it. More or less the motto of his life. And if he wasn't quite feeling his customary level of audacity, he'd fake it until he did.

He had his mouth open to form a greeting when he heard someone speak.

"So has he even got a job? God knows this place is full of people who think they can break into Hollywood. Call themselves actors, but really they only have the right to call themselves waiters or baristas."

Jez instantly hated that derogatory sneer. Didn't help that he was undoubtedly the person under discussion. What had Miguel or Hayden told them? Jez and Miguel might not talk about a lot of personal things, but Jez had told Miguel about every role he'd had, every professional success. If nothing else, to prove to his older brother that his faith in Jez hadn't been misplaced.

Maybe Jez's faith in Miguel had been too generous, though.

"I don't know. According to Miguel, he claims he's got a job. Had jobs. But I looked him up on IMDb. He's not on there."

Jez's stomach roiled unpleasantly. Hayden had looked him up, which could be from interest, but he hadn't asked Jez about his work.

"Did you ask him?" That guy sounded decent. Someone who echoed Jez's thoughts. If Hayden wanted to know about what work he'd done, why hadn't he asked? But he'd completely ignored Jez's professional life. Maybe Jez shouldn't have let him, but he could attribute that to not being his normal self.

"I don't know. I didn't want to embarrass him, especially if he was embellishing his résumé." Oh. Well, that was sort of nice, except the sentiment came packaged with a pretty solid assumption that Jez was lying.

"Hey, I'm just saying you're making a lot of assumptions based on almost no data." The decent guy again. This one he liked.

"So, you banged him yet?" Another new voice, accompanied by nervous grunts, the modern male equivalent of embarrassed titters. Titters. Jez ought to lay off the historical romances, but sue him. He liked a lot of different genres.

"What? No! Why would you ask that?" Hayden didn't have to sound quite so horrified.

"Whatever. Aren't all those actors fags? No offense, Hayden. You're not one of them prancing sissies. Although I still don't understand why you don't like women. Maybe you should try dating Vic's sister. She's hot. She might be able to change your mind."

Change his mind? Like being gay was a jacket that didn't match one's pants. Or maybe a tie that looked more appealing in the store than it did at home. Just shrug on some heterosexuality instead, and you're good to go! But shockingly, Hayden was out to his friends. Jez had met the species before, dude bros with straight-acting gay friends, and they faked being accepting—to a point. Unless they were faced with icky, scary things like two men kissing or hand-holding.

"For fuck's sake, Jordan. Are you even listening to yourself?"

"And fuck you, Jordan. My sister is no man's beard."

Jordan, asshole. Check. Another asshole named Vic. Check. One reasonable, logical guy, as yet unidentified. Check. Hayden, possible asshole, if these were his friends. Check. Was there anyone else?

"Fuck, Kevin, getting married made you into a pussy. Your wife take your balls and keep 'em in her purse after the vows?" The other asshole spoke up.

Kevin identified as definite ally.

"Well, Vic, getting married opened my eyes, that's for sure. And it's pretty easy to see why you've had two failed marriages, if that's how you talk to people."

A crash that sounded like an aluminum can hitting the wall didn't get a rise out of Hayden.

"For fuck's sake. We're not at work, no need for all that politically correct shit, am I right?"

"Can we just watch the game?" Miguel's voice was like a knife to the heart. Not only did Miguel not defend Jez, he didn't defend Hayden, who was in the same fucking room. Had Miguel even heard that garbage?

"Who the hell are you?"

Jez saw his life flash before his eyes; then he spun around and clutched his chest like a Victorian maiden seeing a naked man for the first time. "Jez." It would have been better if he hadn't squeaked out his name. So much for that fucking Xanax. Why hadn't he realized another dude bro had been lurking, sneaking about in the kitchen, tracking down the wily longneck brews?

The large man in front of him nodded. "I'm Marco."

Not even a hint of a smile cracked Marco's stern mien.

"Uh. Nice to meet you?"

"Hayden didn't know when you'd be home. After you." Marco gestured toward the living room, taking away Jez's choice about joining the group. Marco didn't return his halfhearted attempt at politeness.

Conversation stumbled to a halt at Jez's appearance. "Uh. Hi."

Hayden's face was blank, but Miguel didn't look pleased to see him. Jez wanted to stick his tongue out at Miguel. This was the first time he'd seen his brother since he moved.

"Look who I found in the hallway." Marco didn't need to make it sound like he'd discovered a Peeping Tom. Which, okay, Jez had been eavesdropping, but for the time being, he fucking lived here, and the den wasn't exactly in the cone of silence. "Guys, this is Jez."

Three unknown faces turned to him, and only one of the guys stood up and approached. Dollars to doughnuts, this was Kevin.

"Hi, Jez, I'm Kevin." Jez shook Kevin's outstretched hand. "I work with Hayden on the B crew in Pasadena, along with Jordan over there. Vic works with Miguel in an LA firehouse, and Marco behind you is a Pasadena cop."

Cop. Figured. That explained making him do a perp walk into the den. Jez assumed this was the same group that had gone to Vegas with Hayden, then come over here for more together time in front of the TV.

"Nice to meet you all." He gave Miguel a tight nod, but he wasn't particularly thrilled with his brother at the moment. Had he clung to that one family tie longer than he should have?

The thought of losing yet another piece of his life made his eyes burn, despite the Xanax, and he shelved that thought for later. He'd definitely get labeled a sissy or pussy or fag if he burst into tears in front of these men, and at the moment he was too brittle to deal with that.

He settled on an ottoman. "So there's a game on?" It didn't take a psychic or an eavesdropper to figure that one out, but Jez would bet his painfully depleted life savings that whatever game was on wasn't hockey.

Jordan scoffed and turned his attention to the TV.

"Not a baseball fan, I guess." Vic rolled his eyes and sounded as though he'd somehow known and deemed Jez less worthy for the lack.

"No. Not really. I prefer hockey." Although Jayson had managed to take that pleasure away. He hoped by next season he'd be able to put it all behind him, but he'd avoided all hockey news and games so far this season and didn't see any reason for that not to continue.

"Yeah?" Kevin seemed genuinely interested. "My brother-in-law works up in Toronto, and he's been trying to convince me to start watching. Maybe after the Super Bowl."

Football too. Now Jez wanted to roll his eyes, but Kevin seemed like a good guy. How he'd ended up in this isle of misfit troglodytes, Jez had no fucking idea.

No one had answered Jez's question about the game beyond telling him it was baseball, and he was hesitant to ask again.

Then Hayden spoke up. "This game will determine if the Dodgers are going to the World Series again this year."

"Oh. That's exciting." For some. But it told Jez all he needed to know. As a California native, he was well aware the Dodgers were the Los Angeles Dodgers, and he knew the World Series was for baseball what the Stanley Cup Playoffs were for hockey. He didn't know what the semifinals were called in baseball, but he was pretty sure they did best-of-seven series as well. It didn't much matter to him if this was game four or game seven or somewhere in between, because

LA had obviously won three games and hoped to take four wins to go to the finals.

"Guys. Can the chatter. Or save it for a break in play, for fuck's sake." Marco did not sound happy.

Jez didn't want to anger anyone, but as far as he could tell, the game was nothing *but* a break in play. He would sit and socialize for a bit, maybe try to analyze if watching baseball was as dreary as watching football or if it was somehow worse.

The beers kept coming, Jordan and Vic throwing out the occasional homophobic or racial slur when the play didn't go their way. Kevin wasn't happy with their behavior, but Jez couldn't expect him to be the sole decency police when the gay friend, the guy with the gay brother, and the actual fucking police acted as though they hadn't heard anything wrong. The odd throwaway "no offense, Hayden" accompanied by awkward glances in his direction didn't make any of it better. For fuck's sake, they lived in Los Angeles, not the ass end of nowhere. Surely he and Hayden weren't the only gay guys they'd come across. Marco rolled his eyes a couple of times and shot Jordan a glare or three, but it seemed he was more annoyed by the interruption than the comments themselves. Not that he roused himself to say a damn thing either way.

Jez tolerated—barely—the whole thing for a good thirty minutes or so, but it was all too overwhelming.

Jordan called yet another player from the opposing team a fag and gave his almost automatic "no offense, Hayden."

"What about me?" All eyes turned to him, and he resisted the urge to flee even as Miguel cringed. Asshole brother too. Jez was almost certain no one would try to hit him, especially with both his brother and a cop in the room, but he wouldn't want to bet his life on it. But he couldn't just not speak up. He'd already allowed far too much to pass.

"What do you mean? You one of those snowflake libtards? Don't like people who speak their minds?"

So many things in those appalling words, but he was going to continue from Jordan's previous offensive statement. "Just saying 'no offense' doesn't make it better, you know."

"Don't get your panties in a wad. Hayden doesn't care."

"Hayden is not the only gay man in this room. And I take offense."

"I knew you were gay. I told you all actors were fags." Jordan directed that last sentence to the rest of the room.

Jez pressed his lips together. He was in the minority here. Jordan—and Vic—didn't give a damn that they were pricks.

"It was great to meet you all." It fucking wasn't, but Jez could lie better than most. He could think of literally nothing else that he had to do that didn't sound about as convincing as having to wash his fucking hair. Then again, he didn't have to offer an excuse. He didn't want to stay, he didn't have to stay. "I'm going to head up." And he'd wait until they all left before he took Fang out for his nightly pee.

Vic rolled his eyes, Jordan ignored him, Kevin gave him a nod and a pained smile, and everyone else—including his own fucking brother—gave his announcement the bare minimum of attention.

As soon as he left the room, he heard Kevin speak. "Seriously, Jordan? Why are you such an asshole?"

"Those girly gays are always on their period."

Jez wanted to stride right back in there and get on his soapbox, but he was pretty sure karma would make sure neither of those guys found women, firefighters or no. He couldn't imagine any woman willing to deal with that level of misogyny. And that would have to be punishment enough, since apparently they weren't going to lose any friends over it. Except maybe Kevin.

HAYDEN SAT frozen, muscles knotted from stress, stomach roiling, nausea clawing at his throat. What the hell had just happened?

He'd known deep down that letting Jez meet his friends would be a mistake, but he'd never followed that thought through. He should have. He'd seen each poisonous barb with new eyes, seen the train wreck coming a mile away, but hadn't known what to do. He'd spent his entire career training so he could make split-second decisions in life-or-death situations, but he hadn't been able to stop the verbal bloodshed in front of him.

Hayden glanced over to Miguel. He appeared equally uncomfortable and wouldn't meet Hayden's eyes. Hayden had stopped believing in God when his parents had threatened him with conversion therapy all those years ago, unable to recognize the people who'd raised him and supposedly loved him. But he sent a plea out to the universe that Miguel felt as ashamed as Hayden did, and not because Miguel agreed with Jordan and Vic and maybe Marco's thoughts.

He could barely breathe, let alone speak, and he was even more appalled at the way Jordan and Vic fell back into the game, unconcerned that they'd hurt someone, intentionally or not. Hayden had spent so long letting their comments roll off his back, telling himself they didn't mean anything by it. But had they never cared if those barbs left wounds, however minor? Was he right now bleeding out from the death of a thousand cuts on his soul? If so, his parents had inflicted the first slice, and there was no way to get resolution from them now.

Hayden wanted to say something. Kick them out of his house, maybe. But each breath he took preparatory to speaking caught in his chest. Confronting people, getting angry, standing up for yourself. It all resulted in loss. He came out to his parents and lost his home, set adrift from the moorings of his upbringing. He'd lost his grandmother to a terrifying disease where she became more and more a stranger—an angry, volatile stranger—every day. Now he was faced with more loss. He'd spent so much of his life lonely, whether or not he was alone. And if he chose poorly, he'd be lonely for the rest of his life.

He'd never been paralyzed by indecision before, but he now had more sympathy for deer that froze in the face of an oncoming car.

With effort, he uncurled his clenched fists and stared blankly at the television. The only decision he could make right now was to wait until the end of the game, then send the lot of them home so he could think. More inertia than decisiveness, and when his brain unfroze, he wouldn't be proud of that.

He chanced a glance at Kevin, and he couldn't quite place the expression on his face. Pity, perhaps.

Pity. Hayden was indeed pitiful and pathetic, but if the universe hadn't given up on him, this fucking game wasn't going to go into overtime.

BACK IN the refuge of his room, Jez grabbed his laptop and curled up beside his puppy. If nothing else, meeting Hayden's throwback dude bros gave him the kick in the pants he needed. Two hours later, he'd snuck Fang out the front door for a pee and he had a dozen appointments over the upcoming week to look at apartments. Living with Hayden had been a bit of a dream. He'd felt safe here, despite his initial reservations, but that sense of haven was gone. Knowing he could return any time and find Jordan or Vic in the house, with no warning at all? Nope. Unacceptable. With any luck, he'd have a lease signed before filming started, and he could leave Hayden and The stupid Kiss in his rearview.

He was done. Hayden had a different kind of damage than Jayson, but being with Hayden would mean hiding himself in much the same way he'd had to with Jayson, and that wasn't going to happen. He'd fought so hard to become the man he wanted to be, and he needed to be true to that.

HAYDEN WASHED his hair again, stalling. He had to be at work in three hours, and if he'd slept more than three minutes all night, he'd be surprised. But his mind was no longer tangled with unexpected emotions and new perspectives. He couldn't stop thinking about that look on Jez's face. Betrayal, disappointment, and hurt. Until he'd had to sit through that excruciating half hour with Jez reacting to each and

every slur—gay or not—that came out of Vic's and
Jordan's mouths, he hadn't been aware of how much
he'd let slide. Miguel had never spoken up either, not
last night nor any night before—and he'd known all
along he had a gay brother. Hayden was only looking
out for himself, and if he didn't let it bother him, it
didn't hurt anyone. Not really. Or so he'd believed.

But it had hurt Jez. He wasn't sure what he could
say to make it up to Jez, who'd been up already to
take the dog out. The stairs in his house were better
than GPS.

Unfortunately, Hayden didn't deal with guilt
well. It had been the tool his parents had used to try
and get him to deny he was gay. It had been how his
parents had tried to get him to give up the inheritance
his gran had left him after his parents had more or
less disowned him. This time the guilt was of his own
making, not some external force, but that only made it
more uncomfortable.

Hayden sighed and rinsed off. No sense procras-
tinating further, and it was the height of hypocrisy to
take an extra-long shower after telling Jez they should
conserve water. As soon as he was ready for work,
he'd go down and apologize. That way he could make
a break for it if things got uncomfortable. He had no
idea what sort of mood he'd find Jez in.

He'd never dried himself off so thoroughly, or
brushed his teeth with such care, or chosen his clothing so attentively. Eventually, though, he could pro-
crastinate no longer. Not unless he wanted to sit on his
bed and stare at the wall for another couple of hours.

As he headed downstairs, the music from the
sunroom became more audible. A thumping bass beat

vibrated the air, and Hayden recognized the song—
vaguely—as something he'd heard on the radio. The
volume gave Hayden pause. He didn't think Jez had
ever exercised in the sunroom while he was awake
and home. So he either exercised with much quieter
music while Hayden was sleeping, or he just didn't
exercise while Hayden was home.

At the doorway of the sunroom, Hayden opened
his mouth to call out to Jez, but no words came out.
Jez was stretching. And he was so very flexible. He
knelt in the center of the room, back arched backward,
hands flat on the floor behind his feet. Hayden didn't
even know the human body could do that. A faint
sheen of sweat made Jez's skin glisten in the morning light. Hayden licked his lips and breathed heavily.
He glanced away and noticed Fang in a sunlit corner,
sleeping on his doggie bed.

He turned his attention back to the main feature in
the room. Watching when Jez wasn't aware felt wrong,
and yet Jez had never requested Hayden stay out of the
sunroom, and the door wasn't closed. A work of art
as beautiful as Jez should be cherished, and a sense
of admiration swept over Hayden like a tidal wave.
Part of it was simple appreciation of someone's skills.
But a bigger part was the suppressed desire to lick and
bite and savor Jez's body. He'd allowed himself a tiny
taste that one day, and it haunted his dreams. The seal
he'd used to bottle up his desire was cracked and useless, and that genie might never go back in the bottle.

While he'd been busy trying to ignore the lust, he
had fallen in like with Jez. The realization Jez might
not like him very much right now pained him. He enjoyed coming home to Jez—not just any old warm

body, but Jez. How much more fun it was to watch TV and movies with someone else—someone he could discuss plotlines and characters and issues with. Some of the guys at work were like that, but he liked being able to do so immediately rather than waiting until next shift.

Then Jez unfolded himself and started to dance. Not ballet, not ballroom, not anything Hayden could identify or label, but the moves were angry and beautiful, and in that moment Hayden knew that whether or not Jez had been lying about getting work, he wasn't lying about the ability to *get* work.

Hayden leaned against the doorway and just watched. Until Jez spun around midroutine and caught sight of him. Stiff, intractable angles replaced Jez's sinuous grace, reminding Hayden of his unpleasant task ahead. Jez strode over to the speakers attached to his phone and turned off the music. Expectant silence filled the room, and nervousness made Hayden scrub his palms against his pants.

Then Jez turned around, arms crossed, back straight, staring at him without any softness.

"Hey. I wanted to apologize for the guys last night. They were out of line."

Jez curled his lip. "They were out of line? That's all you have to say?"

Hayden grimaced. No, his apology wasn't adequate to make up for what happened. Hayden should have sent everyone home and talked to Jez last night, but he hadn't wanted anyone to know Jez had any influence on him. Instead, he'd pretended nothing was wrong, even though Miguel couldn't look him in the eye for the rest of the night and Kevin had been disappointed. Even though his mind had been a cesspool of painful memories. Marco had been his customary taciturn self, but with an air of expectation. Like he'd been waiting for a particular response from Hayden and it never came.

Hayden opened his mouth, but Jez held up a hand, palm out. "Even before we get to their behavior and how badly it reflects on you, let's first talk about common courtesy."

Hayden blinked. This was gearing up to be a royal ballbusting, but he wasn't sure it was fair to lump all of his sins into this discussion. "What are you talking about?"

"I realize I'm just crashing temporarily, and I appreciate you opening your home to me." That made Hayden suck in a breath. Sure, this was supposed to be temporary, but Hayden had avoided any thoughts about what it would be like after Jez—and Fang—left.

Jez wasn't finished, though. "However, did it not occur to you to warn me there would be a group of strangers in the house? Or what about inviting me to join in? Hell, even just responding to my text about groceries would have been nice."

Shit. This *was* a ballbusting he deserved. Because if he'd done that to his gran while she was still alive, and if she'd known how to text, she'd have been annoyed, upset, and disappointed. Maybe not about an invitation—she wouldn't have cared about joining in—but both he and Miguel were well aware Jez didn't know anyone in LA. Long-planned Vegas trip aside, this wasn't even the first time he'd met up with the guys since Jez moved in. Any one of those times, he could have invited Jez along and didn't. He wasn't embarrassed of Jez—not really—but somewhere in his subconscious, he'd seen this very outcome.

"You're right. I'm sorry. I will try to do better in the future."

Jez blinked at him, stunned. Did he expect Hayden couldn't take responsibility for his actions? Just because he was rarely in a position where he had to apologize to someone didn't mean he couldn't or wouldn't do it.

"Uh. Thank you. As for the rest of it...."

"I'm sure the guys will behave better next time. They know you're gay now."

Jez sputtered. Hayden had never seen anyone do that before, but it made it easy to tell he'd said exactly the wrong thing. He even sort of heard it as the words came out of his mouth. Not fucking this up had been his one job, and he was failing.

"It shouldn't matter if I'm gay or not. You're gay and that didn't change anything. Miguel was there, but that didn't stop the racist comments. I'm sure the presence of any women wouldn't have stopped the casual misogyny. We're talking common decency here, and yet it was like the trifecta of odious right here in this house. And you claim them as friends? Instead of chucking them out of here or even just saying something—*anything*—to let them know they were out of line? No, you let them drink beer and eat snacks and watch TV while both you and Miguel just sat there like bumps on a log. I mean, you do realize those two have no respect for you, right? I'm not sure you have any respect for yourself, and Miguel, well, he apparently has no respect for either of us." The venom in Jez's words struck Hayden like acid rain.

And he sort of understood where Jez was coming from, but these were his friends. Had been for years. Jordan had had his back at work, saved his butt a couple of times. Last night had ripped away the illusion that everything was okay, but didn't Jez realize they were talking about the only people in his life? He'd never been able to get any kind of closure or apology from his parents, as they'd died in a car crash shortly after his grandmother had died, not that he'd ever expected them to change their stance. But if he did anything drastic, he'd have nothing left, and he didn't know if he was strong enough to start over a second time.

"Of course they respect me. I do a great job, and we've been friends since I joined B crew." It sounded like bullshit, but it still came pouring out of his mouth. A part of him felt disloyal just questioning the status quo, but that part was drowning under the weight of his new awareness.

"They may respect the work you do, but they don't respect you—or any other gay man or woman or nonwhite for that matter—as a person. And if they don't respect you as a person, then they are *not* your friends, no matter what they tell you. I sat there for thirty interminable minutes, and I saw that clear as day. Kevin saw it. Why don't you?"

Hayden shrugged, guilt adding more lashes to Jez's words, making his skin feel too tight for his body. "It's just a few words. It's nothing. It doesn't bother me." He'd never allowed it to bother him.

"Doesn't it? I'm not even sure why you came out. You're practically in the closet anyway, as far as I can see. Tell me something. Have you seen those guys with women at all? Wives, girlfriends, even just dates or women they're trying to pick up."

"Sure."

"They maybe kiss or hug or touch them. Hold hands, maybe?"

Hayden nodded. "Yes. That's normal."

"Uh-huh. They ever seen you with a man like that?"

Hayden sucked in a breath. "No, of course not."

"No, of course not." Jez's tone was purely mocking. "Gee, I wonder why. And you told me you'd never had a boyfriend. Could it be that your 'friends' would be giant assholes about it? Could it be you know you'll never find someone willing to put up with that level of obnoxiousness, which will only get more vicious if you're in their face with the scary gayness?"

"I just haven't found the right guy yet." Certainly no one who attracted him like Jez, or whom he liked as much as Jez, but picturing them as a couple, holding hands or being affectionate with each other, while Jordan and Vic looked on? That picture just wouldn't come into focus. He didn't even know why he was arguing. He'd worried about this same thing, but vague worries that he never voiced weren't as real as Jez's sharp tone. He'd convinced himself there wasn't anyone out there for him. How much of that notion had been just another form of denial?

"I call bullshit. Can't you see you're the token 'see, I have a gay friend so I can't be a homophobe' gay? I hope you're happy with your right hand and your echoing, sterile house. I hope friendship with those prime examples of *dickus maximus* keeps you warm at night, because they will chase away any chance at a committed relationship. And fine, not everyone wants that. But I think you do, and even if those guys themselves don't chase away eligible men, your acceptance of their slurs, like you're deserving of them, will. Because if you think you're worthless, you must think the rest of us are too."

Tears were rolling down Jez's face as he finished those last words, and he angrily swiped them away. Seeing Jez's pain hurt Hayden more than anything. Maybe he'd avoided emotional men because he'd been somehow stunted by… years of accepting Jordan and Vic's words. Or maybe his parents had made him believe he wasn't worth any more than casual contempt. Had he truly been stifling himself so he rocked the boat as little as possible?

Pain sliced through his middle, almost making him double over. Those thousand cuts had been numb until Jez woke him up, and now he felt them in a single cumulative stroke that threatened to break him.

Shaking, Hayden stepped forward and pulled Jez close, hugging him. He wasn't sure Jez was going to allow it, but after a moment, Jez wrapped his arm around Hayden's waist and sniffled into his shoulder. The hug wasn't only for Jez, and if not for the admirably strong man in his arms, Hayden might have collapsed to the floor.

"Whatever I've put up with from the guys… please believe me, I don't think you're worthless. I don't think *I'm* worthless, but I'm willing to consider the fact that I need to take stock of what's going on in my life. Assess things." If, as he'd started to suspect, he'd been bleeding for years, he'd be healing the trauma for a long time.

Jez didn't respond, but neither did he let go. Hayden wasn't ready to stand on his own. He dropped a light kiss on Jez's head. "I am so sorry. I hadn't even realized." His voice broke and he drew in a shuddery breath.

Jez stiffened in his arms but didn't push away to speak. "You should be sorry that you've been subjected to it. You should be sorry Miguel never spoke up for you. Or me. Does he… does he ever talk like them?" Even muffled by Hayden's shirt, Jez's fear was obvious, allowing Hayden to gain a precarious hold on his emotions.

"No. God, no." Maybe Hayden wasn't so irredeemable, because he could see how painful it would be—for him and for Jez—if Miguel talked like Jordan and Vic. "He doesn't say anything, and I've never needed him or anyone to stick up for me in my life, so I never expected him to do so in this situation. It would have called more attention to my orientation."

"And?"

Hayden sighed. "And if that caused problems, then they weren't my friends in the first place." As terrifying as it was to contemplate.

Jez squeezed him tight. Hayden wasn't ready for any big moves yet, but his eyes were open now. He'd watch and assess, but not for long. And he wasn't going to have them over here again—even if his place was where they usually watched major sporting events—until he figured out where he stood with them, and where they stood with him. He might lose Jordan and Vic over this, but maybe it wouldn't be a loss so much as cutting out deadweight. He had to hope it got better.

For now, his only priority was making sure Jez didn't hate him. He rubbed Jez's back soothingly and waited until Jez relaxed in his arms.

"I never meant to hurt you," he whispered.

Jez tilted his head back, big brown eyes still shiny with unshed tears. Hayden's eyes burned in response. "I believe you," Jez whispered back.

Jez was warm from his workout, but he still smelled fantastic. Hayden didn't know who moved first, but he should have realized touching each other would spark their explosive chemistry. One moment they were staring into each other's eyes. The next they were kissing. This time there was no gentle lead-up. Just a frantic, hungry clash of lips and tongues and teeth. Hayden clutched at Jez, afraid that if he let go, Jez would change his mind. Hayden would stop immediately if Jez said anything, but oh God, he didn't want to. His dick had been primed for Jez the second he laid eyes on him, and it was already hard and aching, desperate for Jez's touch.

This time, though, Jez sought out skin as he burrowed his hands underneath Hayden's shirt, then flexed his hips, seeking friction for a cock that felt as rebar-hard as Hayden's.

Fuck. Hayden wanted to see Jez wild and untamed. Lusty and loud. He licked down the side of Jez's neck, savoring the salty sting of male sweat. Then he nibbled at the spot Jez seemed to favor. Jez let out a breathy moan, sending an electric shiver down Hayden's spine. God. If just kissing and a little bit of dry humping was this good, he was going to lose his fucking mind once they were both naked. The only real issue was that with their height difference, their cocks didn't line up well. But once he got Jez on his back, he'd be able to make things work.

Naked. As soon as he thought it, he started pulling at Jez's stretch cotton workout gear. "I want to see you," Hayden huffed into Jez's neck. "I want you naked."

The plain speaking made Jez shiver but didn't break the spell of their combined heat. Hayden wasn't sure there was any going back from this, but he didn't care. He was going to glory in the ride.

"You too." Jez tugged at his shirt.

He hadn't ever wanted someone this much in his life. Within seconds they were both shirtless, Jez's glorious chest pressed tight against his, and their hips rutted together. Hayden slid his hands up Jez's torso, giving Jez goose bumps as he went. Then he smoothed his palms inward, the light dusting of armpit hair tickling the edges of his index fingers while tiny flat nipples peaked under the pressure of his thumbs.

Jez explored him right back, hands smoothing over muscles and stroking along his belly. Then Jez dipped his fingers under Hayden's belt, signaling it was time to ditch the rest of the clothes.

Getting rid of Jez's stretchy yoga pants would take no time at all, and despite Hayden's desperation to see how closely Jez's cock resembled any of his fevered fantasies, he waited for Jez to work on his fly and belt. It gave Jez some difficulty, so he looked down, intending to take over, but Jez dropped to his knees with a wicked grin and cupped Hayden's balls through his pants, massaging them and kissing his hard cock through his clothes.

Fucking hell. This was ballbusting of the sort he wholeheartedly approved of. Almost before Hayden could register it, Jez unbuckled his belt, unzipped his fly, and sent his pants sliding down his hips to the floor, all with Jez grinning up at him. Once his cock was out, practically reaching for Jez, Jez dropped his gaze to focus on the cock. He kissed the tip, then slid his tongue all over the head. Hayden groaned and clenched his fists, waiting to see what else Jez had in store.

Jez licked up the underside of his cock, looking up at Hayden, Hayden's heavy cock lying on his beautiful face.

"Jez. More. Please."

Jez smiled, then wrapped his lips around the sensitive head of Hayden's cock, tongue dipping into the slit, teasing out drops of precum. Hayden slid his hands gently around Jez's head, coaxing ever so slightly. Jez allowed the pressure and started bobbing, each time taking a little more of Hayden's length into his mouth.

God. Men should be worshipping Jez's mouth. Hayden was ready to, but he also needed to return the favor. He pulled away and followed Jez to the floor, where he coaxed Jez to his back, then shucked off the yoga pants. Jez lay there, glowing in the sunlight that bathed the room, cock stiff against his belly.

Slender, uncut, just the right length, with…. He closed his eyes and moaned before he reached out and touched the suedelike skin of hairless balls. His fucking favorite. Jez wasn't completely bare, but he didn't have a lot of hair. It took a good deal of manscaping for Hayden to look similar, and he was too much of a coward to wax his balls, but he loved the sensation.

He gently jacked Jez's length while he nuzzled those soft balls, drinking in the sounds of Jez's pleasure. He slid the fingers of one hand below, massaging as he went, and Jez's legs drifted apart. When he hit Jez's hole, he rubbed more but didn't push inside. He wanted to. One day. But they had no supplies down here, and Hayden didn't want anything to jar them out of this wonderful, dreamlike moment. Besides, he'd been on edge for so many days, he wasn't sure he was going to last now that he had Jez in his arms. Judging from the precum slicking his hand and the hitched, breathy moans, Jez was getting close too.

No, he couldn't wait any longer. Hayden shifted, Jez moving with him so they lay on their sides, facing each other, cocks nestled perfectly. Hayden wrapped both of their lengths in his hand and jacked them. Jez moaned and Hayden stretched, just a bit, to capture Jez's lips.

They kissed with the same frenzy as before, a bit sloppier, gusting moans over each other's lips. Hayden moved his hand faster and ate at Jez's mouth, so close, so close. Then Jez yanked his head back and howled, pulsing cum over Hayden's hand and dick, the warmth and slickness shoving him into his own climax. He groaned and jerked, body stiff, as he spurted his pleasure over their bellies.

When they both slumped, breathing hard, Hayden kept his hand clasped over their softening dicks. He smiled at Jez and kissed him gently. Jez smiled back, eyes warm and showing no regrets. For which Hayden was grateful, because he wanted more of this.

Jez yelped and jerked, his eyes wide. "Holy fuck, cold nose in my back!"

Hayden lifted his head to see Fang's sweet, wrinkly face behind Jez. He laughed. "No joining in on this fun, Fang."

"Ugh. No." Jez shuddered. "I guess we should clean up." His gaze darted around the room and Hayden became all too aware of the cum cooling on his hand. When it happened—sexy as fuck. Now—kinda getting gross.

"Yeah, sorry. I didn't know this would happen." Jez's eyes became wary. "Don't get me wrong, I'm thrilled it did. This was not a mistake." Hayden didn't think he'd ever done anything so right. "But I didn't come down here planning to seduce you or anything. If I had, I might have also brought condoms and lube."

Jez chuckled. "Makes sense. Let's use my T-shirt, since I was just going to throw it in the laundry anyway."

They wiped up as best they could. On their way upstairs, both of them naked, Jez dumped his workout gear in the washing machine.

"Mind if I clean up in your bathroom?" Hayden wasn't ready for them to separate. He was afraid the minute he lost sight of Jez, their connection would disappear. "I don't think I need another shower, just some water and a washcloth."

"That's fine. So long as you don't mind if I shower."

"Uh. No. That's good." Or bad, considering how many times he'd dreamed about Jez in the shower. He didn't want to miss out on time together, but he did also have to go to work soon.

Jez started the shower and Hayden rummaged for a washcloth in the linen closet. Standing in front of the sink, he watched Jez in the mirror. God. He might never get tired of looking at that man. He took a deep breath. "Jez, I don't want that to be a one-off. I know yesterday was fucked-up. I'm going to do what I can to fix it, but I… I want to see where this goes."

Poised to step into the shower, Jez twisted about to stare at Hayden via the mirror. If anything, he looked startled. "You mean like… date?"

Hayden shrugged. "Sure. Date. More."

"More." Jez squinted at him. "Relationship?"

"I want to try, yes. I think." Hayden had done all the hooking up he'd ever need. But having Jez in his house, in his space, only illustrated how fucking lonely he'd been before. He'd wanted to share his life with someone. Someone who knew and accepted all of him. But he hadn't known how to go about finding that someone. Then, like a miracle, someone he was crazy about, despite the vegan diet and inability to clean up properly, dropped in his lap. Who was he to question the fates?

"I'm not saying no. I think… I think we could be good together." A wobble in Jez's voice spoke of fear.

Maybe Jez did have fears, ones that were more pronounced than worrying what would happen when friends who knew you were gay had to confront the reality of a boyfriend. Hayden had the impression Jez's last relationship had ended badly. While he wanted to reassure Jez, Hayden didn't know how to be a good boyfriend. Jez was going to have to keep him in line, guide him through it, and maybe that was too much to ask.

"I want to be good together."

Jez smiled and stepped into the shower but left the curtain partially open so they could still talk and look at each other. Hayden worked on cleaning himself up while Jez spoke.

"Here's the thing. Sexual attraction is not enough. We need to have more than that if we're going to have a relationship. That's why people date before they start living together. This is a bit backwards in our case, obviously. There are some things you need to know about me before we start this. We also need to talk more. It'll be tempting to skip that, since we're here with easy access to beds and showers."

"And floors," Hayden interjected.

Jez smiled. "True. But we can't let those temptations allow us to spend all of our time fucking and none of it talking."

Hayden wondered what made Jez so wise beyond his years. He was the novice when it came to swimming these waters. "That sounds acceptable. Necessary even."

Jez nodded as he stepped under the showerhead to wet his hair. When he stepped back into view, trickles of water sluicing down face and body, Hayden had to bite back a whimper. At least Jez hadn't said they couldn't have sex at all while they were getting to know each other.

"Stop it," Jez teased and waggled a finger at him. "I can see what you're thinking." The teasing air evaporated in the wake of Jez's return to seriousness. "We need to get to know each other. I swore to myself I wouldn't get involved again until I knew the person well. We've got a good foundation. But we need to talk before we even decide to do this, and I don't want to rush through before you have to go to work."

"I'll be home right after my shift tomorrow." Hayden didn't want to let this chance slip away. "Will that work for you?"

Jez smiled again, but with underlying tension. "Yes, I'll be here."

Hayden didn't think anything Jez told him would change his mind.

Jez bit his lip. "I think I know why you didn't want Miguel to know about uh... the kiss. And maybe we don't tell him about the sex either. Not yet."

"Yes. Good idea. I may not know much about being in a relationship, but I know having sex with your best friend's baby brother is maybe not the smartest. But if we can make this work, he'll be happy for us."

Jez didn't respond, just started soaping up.

Hayden wanted to kiss Jez goodbye but didn't think a face full of suds would be a good look for work. Instead he pressed a finger to Jez's lips, and Jez pursed his lips, just a bit.

"See you tomorrow."

Flying high on the confidence that tomorrow would see them on their way to a relationship, Hayden fairly bounced into work.

Chapter 6

THE TWIN pleasures of an orgasm and the potential of a boyfriend buoyed Hayden through the first few hours of his shift until he ended up in the kitchen alone, making a pot of coffee, and Jordan walked in with his cup, waiting for the brew to finish.

"You're in a good mood. The princess get over his hissy fit and put out?"

Shit. Now that Jez had opened his eyes, Hayden could hear it. The contempt. The sneering. Jez was right. The second Hayden stopped appearing like a sexless straight man, the knives would come out.

"What are you talking about?" Jordan had one chance to walk that statement back.

"What do you mean? That's the thing about average fags. So fucking emotional and gagging for the cock. Could have had him sucking all of us off, took his mind off that stupid PC crap."

Hayden tightened his grip around his coffee cup, trying to find the patience not to slam it into Jordan's grinning fucking face. Not only had Jordan not walked it back, he'd doubled down on his original statement.

"Jordan. My office, now."

Neither of them had heard the captain come into the kitchen, but Hayden never knocked karma. That was some powerful shit. Jordan scowled and slowly set his mug on the counter before turning and following the captain.

Jordan had been called on the carpet before for offensive language at work, about women that time, and the women on the crew were not impressed. He'd railed frequently about the politically correct gag order when they were at the bar, and Hayden hadn't ever paid attention. But basic decency didn't require a gag order, just one simple tenet: don't be an asshole. Somehow, Hayden had lived with Jordan the asshole and Vic, maybe even a bigger asshole, as he'd coasted along, not wanting to disrupt the status quo. But this status quo needed some serious fucking with. Hayden had been wrong for letting this go on. Every time Jordan or Vic opened their mouth in public, who had overheard those many unkind words and been hurt by them? While Hayden closed his ears, deliberately oblivious.

When the coffee finished, Hayden poured himself a cup and sat at the table, but he didn't drink. The whole reason he'd pushed the issue with his parents and gotten kicked out was because he hadn't wanted to stay in the mold they'd defined, and yet somehow he'd ended up forcing himself into another cramped mold instead of finding people who fit with the man he truly was.

"Hey. You okay?" Kevin walked tentatively into the kitchen. "Cap really laid into Jordan. Couldn't hear the specifics, but it wasn't good. Pretty sure he got suspended from work for today at least, maybe longer."

An evil grin tugged at Hayden's lips. "Good."

Kevin's eyes widened. "Shit. What did he say?" He grabbed a Coke out of the fridge and popped open the top.

"No need to repeat it. But I will say I'm done hanging out with him. And I had a hard time not slugging him."

An equally vicious grin appeared on Kevin's face. "It's about fucking time."

Hayden blinked at him. "Really?"

"Dude. I like you. But just because you, me, and Jordan joined the crew around the same time does not mean we need to be friends with him until the end of time. That guy is just fucking toxic."

"Then you're okay still hanging out with the gay guy?" He had to ask, even if he was afraid to hear the answer.

"Yes, I am." Kevin punched him lightly on the shoulder. The enormous relief almost made Hayden start giggling.

"I'm cutting off Miguel too, unless he stops inviting Vic."

"Oh thank fuck." Kevin sank into the chair across from Hayden. "He's maybe even worse than Jordan, but at least we don't have to work with him. What brought this on?"

Hayden shrugged. "Time to make some changes. Grow up." Maybe Jordan hadn't always been so bad. Maybe the changes had been incremental, getting worse and worse over time. Regardless, Jordan was now intolerable, and it was time to cut that cord.

Kevin smiled. "Yeah. Happens to the best of us. Maybe you and Jez could meet up with me and Maria sometime for dinner."

Hayden's cheeks heated. Guess the reasons he was taking a stand were obvious, but Kevin's assumption pleased him. He had a good feeling about it now that he'd made the first step.

Kevin drained half the can, then stood. "So, pretty much the whole crew knows you were at least peripherally involved in whatever happened. No one's upset or anything, but just giving you a heads-up." He sauntered out of the kitchen.

Hayden's coffee was still hot, so he drank it slowly, preparing for the gossip gauntlet. He'd stall longer, but now he needed to take a leak, so he might as well get it over with.

He washed out his mug, put it on the dish rack, then walked out into the common room.

Usually when someone got suspended for a conduct issue, it put everyone on edge, not just because of being a crew member short. It upset the balance. Firefighting was dangerous, and everyone needed to rely on their fellow firefighters. This time, though? It was like a black cloud had lifted. A black cloud no one had realized was hanging overhead. The laughter was brighter, the smiles were bigger, and while no one gave him the thumbs-up or anything, he felt more welcome. Not that he'd ever felt unwelcome, but more like… his own personal mold was fitting in just fine without conforming to anyone's standards of what a gay man—a gay firefighter—should be.

Shit. Jordan *was* fucking toxic. Jordan might be a dangerous element if he couldn't control his mouth around the station when he got back.

After Hayden took a leak, the captain waved him into his office. Shit.

"Have a seat, Hurst."

The captain waited until Hayden's butt hit the chair—barely. "You may have figured out I suspended Jordan. Three shifts."

Three shifts? That was some serious shit. "Yes, sir."

The captain sighed, scrubbed a hand through his steel gray hair. "This is all in confidence, you understand?"

Hayden nodded. "Of course."

"I've warned Jordan before. And what I heard him say to you was unacceptable. You may have thought he was joking, because I understand you're friends?" The captain sounded incredulous. Hayden was apparently an oblivious idiot. "But I don't think he was. I... I'm concerned for you. Abusive relationships aren't always just with domestic partners or family members, you know."

Hayden closed his eyes. Had he been in an abusive friendship? "Yes, sir, I've recently... figured that out. I mean, that he's not my friend. Not really. I hadn't considered it was potentially abusive."

But he saw the results of domestic abuse all the time. When people called 911, more than just cops showed up, especially if someone was hurt. They'd had seminars, professional development courses, for fuck's sake, for recognizing symptoms of emotional and physical abuse. And yet it had taken one beautiful man and his dog to come crashing into Hayden's life, lifting the blinders he'd worn since he'd come out to his parents.

"Well, that's a step in the right direction. But you may want to consider some additional help. It's not a sign of weakness, you know." The captain handed him a card. Hayden tucked it in a pocket without looking at it. It was either a therapist's card or a number for their insurance, where he could get a referral to one.

"Yes, sir. I'll seriously consider it." His world had undergone some upheaval, and getting a profession-al opinion might set him on more stable ground. He couldn't make Jez do that for him.

"Good. And don't forget, you can submit a com-plaint against him through your union rep."

"Oh. Do you think I should?" Hayden didn't know if he was ready for that.

The captain held up his hands. "Think about it. Discuss it with your rep. That's the best advice I can give, but—and remember this is still confiden-tial—I'm hoping a shift change will improve the situa-tion. When Jordan returns, he'll be on C crew instead."

Hayden shouldn't feel so relieved, but he did. "Thank you, sir."

WHEN HAYDEN got home on Tuesday after his shift, it was too bright and sunny to discuss any heavy topics, and Jez wasn't ready to bring them both down. Hayden took his cues from Jez, and they confined their conversation to small talk. A couple of times Jez opened his mouth to tell Hayden about the appalling apartments, but just as quickly, he bit back the words.

It wasn't like it was a secret, but neither did he want to hear Hayden say anything encouraging about him moving out. He wanted to enjoy his time with Hayden for now, because he wasn't sure this was wise and he wasn't sure Hayden would even want to continue, despite what he'd said.

Instead, they played with Fang out in the yard, and Hayden took a nap. Then they cooked dinner together—although Hayden also broiled a chicken breast to go with the rest of the vegan offerings—and watched a movie while they ate.

It was comfortable and sweet. Idyllic. Little touches, as though Hayden couldn't help himself. Kisses between the stove and fridge. Kisses while Fang chased after a ball and outright didn't fucking bother bringing it back. Everything a new relationship should be, with that coil of awe and desire and hope unfurling in his belly. Jez didn't want to lose it, but neither did he want to get in too deep, because the longer he pretended with Hayden, the more heartbreaking it would be when it all got ripped away.

As soon as the credits rolled on the movie—most of which Jez hadn't even registered due to impending dread—he flipped it over to Pandora and loaded up one of his more soothing playlists. They were stretched out on the couch, Hayden behind him, Fang draped over their feet. Jez shifted as though to sit up, but Hayden kept a firm grip around his waist.

"This is good." Hayden kissed his ear. "Let's at least be comfortable."

At least Hayden hadn't promised that everything would be okay.

Jez let himself rest against Hayden's strong, warm chest. Where to begin? How much detail was truly necessary?

"I had a boyfriend in New York."

Hayden grunted in annoyance, and Jez snickered at the mild expression of casual jealousy.

"I had a few over the years. But it was the last one, Jayson, that I'm talking about. He was big and athletic. I sort of have a type, I guess. Anyway, he was also closeted, at least at work. He was a professional hockey player."

"The one who was with the NHL?"

"Yes. He wasn't on one of the top-tier teams. He played for one of the feeder teams."

"There aren't any of those in New York, are there? Aren't they in Connecticut?"

"How do you even know that? I thought you didn't pay attention to hockey."

Jez felt Hayden shrug behind her. "It's not like I plug my ears whenever it's mentioned. LA does have a hockey team, after all. And I did a little internet research after you said you liked it."

"He lived in Hartford, but his parents had an apartment in Manhattan that Jayson used more than they did. We only saw each other when he was in the city."

"Did you start watching hockey because of him?"

That would have sucked. "No, I got into it in college, even though most of my friends weren't into sports. Probably because I do like the big athletic types. Anyway, I think because I liked hockey, I gave Jayson the benefit of the doubt when I shouldn't have."

"And he wasn't out? Don't they have that program to stop bullying in sports or to help gay players?"

"Yeah, that's what I thought too, but despite the program, I still haven't heard of any out players. Jayson wasn't planning to be the first. Anyway, we started dating and Jayson got serious fast. Too fast."

Hayden's whole body tensed. "Am I going too fast? I really will need you to tell me if I'm doing something wrong."

Jez patted Hayden's hand and linked their fingers together. "This is one of those weird things about relationships. Each one has its own speed. We're doing what's right for us, and if it doesn't feel right, I'll say something. When Jayson started doing all these grand gestures, it wasn't right. I think it might have been because he had feelings for me that I didn't return. Or at least, that I didn't feel as strongly. Everything he did started to smother me. Many of the things he did were things that, on the surface, seemed romantic. Lots of gifts, imported chocolate and wine. Nothing crazy like jewelry, but it was always something. Starting fights because he was jealous. Breaking into my apartment to set up a catered dinner. Breaking into my apartment to spread himself naked on my bed as a birthday gift. He paid my rent one month for no apparent reason. Reams of poetry. Watching me as I slept. It was too much when I knew I didn't love the guy and wasn't sure I ever would. But when he posted some weird shit to my Facebook profile, using my laptop while I was asleep, well, that was it. I broke up with him."

Hayden squeezed his hand. "Sounds reasonable."

"Yeah, you'd think. My friends thought I was nuts, breaking up with a guy because he did too many nice things for me. But it felt controlling, you know? Like he wanted me to be beholden to him or enthralled by him. Anyway, the gifts got bigger. More candy. Bigger stuffed animals. Fruit baskets. Flowers. He sent them to my home, my work. I blocked his number. I blocked him on social media. Then he got a new number. More calls. Calling my work. Showing up at my work. Then it got weird. Things like, I'd order dinner to be delivered, then find out someone else had paid for it. There were no threats, but I felt threatened."

"Is that why you came to LA?"

"Long story short, yes. First, though, I tried to get a restraining order. I got pretty much laughed at. They thought I was overreacting to a lovers' tiff. Told me to stop wasting people's time. I think if I'd been a girl with an ex-boyfriend, they might have taken things more seriously, but as a gay man? They thought I was being silly."

Hayden stiffened behind him. "That's terrible. Did you sue or something?"

"No. But after that, it all stopped. Jayson disappeared from my life. I heard through the grapevine that he'd been called up to one of the New York teams, and I assumed that with his career progressing, he had enough other things to focus on. A couple of months later, things had settled back to normal. I had Fang to keep me company because I wasn't ready to even date again. Then I got a phone call. It was an unknown number. I'd assumed it was Jayson again and was going to ignore it, but then I realized it had a California area code, so I answered. Instead it was a casting director from LA. Said he'd emailed a couple of times and left a voicemail about a job—my old mentor had recommended me—but hadn't heard back and he needed to make a decision."

"Oh. So...."

Jez laughed, Hayden's surprise providing a much-needed break in the tension. "Yes, I really have a job. I'll get to that in a minute."

"Right. Okay, so a job offer in LA."

"This was the first I'd heard of it. I hadn't seen any emails or gotten any voicemails, and told him so. We confirmed my email address, which he'd had correct, and chalked it up the vagaries of the interwebs. The casting director gave me the rundown, and the job was pretty much tailor-made for me, but I loved what I was doing in New York. So I told him I'd need a day or two to think about it."

How had this been his life? One pure moment of chance. They lay there in silence for a few minutes. He'd left out a few details, and a few to come he wasn't going to bother with either, but the bare bones were painful enough.

"I know you took the job, but something happened, didn't it?" Hayden pulled him closer. Surprisingly, Jez was able to take comfort in the warmth of Hayden's big body when he'd sort of expected to have a negative reaction to men built like Jayson for the rest of his life.

"I went home. Opened my laptop. Started digging in my email. I didn't rely on my email for much. I skimmed it every day, but texting and social media, those were my lifeblood, even though I'd been using social media less and less. I guess I was worried about Jayson following me around. Anyway, I couldn't find any of those emails. As I was sitting there, email site open, a new email flashed in with the subject "Need an answer by end of day tomorrow" from Chris, the casting director. I was sort of congratulating the powers that be for finally getting it right when the email disappeared."

"What?"

"Yup. Like, while I was watching. I didn't even get a chance to see what the message inside said. So I decided to check my call logs. I had other calls from that California number, but no voicemails. And it occurred to me—everything that Jayson had done on social media, paying for my deliveries, deleting my voicemails, deleting my emails.... While we were seeing each other, he must have watched me, gotten my passwords for everything." His heart started pounding again like it had done that day, just from the memory of Jayson still controlling him in a super invasive and creepy way. He'd been terrified, sitting there in his apartment, wondering how much access to his life Jayson had.

"Holy shit. That's insane. Sounds like he was trying to gaslight you. Surely the cops could have done something."

"I don't know. Can they do anything if you voluntarily shared passwords? I didn't, but I bet Jayson would say I did. After all, he convinced all my friends that I was the crazy one for breaking up with him. Anyway, I freaked out. I spent the next several hours getting a new email address, then changed passwords and associated email addresses on everything, and I mean everything else. I left the old email alone in the hopes he wouldn't realize what I was doing. Changed my phone number, then called Chris back and accepted the job."

Hayden kissed his neck, making Jez shiver, but it wasn't meant to be a "distract him with sex" sort of kiss. Jayson had tried that many times too, and Jez would have called Hayden on it.

"I sat there in my tiny apartment, sirens blaring as emergency vehicles passed by, Fang in my arms, and I started wondering. If Jayson tried to log into anything besides my email and found out he couldn't? And I remembered reading somewhere that people could be tracked via their social media. I thought I'd locked down all the privacy settings when I changed the passwords, but what if I missed something? I was pretty sure moving to the other side of the country would snap Jayson out of it, but I still had three weeks before Chris needed me in LA. That was a lot of time for Jayson to freak out. I sort of panicked. Over the weekend, I packed up whatever I thought I could move into the van myself, used my neighbor's phone to give crazy short notice at work, citing a family emergency, deleted my social media accounts entirely, then started driving."

"And where did Miguel come into this?"

"Ha. I called him from the road. I hadn't thought out my endgame, and it wasn't until I hit Pennsylvania that I realized I might need some help."

Hayden shifted them so Jez was facing him, sort of half underneath him. Hayden might be a shit interior decorator, but his awesome couch made up for much of his lack. "I am so sorry you went through that, Jez. That's awful. Puts my issues with Jordan into perspective. But that doesn't change how I feel about you. Or trying to make things work with you."

The chapter of his life with Jayson was over. Finally. And he wanted to forget about it as best he could. "No? How about when I tell you I'm in therapy? I have anxiety issues now because of this, and I have problems with crowds. It started out when I was trying to break up with Jayson. I'd go outside and feel like I was being watched."

"Maybe you were being watched." Hayden frowned. "That guy sounds unhinged."

"Obviously. And he wasn't even a goalie." Jez laughed at the complete lack of comprehension on Hayden's face. "I have to admit, knowing that I wasn't imagining things... doesn't make it any better. And now that I have it, I might have to live with it forever. I have meds, but I'll need to find a local therapist soon."

Hayden huffed out a rueful laugh. "Maybe we can go to the same one."

Jez wrinkled his nose in confusion. "What?"

Hayden laid out all that had happened with Jordan at the station, and the part about his boss's support made Jez want to sing. Shit, he'd been worried about Hayden too—he was just glad Hayden had come to the realization that therapy might help on his own. But dancing around for joy might be a little too cheery, considering Hayden had just lost two men he'd considered friends, no matter how horrifically unfriend-like they'd been.

"Going to the same therapist will be very... uh... couple-y," Jez offered instead of pumping his fist. "Might be... well, not fun. But comforting. When are you going to tell Miguel about Vic?"

"Dunno. Next time I see him, I guess."

"Maybe we ought to have him over here. Because there are a couple of things I'd like to straighten out with him, and I think he's been avoiding me."

Hayden frowned. "Funny, I think you might be right. He's been avoiding me too."

"Didn't he go to Vegas with you?"

"Nah. He had that camping trip. He just met us here at the house after we got back to watch the game."

"So, about that night."

Hayden lifted an eyebrow. "Is this not where we start making out? Maybe have sex on the couch? I haven't had sex on this couch, but I think I'd like to."

Jez laughed. Hayden had only been joking, but the thought of sex on the couch sent a surge of arousal blasting through him. An idea to explore later. "Soon. I promise. Miguel told you I was an actor, didn't he?"

Hayden rolled his eyes. "Yup. Talking about your brother. That means no making out. Yes, he told me you were an actor. But have…." He stopped talking abruptly, probably because there was no good way to frame the question of "have you actually *done* anything?"

Jez just pretended he hadn't started to ask. "I'm not an actor. Or at least, not just an actor. I'm primarily a dancer and singer. The roles I get involve acting, true, but I went to college for dance. Modern dance mostly, but I can hold my own in most other disciplines. If you tried to look me up in, oh, say, the Internet Movie Database, you wouldn't find me. I haven't done television or movies. But if you'd checked out the Internet Broadway Database, well, I'm definitely in that. I've been lucky. I've only ever worked on major productions—one of my teachers had a lot of connections and really liked me, so I didn't have to do all the off-off-off-Broadway shows that a lot of dancers need to do to break in."

Hayden started fidgeting, and Jez laughed. "Go on, check your phone. I can see you're dying to."

Before Jez finished speaking, Hayden had whipped his phone out of his back pocket. "Holy shit," he exclaimed a couple of minutes later. "I had no fucking clue. This is amazing. I mean, I've never heard of most of these shows, but wow."

The sincerity in Hayden's voice meant so much to Jez, who'd never had anyone to share the joy of his successes with. Even most of his so-called friends— the ones who hadn't believed him about Jayson—were also his competition for roles, so their congratulations always had an undertone of "why him?".

"Why didn't you tell Miguel about all this?"

Jez grimaced. "I did. I mean, I never told him personal stuff because he didn't seem to care, but I told him about all of my roles. I don't know if he just wasn't listening or if he was embarrassed by his gay brother the dancer. Acting might have sounded more... manly?"

"That's not right. I mean, I made some assumptions I shouldn't have, because I was working with bad data, but Miguel had all the right data. I don't know why he didn't tell me the truth. I'll make sure he comes over the next time we're off on the same night. Hit him with both barrels, see where the shrapnel lands."

A bit of a gory metaphor, but Jez could understand it. This crap with Miguel was an unnecessary waste of time and energy, but he needed to know what his brother was thinking. If it was as bad as he feared, then like Hayden, he'd officially have no family left.

"What show are you working on in LA, then?"

"Funny you should ask that, because this will end up being my first credit on the Internet Movie Database."

Hayden's eyes lit up.

"Don't get so excited. It's not a movie. It's about a fictional reality show that's sort of a cross between *Glee* and *Dancing with the Stars*. The drama of the show is about what goes on behind the scenes as they're creating this reality show. I'm playing one of the choreographers, and I'm also going to be developing some of the choreography for the show. It's the sort of thing I wanted to do eventually, and I can still take theater roles here too, during the show's hiatus."

"Congratulations. That sounds great. I mean, I only saw a little bit of your dancing yesterday, but I was mesmerized."

"Oh yeah? Seduced you right up, did I?"

Hayden's voice lowered. "From the very first minute."

Yeah, that's when Jez had been snared too, even if he hadn't wanted to admit it.

Hayden kissed him gently, then started nibbling at his jaw and neck, sending Jez spiraling into arousal so fast he was almost dizzy with it.

"Wait."

Hayden reared back, eyes wide. "What's wrong?"

Jez cupped his face, rubbing his thumbs over perfect lips. "Got supplies down here? If we're going to christen your couch, we ought to do it right."

"Oh, uh. No."

Jez reached down and smacked Hayden's ass, the sound satisfyingly loud even with the low background music. "Then I guess you'd better go get some."

Hayden shoved himself off the couch, erection tenting the front of his pants, and Jez dropped a hand to his own hard cock, massaging it through his jeans. "Better get a move on or I'll start without you."

Hayden's mock glare only made Jez rub harder and stick out his tongue, taunting Hayden. But that got Hayden running. Great sex with a splash of fun, and a man who seemed to fit like the other half of him. It didn't get any better than that.

Chapter 7

A WEEK later, and after much phone tag, Hayden finally nailed Miguel down, insisting he come over for dinner. It was the night before Halloween, but the pending dinner discussion might be scarier than any horror movie.

He and Jez had fallen into a rhythm, and it was good. They'd gone on a couple of dates—simple dinner and a movie, nothing fancy. Hayden had been nervous at first. Anyone seeing them together would assume they were both gay, and he hadn't known how he'd handle it. People had stared, but for the most part, they'd been admiring Jez. The occasional disapproving look hadn't bothered Hayden nearly as much as he'd expected. Eventually it had become easy to concentrate on the two of them.

When they weren't on dates, they spent their time taking Fang on walks or doing household tasks or fucking. After that cathartic session on the couch, Jez had more or less moved into Hayden's bed. Hayden had never shared a bed for actual sleeping before, but it was good. Great, even. He slept better and deeper than he had in a long while, and he discovered a previously unknown love of morning sex. Having never woken up with anyone, he hadn't realized how enjoyable the sleepy, lazy buildup to orgasms could be.

They cooked together, melding their meals so they had common elements, even if Hayden's had meat and cheese and Jez's had neither. By now, the domesticity didn't frighten him, and he was coming to care for Jez more and more each day. Sometimes that scared him. Could he trust feelings that came on so fast? He had to, because losing Jez would break him.

Tonight Hayden had told Jez they could do a meat-free meal, as long as there wasn't any tofu—that was Hayden's line in the sand—and Jez had put a meat-free chili in the Crock-Pot a few hours ago. Maybe Hayden would be able to test out more of Jez's food, but as far as he was concerned, things that needed a taste "developed" for them weren't worth eating. Maybe for their anniversary, assuming Hayden wasn't jumping the gun, he'd figure out how to cook something vegan that they both loved. He had lots of time to research it.

Hayden was putting the finishing touches on the apple pie for dessert. It would be just for him and Miguel, since the crust was bursting with butter, but Jez assured him he'd be fine with some coconut milk ice cream. Hayden would have to research vegan desserts as well. That might take a *lot* more time than just a vegan meal. A proper dessert without dairy or eggs seemed impossible, but Jez assured him it wasn't. Hell, even standard marshmallows and Jell-O weren't vegan, and that had shocked the shit out of Hayden.

Hayden heard the pipes clank, signaling the end of Jez's shower. They'd chosen to shower separately, because Hayden couldn't be trusted to keep his hands to himself and they didn't want Miguel to arrive in the midst of some good clean—but dirty—sudsy fun.

One last tweak of the crust and Hayden slipped the pie into the oven, then opened a bottle of wine. No reason they couldn't get started on that. A little pregame courage. He poured a bit into two glasses and took a sip before Jez padded barefoot into the kitchen.

He was wearing the exact same outfit he'd worn the day he'd moved in, with the unicorn shitting rainbows and tight jeans.

"Feeling nervous?" Hayden handed Jez the wineglass.

Jez let out a strained laugh. "How can you tell?"

He stared meaningfully at the shirt. "The rainbow shit shirt. You wore that the day you moved in. I'm thinking maybe it's a shirt that… reminds you who you are."

This time Jez's laugh was more relaxed. "Yeah, you're right. I have a couple of shirts that are in-your-face gay, and depending on the situation, it feels a little like putting on armor or something."

"Well, I hope we don't need rainbow armor for this, because I don't have anything suitable."

"Hah. Maybe we can find something for you. Too late for tonight, but there's bound to be future situations that require the might of rainbow shit." Jez grabbed both their glasses and set them on the counter before moving into Hayden's arms and lifting his face for a kiss.

Hayden didn't know how long they kissed lazily, never quite tipping over into frantic and aroused, but he had a half chub when the doorbell rang. Fang skittered to the door, barking wildly, although given his almost silent barks, it ended up being more hilarious than annoying. He wouldn't be scaring off any would-be burglars.

They pulled apart, a tiny frown creasing Jez's forehead. Hayden didn't know if it was because they'd been interrupted or because Jez wasn't looking forward to this either, but he could sympathize. If Hayden could put this off forever, he would, but even without having made an appointment with a therapist, he'd started to see procrastination was one of his primary coping mechanisms, and it didn't help him cope at all.

Hayden left him puttering in the kitchen while he answered the door. "Hey."

Miguel was twitching in just the same way as Jez. Hayden might be the least nervous of the three of them.

"Hey, man. When did you get a dog?" Miguel crouched down and greeted Fang, some of his nervous tension disappearing under the overwhelming onslaught of cute.

"I didn't. Fang is your brother's." For now. Hayden hoped they'd get to a point where Fang would be theirs, but they weren't there yet.

"Jesús has a dog?" Miguel shook his head. "I mean, Jez. Shit, he hates it like poison when I slip up and call him Jesús."

"Yes, Jez has a dog." Unbelievable. Considering how much Jez loved that furry little mite, the fact he hadn't shouted Fang's presence to the rooftops was amazing. "His name is Fang."

That coaxed a snort of laughter from Miguel. "Fang?" He made a couple of ridiculous kissy faces at Fang before standing and brushing off his pants.

Hayden wondered if Fang's name was the doggie equivalent of the rainbow shit shirt. Had Jez intended to give Fang some armor, rather than it being a humorous and ironic name?

"C'mon. Dinner's ready to dish up. Did you want some wine or beer?"

"Beer. Please." Miguel squared his shoulders and followed Hayden into the dining room, where Jez was already setting food on the table. He went to grab Miguel his beer, and then the three of them sat down to dinner.

"You're vegan?" Miguel was aghast. Yet another thing the brothers hadn't bothered talking about. Jez's insistence on communication was starting to make a lot more sense, because it was obvious that the brothers might talk on the phone, but they didn't communicate well. Or maybe Miguel was a terrible listener.

Maybe Jez thought better communication would have made his relationship with Jayson less painful. A noble sentiment, but deluded. After all, no communicating in the world was going to change the fact that Jayson had a screw loose. Getting dumped hadn't pushed him into a mental breakdown. He'd been consciously and methodically spying on Jez to gather his passwords. That spoke of sociopathy at the very least. But now that Hayden was sitting at what might be the most painful and awkward blind date ever between two men who shouldn't be such strangers, well, he knew where Jez was coming from.

After some stilted small talk, the conversation stalled. Hayden was ready to rip off the bandage. "I gotta know, Miguel, why didn't you tell me about Jez's career? Why didn't you tell me he was gay? It wasn't like you didn't know about me. How is it you don't seem to know anything about your brother?"

Miguel took a long swig of beer like he was fortifying himself.

"Are you ashamed of me?" Jez asked.

Miguel wasn't a good enough actor to fake looking that stricken. "*Mi hermano*, no, of course not." He blinked rapidly, eyes shining in the yellowish light of the dining room, the lapse into Spanish startling Hayden. Back when he was a kid, he'd heard it a lot, but once Miguel moved to LA, he'd started to sound a lot more like a surfer or a frat boy. "I was always, always so worried for you. I still am. I guess I thought if I didn't talk about it, if no one knew, you couldn't get hurt again. And when you moved across the country? I don't know, hearing the details of your life... I could imagine how it could all go wrong. And you've met Jordan and Vic. *Pendejos*. If I told them you were an actor, it seemed... safer. God. Seeing you in that hospital bed just about killed me. I never want to see that again."

Hayden straightened up, all senses on alert. "Hospital. What the fuck happened? When was this?"

Jez glanced away. "More skeletons from my closet. I guess I was hoping not to off-load them all in my first month here."

"Please tell me." Miguel's presence more or less faded from Hayden's notice as he focused on Jez.

"It's water under the bridge, I promise. You'd been gone from Willow Ridge for years, but I'm sure you remember, it wasn't gay friendly."

Hayden rolled his eyes. "Uh, no. I'm well aware. Our parents went to the same church, and when I came out, mine threatened me with conversion therapy before I skipped town." A fist of dread lodged itself in his throat. "That... is that what happened?"

"No. Not that. Anyway, I wanted to be a dancer. Forever. The summer before my senior year, I went to New York for a few weeks. My parents thought I'd gone for an internship, but I'd really gone to a dance program at NYU designed for high school students. It was enough to convince me I was good enough to get in, and in senior year, I applied to all the schools my parents knew about, plus a bunch of dance programs that they didn't. I got a scholarship to NYU, and everything was all set. You know my parents. They couldn't read English very well, and they just didn't know. Day after the graduation party, I got jumped by some of the guys from school. Bashed. I'd been indiscreet during the party, starting to loosen up a little, knowing it was all going to be over in a few months. I'd be in New York and free."

The fist of dread moved down to Hayden's gut, and he pushed what was left of his dinner away. He had a bad feeling about what was coming next. "Were you badly hurt?" Stupid question. Yes, since he'd been in the hospital, but Hayden had also seen the man dance, so nothing debilitating. And it was also long over and done.

"*Dios*, I barely recognized him. Face swollen, shattered cheekbone, bruises everywhere, pissing blood, broken arm." Miguel's voice shook at the litany.

"Yeah, I don't remember too much about the attack and immediate aftermath. I needed surgery to fix my cheekbone, so most stuff is a blur until after that. But I remember very clearly my parents and Miguel coming into the hospital room. They knew why I'd gotten jumped, and they'd found out about the dance scholarship at NYU. Mom called dancing 'foolishness,' and my dad said he hoped the guys had beaten some sense into me. If not, he'd have to take care of it later. Miguel, I think, was totally speechless."

Why had Hayden thought doing this over dinner was a good idea? He wasn't sure he'd ever be able to eat again. Miguel looked almost gray, and he'd also pushed his dinner aside. And not because it was vegan either. The chili had been good enough that Hayden could make it at the firehouse and not get bitched at. Miguel had been eating just fine until this had come up.

"I can't believe your parents would say that." Hayden's parents had threatened him with conversion torture, but they hadn't intended to administer it themselves.

Miguel sighed. "I heard them talking at home. About how Jesús—he was still Jesús back then—had been coddled too much. The spoiled baby of the family. They weren't planning to keep him in the hospital as long as the doctors had recommended, but were going to bring him home. Papa was going to get him a job, and they'd decided that the summer he'd spent in New York had given him godless ideas, and if he wasn't going to go to a local school, he

wouldn't be going at all. Dance, of course, would not
be allowed."

Jez finally looked up from his intent study of his
half-eaten dinner to see Miguel smiling at him fondly,
and smiled sadly back. Hayden wanted to hug him so
bad but wasn't sure that was appropriate since they
hadn't told Miguel about them yet. But he was glad to
see that whatever mistakes Miguel had made, it hadn't
been because he didn't love his brother.

"Can we move this to the den? It's more comfortable, and I just can't look at this food any longer." Jez
sounded about as depressed as Hayden had ever heard,
and he intended to make it a life goal to never hear that
defeated tone from Jez ever again. He wouldn't even
insist on the dishes getting cleared right away.

They moved into the den, Hayden sitting in
his regular spot on the couch. As had become their
new normal, Jez sat down beside him and snuggled
up against his shoulder, feet curled up on the couch.
It was impossible to do anything but wrap his arm
around Jez, haul him in close, then give him a kiss on
the temple. Fang followed them up—it hadn't taken
them long to buy a third set of steps so Fang could
navigate the couch—and rested his head on Jez's an-
kles with a grunt. Miguel sat in one of the club chairs,
then twisted in his seat to stare at them, eyes wide.

Hayden tensed momentarily, but an enormous
smile split Miguel's face. "Really? You two are hitting it?" And there was the surfer dude, back like he'd
never been gone.

Jez snorted. "We're not *hitting it*, doofus." *Doofus*. Hayden hadn't heard that word since the last time

he'd been in the same spot as both brothers, when Jez was twelve. "We're...."

Hayden bit his lip to keep from laughing. He wondered how Jez was going to explain it to big brother.

"We're... dating. Intending it to become a relationship."

Eh. Not bad, although in Hayden's mind they were already in a relationship.

"I can't tell you how happy that makes me."

An odd thought snuck into Hayden's brain. "You weren't... you weren't trying to set us up, were you?"

Miguel laughed. "Not intentionally, no. But my two favorite people, both single, and a way to put you in the same place at the same time? I wasn't going to spit in the face of fate."

No, Hayden understood that. And it made him even more confident that Miguel also thought his and Jez's coming together was fate.

"But you hurt my baby bro and we'll have words, *mi amigo*." Interesting. The friend he'd had growing up and the surfer dude combined. That had never happened, but maybe with Jez around, Hayden might see it more.

"I think we're safe." Hayden sighed. "I almost don't want to hear it, but I need to hear what happened after the hospital."

Miguel's expression became serious again, and Jez pressed in tighter.

"I waited until my parents went out; then I packed a bag with anything related to the dance program and as many clothes and such as I could fit, drove to the hospital, and took him away."

"Miguel, that's dangerous! Why would you do that?"

"My parents were planning to do it anyway, and quite frankly, I didn't trust them to let him recuperate at home. I took him to the cheapest reputable motel until I could find a furnished apartment with a short-term lease, and lied to my parents about working extra shifts. I paid for a nurse to come in and check on him while I was working my actual shifts, and slowly, he got better. Maxed out my credit cards too, but it was worth it. Fortunately he didn't need regular nursing for long, because I couldn't afford much in the way of doctor's visits. All the while, I was sending out applications to any fire station in the LA area that had an opening. I wasn't ready to leave California or break entirely from the family, so applying to New York was out, but moving several hours away to be near my best friend seemed like the best solution."

Huh. So Miguel moving near him hadn't been entirely because he'd missed Hayden, but this was an even better reason.

"Didn't your parents wonder where he was?"

Miguel shook his head. "Jez basically up and left, and I don't think anyone even knew I'd been at the hospital. My parents assumed he'd run away, or maybe hopped a bus to New York. I don't know if they realized he was barely well enough for a short car ride. The last thing I heard on the matter was my papa saying 'good riddance.'"

"What about your sisters? Your brother? Didn't any of them worry?"

"Not that I ever saw."

Hayden half expected Jez to flinch at that stark response, but he didn't react at all. Then again, he'd had years to come to terms with his family situation. "They didn't even come to the hospital. That day in the hospital was the last time I spoke to anyone in my family, except for Miguel."

That made Hayden flinch. Fucking hell. Hayden's family might have been small, but a full third—his gran—had been supportive.

"And the scholarship?"

Jez drew random patterns on Hayden's thigh, far enough down that Hayden's stupid cock with its one-track sex mind didn't get the wrong idea. "I wasn't sure I was going to be well enough to make it. A week before school started, Miguel flew us both out there, helped me set up my dorm room, and made sure I had doctors through the school who could continue my care and provide documentation that would help me keep my place in the program until I was done healing and got my strength back. The school was horrified by what had happened and made allowances for me. And I'd had all summer to recuperate. It was only a few more weeks before I was back to a hundred per-cent. I didn't think so at the time, but I was very lucky. If those guys had busted my knees or dislocated my shoulders, most likely I wouldn't have a dance career. But a couple of broken bones, one of them in my face? Yeah, that was about the best-case scenario."

Thing was, Jez was wrong. A busted knee wasn't the worst-case scenario. Jez could have been killed, and Hayden would never have gotten to know him. That sparked a whole new brand of fear Hayden hadn't experienced before.

"Anyway, the scholarship covered the bare min-imum of school and living expenses, but Miguel still sent me a bit of money and presents now and again until I finally got my first paying job."

Hayden hugged Jez and rocked him gently. He didn't bother to ask if the guys had been arrested. With Jez disappearing from the hospital and the Perezes unlikely to press the issue, any investigation would have petered out.

The silence lengthened, broken only by Fang's breathy puppy snores. As painful as this discussion had already been, they weren't done yet.

"Look, Miguel, I'm done with Jordan. He's said too much that I can't forgive. And I know Vic is your friend, but I can't deal with him anymore either. You are always welcome to come over and whatever, but only if Vic isn't with you."

Miguel's cheeks got dark and blotchy in a way Hayden saw only when he was extremely embarrassed. "*Dios*. He was awful last week. He's not so terrible at the station, but he just feeds off cues from Jordan. I understand totally. I haven't been hanging out with him as much lately because he is just so angry all the time."

"Why didn't you say anything?" Jez's voice was small and hurt. "He and Jordan were saying awful things, and even if they weren't directed at me personally, they could have been."

The flush got worse. "I am so sorry. Maybe it wasn't smart, but I thought if I didn't draw attention to it, if no one knew, then maybe no one would get hurt. Not just you, but I worried about Hayden too. If they were reminded too strongly that Hayden was also gay, they might have done something stupid. I hate every time Hayden goes out to a gay club because it scares me. I know he can take care of himself, but I'm always afraid he's going to get bashed."

Huh. That made Hayden feel better. Miguel needed to stop that shit, but at least it wasn't because he was weirded out by Hayden having a sex life.

"Don't you understand? Talking about it, shining a light on it, letting them know that sort of behavior isn't acceptable, is the only way to make sure no one gets hurt. Those guys that attacked me started out bullying me just like Vic and Jordan. And no one cared. No one stopped them. So they felt free to attack me physically."

All the color drained out of Miguel's face as he gaped at Jez. "You mean you know who attacked you? Why did you tell the cops you didn't?"

Ah, so that's what had happened.

"I was afraid, Miguel. My own parents thought those guys had done me a favor. But once I was better and living in New York, I got angry. I wasn't going to hide, and I wasn't going to let bullies dictate my actions. It got me roughed up a few times, but I learned to fight back, and I never got hospitalized again."

Holy fuck. Hayden's vision swam and he got light-headed. He wasn't going to faint, was he?

A few deep breaths and he was back to normal, and saw Miguel was as horrified as Hayden was.

"Baby, look at me." Hayden tapped Jez's side to get his attention.

"You've never called me that before." But getting lost in Jez's soft, warm eyes was not an option.

"I will again, don't worry. But please, Jez, please. Don't deliberately put yourself in danger. Just listening to all this has taken years off my life." Miguel snorted in agreement. "You forget that I see what can happen, what angry people can do to one another. And I couldn't bear it if something bad happened to you."

"I'm sorry. I won't deliberately put myself in harm's way. But neither am I going back in the closet."

"Thank you, baby. And I'd never ask that of you." Hayden kissed him, quick and fast, because anything else would distract him and give Miguel too much information.

But Jez didn't completely relax. "Why have you been avoiding me?"

Miguel shifted uncomfortably. "It was stupid, but I... it's been so long since I've seen you. After all the money I spent to get you well, I just couldn't afford to visit you, and I couldn't get any help from the family. I was just afraid... we'd be strangers. I know I've seen your pictures on social media and all, but I was also worried I wouldn't even recognize you. The last thing I wanted was to see you and have it feel like an awkward first date or job interview. Putting my head in the sand and pretending things were fine seemed like the easiest solution."

Jez let out a bark of laughter. "Hoping problems go away if you ignore them must be a family trait, because I've done that a few times."

Miguel grinned at him before standing up and pulling Jez into a giant bear hug. Hayden, almost like one of the family, pretended not to notice the brothers had teared up.

"Right, so am I being reamed out for anything else? Because I think I saw a freshly baked pie that has my name on it!"

Yes, Hayden knew his friend well. "Let me clear off the table and get dessert. Jez, you stay here and chat with your brother."

Chapter 8

BY THE time Miguel left, Jez had lost that brittle edginess that had infected him since Hayden had invited Miguel over. Hayden understood. Jez had left behind his entire support network to start a life in a new state. The resolve he'd gained from his attack meant that Miguel might be the last of his family still talking to him, but he sure wasn't sacrosanct if Jez thought Miguel had started thinking like his parents. Hayden admired that strength, and his enforced independence at seventeen probably accounted for Jez often seeming older than his years. In attitude and thought process, definitely not in looks.

Hayden was fucking exhausted, and there was no way Jez wasn't just as beat. He finished putting the dishes in the dishwasher while Jez took Fang out back for his last pee of the night.

The door opened, and Hayden heard the jangle of Fang's collar and leash before the door slammed shut again and the lock engaged with vigor.

"Ready for bed?" Was it normal to take so much joy in these domestic tasks? Even when he'd lived with Gran, he'd sort of envisioned himself as a lone wolf, not trapped in a cage of his own making. On a personal level, anyway. He'd wanted to be a firefighter since he was a kid—it was what had initially bonded him and Miguel at the age of five. They'd helped each other toward that goal, but once they'd attained it? Hayden hadn't fully recognized his need to make a new family for himself, starting with a boyfriend.

Jez plodded into the kitchen, a tired smile on his face. "I am." The smile flattened. "I don't think... I'm not up for...."

Hayden shook his head. "I realize this is new for us and we have been doing our best impression of stags in season, but we're also adults with lives. Shit happens, and I'm pretty sure a relationship means not having sex every night. It's not a deal breaker." Besides, there was always morning sex, when Jez was sleepy and warm and hadn't woken up enough to remember everything that was weighing on him.

Jez's smile returned, wider than before, and he gave Hayden a sweet little kiss. Mentally, Hayden gave his cock a stern talking-to. *Everyone* was too tired for fucking. Overenthusiastic piece of flesh also loved this new domestic arrangement.

Exhaustion didn't stop him from letting Jez go first up the stairs so he could admire his ass. Didn't take any effort to gaze lovingly on a work of art.

As they undressed, Hayden's cock perked up a bit at the sight of a naked Jez—he'd have to be dead before he stopped responding to that. Curling around Jez's slim, muscled body was a joy he'd never known he'd been missing, and it was already a habit crucial for a good night's sleep.

Lying there in the dark, he stroked Jez's shoulder, expecting him to drop off right away, but Jez's breathing didn't change to that breathy sleep sound.

"Your parents really wanted you to go through conversion therapy?"

He'd had a long time to come to terms with that. "Yeah. It sucked."

"Is that why you never came back to Willow Ridge again after you moved away? Not even for Christmas or Thanksgiving or anything?"

"Pretty much. After my parents died, I came back a few times with Miguel and spent the holidays at your parents' place. You were already living in New York, and I assumed that was why you were never there. It never twigged that no one talked about you, although I was always careful to keep quiet about being gay while I was there. It's possible your parents knew, but I'm guessing my parents wouldn't have told anyone, and we both learned that Miguel is far too good at keeping secrets, so I know he didn't say anything."

"But your gran was okay with everything?"

Aside from the steadily deteriorating mental health? "Yeah, she was fine with me. I called her as soon as my parents started raving, and she immediately sent me money for bus fare. Told me I'd have a safe place with her." He smiled in the darkness. "You know, she would have liked you. She was a professional ballerina for several years but quit when she was pregnant with my dad. A few years later, she divorced my alcoholic grandfather, and then she moved into acting. She had a few decent movie roles—mostly made for TV and miniseries—as well as a bunch of bit parts on shows like *Columbo* and *Fantasy Island* and *Murder, She Wrote*."

Jez half sat up, resting his weight on his elbows. "Oh my God, really? That is so cool."

Hayden didn't know why it wouldn't have occurred to him that Jez would be interested in his gran's accomplishments. "She wasn't famous or anything, but she knew a ton of people and had stories about everyone. She never could figure out how she'd somehow birthed an ultraconservative Republican." Probably some sort of weird rebellion against Gran's liberalism. Or acting out against her divorce. Whatever it was, his father had been a dried-up sour lemon compared to Gran's lemon chiffon pie personality. "Her memorabilia is packed in those boxes in the third guest room."

"Shit. That's a lot of memorabilia."

"It's not all memorabilia. Acting didn't take up all her time; she also loved sewing and cross-stitch and knitting." And a ton of other fabric-related things he didn't know the names for. "Those things in the boxes were all the things that she loved best." Because Hayden refused to believe his gran loved the stacks of newspapers, and collection of broken porcelain dolls, and myriad jars of old buttons as much as she loved sewing and being an actress. No matter what she'd claimed in those final years.

"Why is it all in boxes, then? Surely you're not planning to get rid of it?"

Hayden blinked. "No. I just don't know what to do with it all." Besides worry it was the kernel from which he'd grow his own hoard.

"I know." Jez sighed. "Too girly, right? Putting it right out there would mark you as obviously gay, and with the guys coming over all the time, you couldn't have that."

"Yeah. That's part of it, for sure." It was also messy. Too messy for Hayden to be comfortable with.

"Don't worry. We'll figure out a way you can keep your memories without it looking like the back room of a warehouse in there." Jez relaxed on the bed. "Are they, like, private? Or would you mind if I opened a few boxes, just to see what's in there?"

Hayden sucked in a couple of breaths. "They're not private, but... please don't make a mess." He wasn't sure he and Jez defined "mess" the same way, but he'd packed the stuff away once; he could do it again if necessary.

His eyelids started to droop, and he was almost ready to drift off when Jez asked another question, something about going to see a movie, but it brought him mostly back to wakefulness. "Baby, can we talk later? I gotta get to sleep. Working the Halloween shift is always shitty."

"Oh. Yeah, I guess that makes sense. It wasn't important."

Fang settled in at the bottom of the bed, silence descended, and Hayden heard Jez's breathing change. All was right in his world, and he'd sleep better for knowing it.

JEZ CIRCLED the block around Tyson's place a couple of times, looking for street parking. His Prius was super compact, but for someone who'd gotten his driver's license only a year before taking an eight-year hiatus from driving while in New York, parallel parking was more stressful than opening night. He needed a big spot soon, or he'd still be driving in circles when the kids started trick-or-treating. One of the main reasons they'd agreed to meet up so early was to avoid any of them driving during the kiddie portion of the evening. Scary movie, dinner, another scary movie, then pregame some drinks while putting on their costumes. Jez couldn't wait. What was more fun than a packed gay club on Halloween? He and Hayden were exclusive, as unbelievable as that was, so for the first time since he was legal—since he'd lost his virginity to a fellow dance student his first September in New York—Jez wouldn't be getting laid on Halloween. Night. They'd had a very good Halloween morning, though, before Hayden left for his shift.

Paul had just gone through a bad breakup and was ready for all the cock he could handle, and Tyson, well, Tyson was pining after one of Jez's costars and might end up as celibate as Jez tonight. According to his new friends, they were going to hit a couple of the best bars in WeHo, and Jez was fucking ready. It felt like forever since he'd been to a club. He was also nervous. Living in a different city from Jayson helped, but anyone could have faulty wiring in their brain.

No. Jez shook off that line of thought. Clubbing, dancing, and fun. Some drinks to relax.

On his third time around the block, like magic, a car pulled out, leaving a space plenty big enough for Jez to zip right into without any futzing with reverse.

He grabbed his bags, then trundled up the steps. Tyson's apartment was one of six units in a large house that had been cut up into functional living spaces. It was pretty cool—very classic Hollywood. He followed a path around to the back of the house and knocked on Tyson's door.

"Hey there!" Tyson gave him a hug and two air kisses. "Paul just got here a few minutes ago. We can get started."

"You got any kids that'll come to the house?" Jez had sort of forgotten about that part of the night, and Tyson hadn't mentioned it when they were making plans.

"Nah, not since I'm at the back of the building. I've got a couple of bags of candy in the kitchen just in case, but I'd be surprised. I've lived here six years and only ever gave out candy two of 'em. To a grand total of eleven kids. So I made sure to get candy I like." Tyson winked at him and Jez laughed.

Tyson hustled him into the living/dining room, where Paul was mixing cocktails. At least he knew with these guys—unlike with Hayden's beer—the cocktails, for all their brilliant color, would be as low calorie as possible. Big strong firefighters with lots of muscles didn't have to worry about empty calories and getting fat, unlike the rest of them.

"Hey, boy, how's it going?" Paul offered a glass with lurid green liquid in it and a floating gummy brain. Jez wrinkled his nose and reached to pluck it out.

"Vegan gummies. You can have a little cheat."

Ooh, he just might cheat for that. "You guys are so good to me." And they were. Every time they'd gone out—which hadn't been all that often, since Jez had just met them—they were careful to choose places that had plenty of vegan options. That buffalo cauliflower in Silver Lake had been to die for.

"I'm surprised you wanted to leave the new boyfriend to come out for a Halloween extravaganza with us."

Jez's ears heated a bit. The moment he'd had the exclusivity talk with Hayden, he'd texted them both like a teenaged girl. Fortunately, they'd been every bit as excited for him, just like a teen girl posse. "He's working tonight. Says it's usually rough."

Tyson made a face.

"What's that supposed to mean?"

"Nothing much, but honestly, your man works in Pasadena. There's places in LA where cars get set on fire as Halloween entertainment."

"You know what? I am okay with that. The fewer times he's in danger, the happier I'll be."

"I'll drink to that," Tyson said and lifted his glass. "When do we get to meet this man?"

Huh. Jez had already met some of Hayden's friends, which hadn't gone well, but that didn't mean he shouldn't try to introduce his new friends to Hayden. "I don't know. I'll talk to Hayden and see. Maybe we can have a barbecue or something?" After so many years in the northeast, it seemed almost ludicrous to offer a barbecue for some future time after Halloween, but it hadn't cooled off much, and Hayden had one of those outdoor space heaters for the patio in case that changed.

"You do that."

"What are we watching tonight?"

Paul giggled. "Got a movie about a serial killer preying on poor WeHo gays on Halloween. Get us in the right frame of mind."

Jez rolled his eyes. It was bound to be terrible, but in a good way. "Let's bring on the horror."

The three of them sat in a row on Tyson's plush couch and started their Halloween celebration.

THE SECOND movie finished around nine thirty. Perfect timing. They'd have time to get into their costumes and head out, and they'd arrive at the first club just as things were heating up.

They got dressed in separate rooms so they could have a mini fashion show. Since Tyson's place was a small one bedroom, that meant one of them in Ty's bedroom, one in the living/dining room, and the third in the bathroom. Jez took the living/dining room because he didn't need too much primping with his costume, aside from some guyliner, and the mirror by the front door would suffice.

Jez had chosen a fairly sedate—for a WeHo Halloween club party—sailor costume. The base was super clingy black fabric, with full-length pants and a sleeveless vest with a vaguely nautical neckline and accents. Also a little sailor cap, which Jez expected to disappear over the course of the night. If he'd been aiming to hook up, he'd have worn a jock, but since he was planning for his cock to remain tucked away, he put on a pair of tiny briefs before pulling up the pants.

"You guys ready?" Tyson called out. Both Jez and Paul replied that they were.

Within seconds, his friends had joined him by the couch.

"Oooh, Sailor McSlutty," Tyson exclaimed. "I'd take a ride on your submarine."

Jez laughed and rolled his eyes. "I love the gladiator costume." Tyson was wearing a leather… skirt? Kilt? Jez didn't know what gladiators called the lower half of their outfits. The leather wrist cuffs and collar looked a little more BDSM fetish night than Roman gladiator, but it was still a good look for Tyson. And if Jez wasn't mistaken, parts of the costume might have been culled from a movie set. Tyson had some good connections.

"Thank you." Tyson twirled a bit, letting the hook of his ass peek out from under the kilt.

Then they both turned to Paul.

"Um. Boy." Tyson bit his lip while Jez tried to piece it all together. It was orange and looked a bit like a wrestling singlet, but with about half the material. The front scooped down low enough to confirm Paul had waxed it *all* off.

"Are you a wrestler?" Jez asked tentatively.

Paul scoffed and twisted his hip. "No. Check out the handcuffs."

"Handcuffs," Tyson repeated. There were indeed plastic handcuffs hanging from Paul's hip.

"I'm sorry. I still don't know." Nothing about it screamed sexy cop. No cop he'd ever seen had worn pumpkin orange.

"Sexy prison inmate. Honestly, you guys."

"You do know they don't just hang handcuffs from prison jumpsuits, right?" Tyson asked, only slightly mockingly.

Paul rolled his eyes. "Artistic license. Obviously."

Oh, obviously. "Paul, I don't know what kind of prison porn you've been watching, but you look great." Getting prison inmate out of that scrap of fabric and plastic was a bit of a stretch, but Paul was not going to have any problems getting under a new man tonight.

Chapter 9

HAYDEN SWUNG out of his truck feeling every one of his thirty-one years—times two. Working Halloween was the fucking worst. Nah. Maybe it was third-worst. The Fourth of July and New Year's Eve were the worst.

As much as he'd like to get Jez to model his Halloween costume—the selfie he'd sent last night from Tyson's had been a total tease—Hayden was too beat. Maybe after a nap.

He opened the door to find Fang lying near the door. Was it possible for a dog to look chagrined?

"Hey there, little man. How's my Fang?"

Fang gave him a halfhearted butt wiggle and a grunting bark but didn't move.

"Are you okay?" Hayden's heart started to thump. Had Jez chosen a vet yet? If not, what was the closest one? He didn't bother taking off his shoes, just stepped fully into the entryway. "Jez? What's wrong with Fang?"

There wasn't an answer. Frowning, he looked back outside, but Jez's red Prius was nowhere in sight. He pulled out his phone and started pacing as it rang. Just when it went to voicemail, his heel skidded on something slippery.

"Call me," he barked into the phone before disconnecting and staring at the floor. A puddle. Was that pee?

"Fang? Did you do this?"

Fang whimpered, and Hayden couldn't find it in his heart to be upset. At least he'd peed on the tile. Hayden kicked off his shoes—they'd need cleaning later—picked up Fang, and carried him right out to the backyard.

Almost immediately, Fang squatted. After, he perked up, relieving Hayden. Poor pup just needed to go to the bathroom, he wasn't sick. Hayden let out a sigh, amazed at the burst of adrenaline that concern had sent through his system.

Now he just had to worry about Jez. He'd been planning to crash at Tyson's last night, but Hayden had expected him home by now, if only because Fang couldn't hold his bladder for so long.

He checked his phone again while Fang frolicked, but the selfie of Jez in sailor garb was the last message he'd had.

"Okay, buddy, let's go inside and get you fed." And get the pee cleaned up before it did anything permanent to the tile or his shoes.

His phone rang as he was washing his hands after dealing with the pee. He wiped his hands quickly on the towel before grabbing the phone, frantic to answer before it went to voicemail.

"Jez? Where are you?"

"Funny you should ask that," a voice that was not Jez replied.

"Who is this?"

"Marco, you idiot. Surely you have caller ID?"

Hayden blinked, recognizing Marco's voice now. "Oh. Yeah, sorry. Long night last night. I just got home."

"Well, buddy, it's about to get longer."

Then it registered. Marco was a police officer, and he seemed to be aware Jez wasn't home. The adrenaline spike he'd gotten from worrying about Fang returned with a vengeance. "Shit. Marco. Is Jez okay?"

"Yeah, bud. He's fine. In the sense that he's alive and unhurt."

Hayden squinted as he processed those words. "And what other sense would he not be fine?"

"He's been arrested. I think it can be cleared up pretty quick, but you're going to have to come to the station and fix this in person."

"Arrested? Why would you arrest him?"

Marco snorted out a laugh. "I didn't do it. I just got here, and you're lucky I even noticed he'd been detained. He was arrested, well, breaking into your house."

"What? That doesn't make sense."

"I just skimmed the report. He was drunk, lost his keys somewhere, decided to break in, and one of the neighbors called the cops."

"Did he get mugged or something? Where was his ID?"

"Oh, he had ID, but it was a New York driver's license. Didn't have anything with your address, so the officer who responded arrested him. For B and E."

"Can't you just tell them it's a mistake?"

"No can do, bud. It's all official-like now. As the homeowner, you're the one who's going to have to fix this mess."

He didn't know why Jez wouldn't have called him when this all happened. Maybe it wouldn't have had to get to the point of being all "official-like." But he supposed getting arrested was a good reason for not being home. After filming started, he'd have to get used to Jez not being there when his shift ended, but this was a ridiculous test run.

"I'll be there in a few minutes." At least he'd been arrested in Pasadena, so Hayden didn't have far to go.

"Be good, Fang, I'm going to get your daddy."

Fang wagged his little corkscrew tail before waddling upstairs.

HAYDEN TEXTED Marco as soon as he arrived, and Marco met him at the door. Hayden waved and nodded to a number of officers he knew either from social events or from coming across them on the job, but how many of them knew why he was here? Obviously it was all some big misunderstanding, but that didn't stop it from feeling like a walk of shame. Poor Jez. This would be a hundred times worse for him.

Marco led him to a small room with a table, a couple of chairs, and some filing cabinets lurking in the corner.

"Where's Jez? Don't I have to sign something?"

"Sit down for a minute. I'll get you the paperwork, but I wanted to talk to you about something first."

Now he had Hayden concerned. Again. At this rate, he was going to have adrenaline poisoning before he managed to get a nap. But he sat, because it would be the fastest way to spring Jez and get back home. One day this would be funny. He hoped.

"Talk, Marco."

"How well do you know this guy? I mean, sure, he's Miguel's brother, but I hadn't even heard that Miguel had a brother in New York until he was living with you."

"Is this an interrogation?" Hayden was incredulous. What the fuck was going on?

"No, no. Sorry. One of the hazards of, well, interrogating people."

"Why do you want to know? I mean, I hadn't seen him in years when he showed up, but he's Miguel's brother. I've known him since he was born. And although he was a gangly, awkward preteen the last time I saw him, there are enough similarities between that kid and the guy who showed up on my doorstep." Even Miguel wouldn't have faked that, some random guy pretending to be his brother.

"Just, when they were running his information, a record of a protection order came back."

Hayden frowned. "Protection order."

"Restraining order."

"Huh. He told me he tried to file one against an ex-boyfriend but got laughed out of the police station. Would it have gone through without him knowing?"

"No, man, I mean someone took out a restraining order *against Jez*."

Hayden started shaking his head before Marco had finished talking. "That can't be right."

"I don't know what to say. It's public record. Guy named Jayson Bain. It has nothing to do with this arrest, and as long as you sign the appropriate paperwork, the arrest will all go away. But this restraining order worries me a bit. If Jez is a stalker, well, they don't tend to change their stripes. And it doesn't take much to get one fixated. Be careful. Don't get too involved with him."

Right. A little late for that. He'd need to talk to Jez about it, but when? Jez wouldn't be happy, at all, about more doubts directed at him. But the coincidence with the guy Jez told him about and the one who'd taken out the restraining order both being named Jayson? That was a little too much to ignore.

Whatever had happened, it seemed like Jez was over the relationship with Jayson, and Hayden didn't see anything scary about Jez. In fact, being with Jez was turning out to be the least scary thing he'd ever done. Just like the arrest for breaking and entering, the restraining order must be some sort of colossal misunderstanding.

"I'll keep your advice in mind. Where's the paperwork I have to sign?"

Marco gave him a stern cop stare like he could hear Hayden's thoughts and that he wasn't taking the whole thing seriously. He was, but Marco was acting like Jez was one step from being a serial killer. Whatever a typical "stalker" was, Jez wasn't it. There was a good explanation for this, Hayden was absolutely certain.

"I'll go get it."

The paperwork took far longer than he expected, but finally Marco led him to an interview room. Hayden opened it to find Jez, still wearing his costume, a little worse for wear, slumped in a chair, elbows on the table, head resting in his palms.

"Hey," Hayden said softly. Jez jolted to attention and looked at him. His eyes were bloodshot, his color not good, and smudged eyeliner gave him a distinct "raccoon with a hangover" look. Scratch that, a *seafaring* raccoon with a hangover. Hayden couldn't help himself.

"C'mere." He held his arms out, and Jez leaped at him, wrapping his arms tightly around Hayden's waist.

Holding him close, he let Jez shake and sob. Mistake or no, this had to have been scary. Hayden would have been scared, spending the night in jail. He stroked Jez's back and made soothing noises. Once they got home, he'd figure out what had happened. For now, all that mattered was that Jez was coming home with him.

As soon as they got home, Fang nearly levitated in his joy at seeing Jez. Jez sniffled and apologized to the pup in baby talk, and then Hayden sent Jez upstairs to shower while he heated up some minestrone soup and made sandwiches—grilled cheese for him, hummus and cucumber for Jez.

His eyes were practically grainy with exhaustion, but they'd both sleep better once Jez had told his story.

Hayden dashed upstairs to change into sweatpants and was back in the kitchen, dishing up lunch, long before Jez returned, clean, damp, and wearing pajamas.

Hayden didn't begrudge him one ounce of hot water.

They ate in focused silence at the kitchen table before Hayden ushered them into the den. He needed Jez in his arms every bit as much as he suspected Jez needed to be there.

If it weren't for the limb-deadening exhaustion, Hayden would take them up to bed, but the second he was horizontal, he'd be out cold. Marco hadn't been kidding when he'd said Hayden's day was gonna be long.

Hayden tucked Jez into his side—he didn't dare even lie down.

"So…," Hayden prompted.

A gusty sigh erupted from Jez. "I am so, so sorry. I can't believe everything went so wrong."

"What the hell happened?"

"Fuck. I mean, it was so fucked-up I hardly know how to begin."

"Just start somewhere."

"My costume had only one tiny pocket, and I was planning to crash at Tyson's. Paul wasn't sure—he wanted to hook up, maybe a couple of times, so he didn't know if he was going back to Tyson's, but I definitely was."

Hayden had no idea where Jez was going with this, but then, he couldn't envision any scenario that ended with Jez getting arrested for trying to break into his house.

"My car was at Tyson's, and we weren't going to drive to the bar, so I left my keys with my wallet and change of clothes at Ty's. I only brought my ID, my phone, and a bit of cash for drinks. But, see, Tyson and I have the same phone, and at some point during the night, we accidentally swapped. Tyson hadn't been planning to hook up, but he did, and just after midnight I found myself tipsy, tired, and alone. So I decided to leave. Tyson had told me that if we got separated for whatever reason, I could just head back to his place and let myself in with the key in the fake rock by his door."

So far, Hayden was following. "And why didn't you go there?"

"Well, I told you I had Tyson's phone. I was drunk, you realize. Fortunately his phone wasn't locked, so I was able to call an Uber, but I couldn't remember his address. I had the bright idea that I would just come home and pick my car up in the morning. Sounded great, but after the Uber left, I realized I didn't have any keys. And I still didn't remember Tyson's address. I tried calling my own phone, but no one answered. And I was just too out of it to try and figure out on Tyson's phone where the fuck he lived."

"And breaking in was the answer?"

Jez lifted a shoulder in a halfhearted shrug. "I couldn't remember your number, so I couldn't call you. And Fang had a little accident in the bedroom, so I'd opened the window. I was pretty certain that the window was still open, and I was also certain I could hoist myself up to the roof of the porch, then use that to walk over to the bedroom window."

And Hayden saw precisely when this little caper had veered out of control. "And that's when you got caught?"

"More or less. It took me... a large number of attempts to get on top of the porch, and I don't think I was particularly quiet. It never occurred to me that the optics of the thing were incredibly damning."

"They sure were. I guess it wouldn't hurt to let the neighbors know you live here now."

"Ha. Maybe." Jez sounded a bit more like himself. "Anyway, I guess you know the rest. I tried to explain I lived here, but without any proof, and no one I could call on Tyson's phone who could vouch for me, the cop booked me."

"Well, I guess we can't blame him for doing his job. I'm just glad you're okay." Because the night could have gone far worse. "Did you at least have a good time?"

"I did. It would have been more fun if you'd been there."

Hayden smiled and gave Jez a little kiss. "Next time."

"Yeah. Next time. Paul and Tyson want to meet you, by the way. I said maybe we could have a barbecue or something?"

"We'll definitely plan something. Maybe have Kevin and Maria over. Your brother. Make it a bit of a party."

Jez hugged him. "Sounds like fun."

It did. Hayden was looking forward to hosting a party with his boyfriend. And there would be no sports. Not that Hayden was swearing off sports—far from it. But he didn't want to backslide into the types of caveman events he'd had before.

"Was your night as bad as you thought it would be?" Jez's voice had a sleepy note, and if they weren't careful, they'd pass out down here.

"It was busy, sure, but it was coming home finding a Fang puddle and you not here that made things really bad."

"I'm so sorry. I can't apologize enough."

"No need. It was one of those things. I mean, your judgment was maybe a little suspect, but not bad enough you deserved a night in jail."

Jez yawned loudly.

"Well, I'm ready for a nap, and I think you didn't get much sleep either."

A bitter laugh told Hayden all he needed to know. They got up from the couch, only to hear the faint sounds of "You Think You're a Man" by Divine.

"That's Tyson's phone." Jez dashed to the table in the front hall where they'd left it. "It's Paul." Jez was positively gleeful.

"Hello? Oh, hey, Tyson."

Hayden waited. Paul must have ended up back at Tyson's the way Jez should have.

"Yeah, I ended up going home instead." Jez smiled at Hayden. "Yes, I know. It's a long story, and I'm about ready to crash. I don't need my stuff until tomorrow. Are you okay to wait until then to swap phones?"

There was another slight pause.

"What? You've got to be kidding me."

Hayden frowned. What else could have happened last night?

"Thanks. I'll be over as soon as I can."

Jez disconnected the call and grimaced. "So, how do you feel about postponing the nap?"

God no. "Like maybe I want to cry? Why, what can't wait until tomorrow?"

"Tyson brought a hookup home. He wasn't awake when the guy left, but he thinks the guy slashed my tires."

Lack of sleep was making Hayden delirious. "Are you telling me the tires on your car are slashed? Why does Tyson think his hookup did it?"

"Dunno. Said his neighbors are good people and he didn't even know the guy's name. Might have taken his phone number, except he didn't have his own phone, so there's not even that lead. I need to get over there and get the car towed or something. Do you think I should call the police?"

"Probably nothing they can do to catch whoever did it, but I'll drive you over there and we can call Marco while we're waiting for the tow truck."

"You know, I can Uber over. I know you're exhausted and this wasn't what you wanted to do with your day."

"Nope. I may not know much about relationships, but I'm betting a good boyfriend would go with you, despite turning into a zombie from lack of sleep."

Jez smiled. "You're a good man, Hayden. I'm glad we found each other."

"Me too." Bringing up the restraining order was pointless. Jez had too much on his plate right now, and Hayden didn't believe it was an issue anyway. "Hey, on the plus side, this will end up being a super memorable Halloween."

"Too true. Right, well, let's get changed and head out. The sooner it's done, the sooner we can sleep."

Jez led the way upstairs, his butt every bit as mesmerizing in pajamas as it was in jeans. Hayden would have to make sure not to even look at the bed, or his chivalrous resolve to keep Jez company would fall by the wayside as he dove into the pillowy goodness of his mattress.

JEZ COULD not shake the feeling someone was watching him. It had intensified after Halloween and getting his tires slashed. In the days since, there hadn't been another damned suspicious person or incident. He was trying desperately to believe it was nothing more than bad luck, and each day nothing happened got him closer to that belief.

It was easier when Hayden had his four days off, though. Work helped too, but here he was, Friday night, all alone in Hayden's house. A man's shout made him flinch. Had to be one of the neighbors.

Jez turned up the volume on the fluffy rom-com he'd selected, his e-reader on the couch next to him. He was going to need both for company tonight. He'd rather not take a Xanax if he could avoid it. He'd had a healthy supply when he left New York, but if he ended up taking it every day, he'd run out before he found a new therapist. He'd found a few possibilities, but he hadn't decided if he should choose one close to work or close to home. As comfortable as he was with Hayden and as much as he was coming to love Pasadena, their arrangement wasn't permanent, and Hayden hadn't dropped any hints about making it so. Having to drive a long distance in shitty LA traffic to see a therapist would cause even more anxiety. But he couldn't put off the therapist decision much longer.

Paul and Tyler were both busy, and Miguel was on shift tonight too. A commercial flicked on, and Jez hopped off the couch to check the locks again, then pulled the blinds down on all the windows.

He didn't care if Hayden laughed at him in the light of day tomorrow morning. Since the tire incident, Hayden would sometimes get this speculative look in his eyes. Like Jez had done something inexplicable, and not necessarily good. It wasn't even anything tangible, nothing he could explain to friends to get a second opinion. Maybe Hayden was questioning Jez's sanity.

Sometimes Jez questioned it. No reason Hayden shouldn't worry about it too. Tonight, he'd wigged himself out enough that he'd even spread a puppy pad by the door, in case he couldn't bring himself to take Fang out for his before-bed pee.

Jez's phone rang, startling him.

Fucking hell. Now his phone was scaring him. He snatched it up. "Hello?"

"Hey, babe. How are you doing?"

Jez breathed easier. Even if he wasn't imagining the weird looks Hayden had directed at him, at least Hayden still cared. Knew Jez was worried, even if Hayden thought he was crazy.

"Doing okay. Watching a movie. Guess it's been a quiet night for you?"

Jez settled back into the couch and pulled the fleece throw over his legs and partially over Fang. He wasn't alone, and that made all the difference. Fang helped some, but he wasn't guard-dog material.

They talked for almost an hour, and as soon as Jez hung up, he dozed off.

Chapter 10

JEZ COULD hardly believe he'd been living in Hayden's house for almost two months. The house felt like home, but he was still checking out apartments. Although he hadn't slept in the guest room in weeks, Hayden hadn't mentioned making living together a permanent thing. It was all well and good to talk about the benefits of communication, but he couldn't invite himself to live there forever. And honestly, that might be moving too fast. Getting a place of his own might still be smart, even if he was becoming more reluctant each day. The more he came to care for Hayden, edging perilously close to love territory, the less he wanted to leave. They felt more solid as a couple than Jez had ever experienced with a boyfriend. Maybe it was because Jez was getting older and wiser. Or maybe living together for two months was the equivalent of dating for a year. Sort of a relationship fast track.

The sensation of being watched still lingered, but with no other incidents, Jez was able to mostly ignore it. He didn't think Hayden could, though. Those speculative looks cropped up every couple of days, and sometimes he thought Hayden wanted to ask him a question but changed his mind. Didn't feel like an invitation to live together, unfortunately. But it unsettled him enough to keep him searching for apartments. Not frantically, but he went to see a couple every few days, while Hayden was on shift.

It was hard to find anything that compared to the amenities he had in Hayden's house, and that didn't even include the frequent and utterly bone-melting sex.

Despite those few niggles, they were hosting their first party, a Black Friday dinner. Hayden had popped out to grab a few things they'd missed when they'd done the big grocery shop earlier in the week, and that gave Jez time to call and make some appointments to look at more apartments next week. Then he could enjoy the party and the weekend with Hayden, who'd started his four-off today.

HAYDEN'S SHOPPING trip had been a disaster. He'd only popped out to pick up a few things, but the universe had been pissed off about something.

Lentils. Who know they came in so many varieties? And tofu. Jez had specified exactly what he'd wanted, but Hayden hadn't been able to find it among the soppy, soggy, juicy bricks of processed soybean. And Jez hadn't answered the three texts Hayden had sent. If he hadn't grabbed an appropriate alternative, Jez was going to have to get it himself or do without. To make matters worse, an old woman in the checkout line patted his ass, and his beloved truck hesitated alarmingly when he started it up in the parking lot.

Fang bounced around his feet while he put away the few groceries, and Hayden patted him on the head before seeking out Jez. What he needed was a bit of loving attention from Jez to smooth over his spiky mood.

Hayden rocked to a stop outside the den. Jez was on the phone, and Hayden couldn't believe his ears. Hell, he'd have had an easier time—maybe—accepting that Jez was cheating on him. This... this was a betrayal he'd never seen coming.

But he waited until Jez was done. Waited and listened and heard enough to know he wasn't imagining things. Wasn't blowing things out of proportion.

They were expecting guests in a little under an hour, but Hayden didn't know how he could talk and laugh and mingle with this hanging over his head.

"Thanks. I'll see you then." Jez dropped his phone onto the coffee table with a clatter, stood, and saw Hayden. And Hayden saw the guilt, clear as if someone had Sharpied it across Jez's forehead.

"You're moving out." That hurt, pained voice couldn't belong to him. And yet the words were his, jagged shards of ice simultaneously slicing him to ribbons and freezing the warm place inside that loved Jez.

Jez rounded the couch. "No. I'm not. Not really."

Hayden pressed a fist to his stomach. Jez was the best thing that had ever happened to him, and he'd failed. Failed to make a go of the relationship. But why hadn't Jez told him? Hadn't he promised to help Hayden through the mire of relationship pitfalls? "I heard you."

"Well, yes, okay. I've been looking at apartments. I've been looking since my first week in California."

"But why?" If Vic and Jordan could see him now, they'd be utterly disgusted, but Hayden was ready to drop to his knees and plead for Jez to stay. He wanted to ask if Jez wasn't happy, but how could he? They—Hayden—didn't talk about feelings much. He knew what he felt for Jez was big, so big it overwhelmed him sometimes, but that had been okay. Because he'd been sure Jez was right there with him.

Now he knew he was wrong. Jez had been… killing time? If nothing else, that should negate Marco's theory that Jez was dangerous—in the stalker sense. But he was going to destroy Hayden nonetheless.

Jez shook his head and reached out for Hayden, but he flinched back. The look on Jez's face was like Hayden had slapped him. Pained and surprised all at once. Hayden didn't want to hurt Jez, but he couldn't process his own hurt, never mind assuage Jez's.

"Do you want me to stay? I mean, the plan was always for me to get an apartment, wasn't it?"

Hayden grudgingly lifted a shoulder. "Dunno. Maybe. But then we had sex."

"Oh? And you invite all your hookups to come and live with you, do you?"

Those words seared him like he'd walked into a three-alarm blaze wearing nothing but bunny slippers. Their first time had been special… to Hayden. Apparently Jez had thought it was only a hookup. And ever since then, what? Just an endless series of hookups? Had he agreed to be Hayden's boyfriend because he hadn't found somewhere else to live?

"If I did, I'd expect them to pick their clothes up off the floor and put their dirty dishes in the dishwasher."

Jez gaped at him, and Hayden didn't even know why he'd said that. It had nothing to do with what they were talking about, but he'd wanted to fling something back. Something that might hurt in return.

"What are you even talking about? I clean up after myself."

Hayden rolled his eyes. "You did not get the gay neatness gene. The only reason it looks like you clean up after yourself is because I do it for you."

What was happening? How had this veered so badly off the rails? And yet, Hayden was mad and hurt and had no fucking idea how to stop lashing out with the wild fire hose that was his mouth.

"Oh, if we're going to fling stereotypes at each other, you didn't get the decorating gene. Why on earth would you paint everything white? It's like a blank canvas for *The Matrix* or something. Or a hospital. A morgue."

God. Getting slammed in the balls wouldn't hurt like this. Hayden could barely drag in a breath. "Then maybe we ought to cancel the party. Give you a head start on apartment hunting. I wouldn't want to keep you in the morgue any longer than I have to. Don't worry, I won't expect you to hook up with me so you'll have a place to stay until you find an apartment." Hayden's voice was raw with unshed tears, but he'd be damned if he let Jez see how badly he'd been eviscerated.

He turned and strode as fast as he could without actually running to the bedroom. His, not theirs, as he'd been considering it. Hayden slammed the door behind him.

But the room was no longer the haven it had been. How would he hide what had happened in this room? There was no way to get more blank than white.

Angrily he scrubbed at his eyes and started yanking the blankets off the bed. If he was going to be alone from now on, he couldn't do it if his sheets smelled like sex and Jez.

The door to the bedroom blew open, Jez standing there like a sexy, heartbreaking avenging angel. Hayden froze, waiting for yet another attempt to carve out his heart.

"What the fuck was that?" Jez had never sounded so angry. "Wait, are you crying?"

Jez rushed over to him and Hayden sat on the bed, face averted. "No."

"Okay, I don't know what happened down there and I'm starting to think you don't know either." Jez sat beside him and grabbed his hand. "I think we need to talk. Calmly. Because I know I said some things I shouldn't have, and from what you said back to me, you took those things in the worst possible interpretation."

Hayden didn't think he could speak without his voice breaking, but Jez didn't seem in any hurry to do anything but rub Hayden's hand with his thumb.

Fang came into the room and bounded up the doggie steps to wedge his way onto their laps. Hayden used his free hand to pet the soft fur, a calming lassitude descending. His swollen eyelids burned and his nose was all stuffed up. But the rage had drained away, leaving only a gaping maw of pain, one he suspected might linger for a long time, like a second-degree burn that hurt to even shower with for days and weeks after the injury.

This time Jez wrapped his arm around Hayden's shoulder and tugged him close. It wasn't perfectly comfortable, but Hayden twisted to make it work, getting his nose into Jez's neck, inhaling that sweet spicy chai scent he loved so much and was going to have to get used to not having in his life.

"Let's start with the big-ticket item first. Which I think is apartment hunting."

"Do we have to rehash this all?"

Jez stiffened. "I don't know. I thought we were boyfriends. In a relationship. Who had a fight. I…. Do you not want to be with me anymore?"

A slow twisting started in Hayden's gut. Had he so badly misconstrued this? "I do want to be with you. I thought you didn't. That wasn't… that wasn't us breaking up?"

"Holy shit." Jez breathed the words out, sounding awestruck. "I hadn't realized when you said you'd never had a relationship, you'd never had a relationship. Didn't you and your friends ever disagree on things? Or your parents? Say things you regretted?"

Hayden shrugged. "I don't remember ever fighting with my parents until I came out to them. The closest Miguel and I ever came to arguing was the other night when he came over for dinner."

"What about Jordan and Vic? I mean, I'm glad you're done with them, but over the years you must have disagreed with them about something."

"Yes, but I never told them. Now that I've told them…." That hadn't been a fun conversation when

Jordan was done with his suspension. Even after Miguel had talked to Vic, Vic had called Hayden up and Hayden had to have the same conversation he'd had with Jordan. "Anyway, I'm glad they're gone too, but that was the first time we'd ever had anything close to an argument."

Jez hugged him, and Hayden allowed himself to believe that maybe things weren't as dire as he thought.

"Right. So, the only big blowups you've ever had with anyone… have been followed by you losing them. Your parents obviously set the stage for your avoidance of conflict, but we need to find ourselves a therapist, because you need to be able to speak your mind without fearing everyone is going to leave you."

Hayden bit his lip. "So just to be clear… you're not leaving me?"

"No, I'm not leaving you." Jez's words rang with conviction. "Hayden, I love you."

Oh. Hayden hitched a breath before his eyes started to burn again. "I… I love you too."

Jez wrestled him to the bed so they were lying down, pressed together, and Hayden got a full-body hug.

Hayden hugged Jez back but couldn't stop himself from whispering into his hair. "If we love each other, why don't you want to live with me?"

"Hayden, I do want to live with you. I've been loving living with you. But this is… unusual. I mean, we started living together, then having sex, and then dating. We've done everything backwards, and it's been… making me nervous. Like we missed a vital step."

"Uh-huh. And how has following conventional rules worked out for you so far?"

Jez sputtered out a laugh. "You've got a point. Maybe we just need to do what's right for us. If you want me to live with you, no reservations, then I will stop looking for apartments."

"I want that. Except… not if you think this is a morgue."

Jez's lower lip pushed out and he stroked Hayden's arm. "I don't. It was just a figure of speech, I swear. But it is very, uh, plain. I haven't done anything to change it so far, but if you want this to be my home too, I'd like some say over the decor."

Heart racing—and not in the way it usually did when he had Jez in bed—Hayden tried to breathe deeply, to calm himself. But the breaths kept coming faster and faster and his vision narrowed and Jez pinched his arm.

"Ow."

"Shit, Hayden, you were starting to hyperventilate. Look, I get that you're obsessive about cleaning and neatness, and I promise to try and be better about that, but what freaked you out so badly?" Jez seemed truly concerned, and to be honest, Hayden hadn't quite realized how affected he'd been.

"Uh, so, you know I lived here with my gran, right? She had this place decorated the way she liked it. Busy Victorian-style fuzzy wallpaper with intricate patterns. Knickknack tables and shelves filled with collectible porcelain figures and spoons and thimbles. Sometimes it was hard to get around, but everything had its place, and she loved those things. She also wasn't like other grandmothers. She had her own computer and she knew how to use it. She'd bid online for estate sales and auctions and Etsy and tons of other places. Get stuff delivered. It was manageable, or so I thought, until oh, I think I was about twenty-two or so. That's when most of the closets were filled. Then the deliveries became odder. Reams of old newspapers and magazines. Broken dolls and ripped stuffed animals that she was sure she could mend. But they all just sat around, and then encroached on the living space."

Jez's eyes were wide, focused on him, but Hayden couldn't hold his gaze very long. "I was still pretty young. I didn't know what to do about it, and if I tried to get rid of anything, she'd cry or scream or both. But as long as she had her stuff, however junky and weird it was, she was good."

"And no one knew? Not even Miguel?"

"Miguel hadn't even moved here when Gran started buying stuff. When he showed up, things were getting bad. I... have to admit, he seemed a little pre-occupied, and I wasn't a good enough friend to find out what was wrong. Now, of course, I know he was worried about you, but at the time, I think we used each other as a distraction from our family issues, rather than gaining true support. What I should have done was gone to talk to my supervisor—he's captain now—but it never occurred to me, and I had no one to ask." Yeah, his captain would have helped or figured out who could. Hayden had never appreciated what a good man he was, what a good leader he was, but as with many other things, the blinders of oblivion had been lifted.

"I'm so sorry, Hayden. I wish I could have been there, but I wouldn't have been any help either."

Hayden swooped in for a quick kiss, taking comfort in his boyfriend. Who was going to live with him.

"Thanks. I appreciate that. Anyway, so long story short, a few months before her death, the arthritis became so bad I was alternating between my shifts at the firehouse and being an almost full-time caregiver. Stuff wasn't stacked up to the ceiling, but there were only defined paths between piles, and only our beds and a couple of chairs escaped getting buried. After she passed, it took me two years to get everything cleaned out, and when I got down to that busy curlicued wallpaper, it had almost all been damaged by mold. I had to have the house fumigated, repaired, and repainted. Fortunately there were no cockroaches, but there were spiders and silverfish."

"Yikes. Okay, I get it. I do. But I'm hoping we can still work out a compromise here. I don't want to bring in a bunch of new stuff. I'm hoping for some color. Paint a few accent walls, get some colored throw pillows or curtains to go with those utilitarian white Venetian blinds. No wallpaper, I swear. Anyway, just think about it. Think about simple changes and see if you think you'd be able to handle it. Or wait until you set up some therapy. Talk it over with the therapist. Now that I know why things are the way they are, I'll stop pushing."

Hayden cupped Jez's cheeks. "I like when you push. You've made me see things I was blind to, and made my life better by being in it. Please continue to push." He dropped a small kiss on Jez's lips. "But gently. I'll think about it. I couldn't bring myself to get rid of Gran's movie and sewing stuff. I think she retained some small spark of that love, because she closed off that room without storing any junk in there, and it was the only room besides the kitchen that escaped the mold. I'd love to be able to do something with the things she truly loved, but every time I think about opening those boxes, I break out into a sweat."

"We're quite the pair, aren't we? And there's no rush on your gran's things. They'll be there when you're ready for them."

Hayden lowered his voice. "You know what?"

"What?" A breathy hitch told him Jez was thinking about them being a pair in other ways.

"I love you."

"I love you too."

"HEY, ARE you in here?"

Jez stared at Hayden, heart racing. It couldn't be.

Miguel stuck his head in the open door, and his eyes widened. Jez jerked the sheets to his chin like his brother hadn't already seen his very naked ass. Miguel's gaze flew around the room before he stepped back out into the hallway, but he didn't leave. "Oh my God. What is wrong with you two? No one fucks right before having guests over. Get dressed. I'm not the only one here."

"Guests," Hayden mouthed at Jez.

"Uh, how did you get in?" Jez called out even as he gathered up his clothes and started pulling them back on.

"Key, dumbass. I've had a key for years."

"That doesn't mean you just walk in." His voice got shrill, like when they'd used to fight as kids. "Normal people knock."

Had Miguel left his date, an engineering professor from Cal-Tech, downstairs? That was super embarrassing. And apparently he'd been dating her for a while, just wasn't willing to introduce her to the group while Jordan and Vic were a part of it.

Jez groaned as the elastic on his briefs snapped against drying cum. Miguel had him so flustered that he'd forgotten to clean up. That was almost as uncomfortable as unloading in your pants.

"I did knock. And I rang the doorbell. Called. Texted. Then two more of your guests showed up and I just unlocked the door and let them in."

God. Who could that be? Kevin with his wife? Marco, with or without a date? They were also expecting Paul and Tyson, both with dates, although Paul was bringing someone he called "arm candy boy toy." Jez was a little worried how a twenty-six-year-old would define "boy toy," but he guessed they'd find out. Tyson had managed to snag Jez's costar, Darin. Jez worried about the state of everyone's makeup if they broke up, but for now, Tyson was on the fucking moon, right there with Jez.

"Why are you all here early?"

Hayden waggled his hands like he expected Jez to suddenly be able to understand his made-up emergency sign language.

"We're not early. You're late. Dumbass. Get downstairs."

Fuck.

"If you shut up and leave, maybe we can."

"I'm going, I'm going."

The creak of the top stair signaled Miguel's retreat. "Offer them something to drink. We've got beer or wine," Jez called out.

He was almost certain Miguel snorted, but whatever. He was family, might as well make himself useful.

Jez shucked his briefs and darted into the bathroom to perform the quickest cleanup in the history of sex. When he came out, he pulled a fresh pair of briefs out of his side of the dresser. Then he paused and smiled.

"It makes me smile when you stand around naked, but what's your reason?" Hayden asked.

"Oh, I see you found your tongue," Jez sniped in a playful way. "Did you think if you were mute, Miguel wouldn't realize you were in here naked with me? He saw you."

Hayden hadn't required the same amount of cleanup and was already wearing jeans. He shrugged. "I don't know. It just felt weird, talking to your brother when we were both naked."

"And how do you think I felt?"

"Eh, you did fine." Hayden sauntered close and placed those large hands on Jez's shoulders before kissing him. "Maybe they can amuse themselves for a little longer."

Jez's still-sensitive cock brushed against the stiff denim, the atypical friction coaxing blood back into his groin. With a groan, Jez pulled away instead of pressing close and humping Hayden's leg. Being naked while Hayden was dressed felt so decadent, but they definitely weren't fucking again, with an audience this time. He pulled on his briefs quickly to help him avoid temptation. "Anyway, to answer your earlier question, I've already moved in. For real. I don't just sleep here, I keep my clothes here. My toothbrush is sitting next to yours in the bathroom. My bodywash is in your shower. I guess you're not the only one who's had some temporary blindness."

"Dammit, Jez. Now I want to throw you back in that bed even more."

"No. You save that for later. We'll have a little celebration after everyone leaves."

"I will do that." Hayden leaned in and bit his neck.

"Sneaky bastard. I'm not changing my mind." Although Hayden had come very close to convincing him. Jez danced away and pulled on more protective gear in the form of jeans and a snug bright purple dress shirt. "I can understand us missing a knock on the door, and our phones are downstairs, but how did we not notice the doorbell?"

"I'm just that good, baby."

For a man who claimed never to have brought a man home to his bed, Hayden was fucking spectacular, but Jez hadn't been insensate or in an orgasmic coma. He tilted his head to the side and squinted.

Hayden laughed. "When I was doing all the repairs to the house, I redid the doorbell. It doesn't ring up here at all."

"It doesn't? Why not?"

"Shift work, baby. I sleep at odd hours, and I figured out early on anyone who'd be ringing the doorbell while I was sleeping was never, ever anyone I wanted or needed to talk to. It only rings in the den, the office, and the kitchen, and not loud enough for me to hear when I'm in bed."

"Clever. Okay, lover boy, let's get downstairs and be good hosts."

By the time they got downstairs, all of their guests had arrived, and had been there long enough for Miguel to share, or rather overshare, about his sighting of Jez's ass.

But the teasing was good-natured, and the evening ended up being a million times better than the last time guests had been over. Jez didn't even shudder when Hayden turned on the television—briefly—to check a couple of football scores.

Living with a boyfriend was a new step for him too, but this felt right. The way it was supposed to be.

Chapter 11

JEZ PUTTERED around the house, mentally planning where he'd put up Christmas decorations. As soon as he got the nerve to talk to Hayden about it. And assuming Hayden could handle them. High on the success of their Black Friday party and the relationship breakthrough they'd had, they'd finally taken the plunge and booked appointments with the same therapist—at different times, because they weren't going to couples therapy, but it still felt super couple-y in a vaguely modern but possibly dysfunctional way.

Hayden had had one appointment already, and Jez's was upcoming. But he didn't know if Christmas decorations would set off Hayden's clutter issues.

Once he had a plan together, he'd broach it with Hayden. He turned up some music and danced around the den, the living room, and the dining room, imagining what he'd like. Good thing he was a fan of sleek and modern, because that had a better chance of finding acceptance with Hayden. The trick, of course, would be finding sleek and modern that also complemented the excellent but old-fashioned homey bones of a Craftsman house.

"Hey," Hayden called out from behind him.

Jez shrieked and whirled around. "You scared the crap out of me."

"Yeah, I gathered that." Hayden lifted the corner of his lip in a halfhearted smile. And frightening a year off his life ought to be worth a full-on smile, at the very least.

"What are you doing home?" Jez glanced at the clock on the DVR. "You're supposed to be at work."

"So are you, aren't you?"

"Nah, I got all the way to set and found out they switched to a night shoot and forgot to send me and a couple other people notices."

"Shitty."

Jez shrugged. Sometimes shit happened. "But why are you home?"

"Packing a bag. We're sending a crew up north to help out with the wildfire, and I'm on it."

"You mean the one that was on the news last night?" Jez shivered. Against the backdrop of a stretch of Northern California forest, the fire had glowed as ominously as an active volcano. It wasn't all that far from Willow Ridge either.

"Yeah. That one."

"Uh. Will it be dangerous?"

Hayden gave him a serious look, and Jez shivered again. By all accounts Hayden was good at his job, but he'd shared enough stories with Jez to drive home the point that the job was dangerous no matter where the fire was located.

"I'll be careful. I promise." His lips quirked in an almost full smile. "I have someone waiting for me at home now."

Fang barked and wiggled his butt. Mere minutes ago, he'd been asleep in the sunroom, but he must have heard Hayden's voice.

"Make that two someones at home." Hayden picked up Fang and accepted a few doggie kisses on his chin.

He carried Fang upstairs, and Jez abandoned his decoration plans to follow Hayden up and into the bedroom. The sheets were mussed, and the musky scent of their morning sex still hung in the air. The fact that Hayden didn't even flinch when he glanced at the unmade bed gave Jez hope that whatever had been triggered by his grandmother's hoarding wasn't too far gone. If he had to live inside a featureless white house for the rest of his life, he would, but he loved red. And blue. Lavender.

God. He had more important things to think about, however scary. Jez sat cross-legged on the bed while Hayden pulled out a duffel bag and methodically filled it. He'd definitely done this before.

"How long will you be gone?"

"One week. Maybe more, but won't be less."

"I still don't understand. It's December. I thought the wildfires were only in the summer."

Hayden gave him a pitying glance. "You lived in California for your first seventeen years. How could you not know about the fire seasons?"

"Dunno. I guess I spent most of my time trying to practice dance moves where no one would see me. And you said seasons, as in plural?"

"Yup. May more or less separates Santa Ana fire season from the summer fire season. Summer and Santa Ana switch off in October."

Jez swallowed around a lump in his throat. "You mean there is one month a year that isn't part of a fire season?"

Hayden shrugged. "Pretty much, yeah. And I'm guessing climate change will put paid to that sooner or later. Right now Pasadena doesn't get quite as much activity from the Santa Ana winds as other parts of the state, but yeah, fire season is more or less year-round."

Well that was fucking terrifying. How was it he'd never realized that?

All too soon, Hayden was packed up, and for the first time, it fully struck Jez that Hayden could be severely injured or even die doing his job. Fighting wildfires was even more dangerous than urban fires. This was a big, scary commitment, one that he'd made lightly, and now it was too late to undo it. He loved Hayden, and that wasn't ever going away. He was just going to have to learn to deal with his fear—and not with Xanax—whenever Hayden ended up in a dangerous situation.

"I was thinking."

Jez waited, not sure that ever prefaced anything good.

"If you want, while I'm away, you could start to redecorate one room. Not our bedroom. And we'll see how I handle it." He grinned ruefully. "I still have a few gallons of white paint in the storage under the stairs, just in case I freak out."

"Oh." Jez had not been expecting that. "That sounds like a plan." He wasn't sure whether Hayden had come up with the suggestion to test out his clutter phobia or if he was trying to find something for Jez to keep himself occupied and not worrying, but since it would work toward both ends, Jez was going to take it.

"Good. I, uh, have to get going."

"What if I hadn't been home?" He might have missed Hayden leaving.

Hayden gave him the sweet smile, the same one he wore every time he told Jez he loved him. "I was planning to stop by the set on my way out of town."

Best fucking boyfriend ever. Except for this whole running into raging fires thing, but Jez could hardly call such a heroic characteristic a flaw, even if it was going to scare the crap out of him from now on.

"Uh, maybe you could see if Maria wants to help you with the decorating?"

Oh. Yes, it was definitely intended as a make-work project, and Kevin must be going up north with Hayden. That didn't mean Jez wasn't going to do it, though. He adored Maria and was super glad Kevin wasn't a giant douche-nozzle like the friends Hayden had ditched, because that meant he got to keep Maria.

"I'll call her. Thanks for the suggestion."

Hayden stalked over to the bed and kissed Jez so thoroughly he was light-headed when Hayden pulled away. He cleared his throat. "Promise me you'll be careful."

"I promise. I'll call or text when I can, but I've done this before. It's exhausting and when you're not busy, you're sleeping, so I'll do what I can, but don't expect much."

Jez nodded. And then, with a creak of the stairs and the slam of the front door, Hayden was gone.

He didn't even know if Hayden had made him an emergency contact. That was going to be first on the list when Hayden got home, if Jez had anything to say about it.

Biting his lip, Jez lay back on the bed and curled up in sheets that still smelled like Hayden. He wasn't quite ready to face a big house that was going to feel extremely empty for the next week.

TWO WEEKS had seemed so long, with Hayden promising he'd be home before Christmas for sure. He'd even sent Jez a little present, which was so sweet, considering how focused he needed to be on his job. But today was the day. Jez couldn't believe they'd switched the filming schedule just for him, but he'd become friends with a number of people involved in his show, and he'd shared his fears about Hayden fighting the wildfires up north with just about all of them. It didn't hurt that the fires had continued discussion on the news since Hayden had left. When he'd told the director yesterday that Hayden would be home sometime today, he'd immediately shifted the schedule to give him two days off. He had no doubt that in the future it might be his job keeping him from greeting Hayden at home, but he was immensely grateful he had the chance to do so now.

He'd already tuckered out poor Fang, who'd followed him all over the house as he'd checked the guest room he, Maria, and some of the guys from the set had decorated. With Hayden away for two weeks, they'd almost finished. In between paranoid rechecking of the room, he paced all over the house, making sure he hadn't left any other sort of mess that would get under Hayden's skin.

Everything had to be perfect.

The door opened, and Jez ran down the stairs, flinging himself at Hayden, who dropped his duffel bag in time to lift Jez up in a giant hug. Jez buried his face in Hayden's neck, brushing up against some heavy-duty stubble that bordered on beard territory. Although he'd showered, the cloying scent of smoke lingered to the point Jez suspected whatever clothes Hayden had taken with him would have to be thrown out or soaked in bleach.

Hayden set him down and kissed him, Jez just opening up like the first time they'd kissed, except this was better, a million times better, because he'd been so fucking worried.

Then Jez stepped back and took a good look at his man. They'd worked him hard—in two weeks he'd visibly dropped weight, and he had dark smudges under his eyes that weren't soot. The pseudobeard only added to the rough mountain-man look. He had a few scabs on his face, and Jez dropped his gaze to the white bandages on Hayden's hands.

"What happened?"

Hayden followed his gaze. "Stray embers. As burns go, they could be worse."

"Weren't you wearing gloves or something? Protective gear?"

Hayden shrugged. "Shit happens, and when you're fighting wildfires, shit happens fast and unpredictably."

Jez pursed his lips. He suspected Hayden wasn't going to tell him any more than that, likely because Jez might—definitely would—freak out.

"I'm glad you're home. The chocolates weren't necessary at all, and they're way too much for just us, but thank you anyway." Jez hugged him again, but gently, as Hayden winced. However minor Hayden claimed his injuries were, the past two weeks had clearly taken a physical and mental toll. Fortunately, according to the news, no firefighters had died, which was probably as good for Hayden's sanity as it was for Jez's.

Hayden frowned at him. "What chocolates?"

"The ones you had delivered. Didn't you? They came today. I assumed they were from you." Jez's mouth dried out as Hayden continued to frown in confusion.

"I didn't have anything delivered."

Jez whirled and strode into the kitchen, Hayden on his heels. "These." Two pounds—a ridiculous amount for someone who had to watch almost every calorie he put in his mouth if he wanted to keep his job—sat on the counter. And he wouldn't have eaten them anyway, as they weren't vegan; he'd assumed Hayden had forgotten that most chocolate had dairy in it. But now they lurked rather than sitting innocuously as they'd done not thirty minutes prior.

"Did they have a return address?"

"No. A delivery guy showed up and handed them to me."

"What about a card?"

Jez shrugged. "I didn't see one, but I couldn't think of anyone else who would send me something like this." Or at least, no one who knew his address. Jayson was long out of his life and living clear across the country. This had to be some sort of weird, uncomfortable coincidence.

Hayden picked up the box and looked underneath. A white envelope was stuck to the bottom. Hayden yanked it off and ripped it open.

"From your secret admirer."

Hayden turned the paper over in his hands, frowning. Jez stumbled to the kitchen table and fell heavily into one of the seats.

"It can't be."

"What can't be?"

"Hayden, this is how it started with Jayson. He sent me all these gifts, supposedly from my secret admirer. It was this coy little deception that amused the crap out of him."

Hayden brought the chocolates and card over to the table.

The chocolates were still sealed, but that didn't make a difference to Jez. They were going right in the garbage. In an earlier, more idyllic time, food items from a secret admirer would have been sweet. But even without his experience with Jayson, eating something from an unknown sender seemed about as smart as accepting a drink from a guy in a club when you hadn't watched the bartender mix it up yourself.

"Maybe it's nothing." If Jez had been on film that second, no one would have bought his conviction. This was something, he just didn't know what.

Hayden pulled out his phone. After a few seconds, he lifted his head, expression serious. "What was that guy's name again?"

"Jayson. Jayson Bain."

Hayden flipped his phone so Jez could see it. An article dated October 30 spoke of several hockey trades. Jez clutched the phone and scrolled to find the list of players' names. Jayson fucking Bain. Jayson had been traded to Los Angeles. That couldn't be a coincidence. It hadn't been headline news anywhere because Jayson hadn't played enough to have any name recognition, and Jez had deleted his hockey app weeks ago in an attempt to pretend Jayson had never been a part of his life.

Jez wrung his hands, fingers chilled and bloodless. "How did he find me? What is he *doing* here?"

Hayden wrapped both of his large hands around Jez's smaller ones, and they radiated heat and comfort. "First, this could be a coincidence. It's a weird one, I grant you. But that doesn't mean it's not true. I think we should wait and see."

Jez nodded, but he didn't believe that. For whatever reason, Jayson had followed him to California. It had been months of radio silence. The restraining order should have been the end of it.

"I'm going to call Marco."

Panic spiked, making Jez shaky and tense. "No, you can't."

Hayden squeezed his hands. "Hey. We can wait if you want, but I think it would be a good idea. But first, maybe you ought to tell me how it is Jayson took out a restraining order on you. Did you… I don't know, retaliate in some way after your request for a protection order was denied? You can tell me anything, I swear."

Jez hung his head. He'd hoped with all his soul that he'd just be able to forget all the crap with Jayson had ever happened. But that was not to be.

"I'm sorry. I should have told you everything. But I was afraid you'd think I was crazy. It sounds fucking crazy, so fucking crazy I ditched all my friends, who didn't believe me, and it's why I ended up needing antianxiety meds. How long have you known about the protection order?"

"Since the night you got arrested."

Jez stared at Hayden. In other words, weeks. Hayden had known weeks and not only hadn't demanded to know what was going on, but hadn't treated Jez any differently, despite the occasional quizzical glance. Hell, Jez had never been so pampered as he'd been when Hayden brought him home from the police station.

"Thank you."

"For what?" Hayden genuinely had no clue, and Jez didn't know how he'd gotten so lucky.

"For believing in me. If you didn't, you would have demanded that day to know why I'd lied. Or at least left out part of the story."

"I loved you even then. And I was sure whatever happened, you weren't crazy."

A bitter laugh escaped his throat. "I'm glad you think so, because sometimes I'm not so sure." He dragged in a fortifying breath and tried not to grimace at the taste of soot that accompanied it.

"So, everything happened the way I told you. But then, when I thought Jayson had stopped, given up, he'd been sending himself gifts. That were supposedly from me. He had a burner phone and used that to call his own phone at weird hours. Gushy emails from a generic JB1993 email address that he also claimed was mine. And then he went to the cops and got his own restraining order against me. I assumed it was partly because he was mad at me and partly because he'd gotten called up to an NHL team. I figured he'd use the restraining order as a way to prove his straightness and to support his argument that I was only a crazy fan, not a boyfriend. And he didn't get laughed out of the station, because he was rich and a minor celebrity with a great athletic career in his future."

"That's messed up."

"I even tried to explain that I hadn't bought those things, that the email wasn't mine, but it didn't matter. No one was going to subpoena financial records for a protection order, especially when I had no intention or desire to get within fifty yards of Jayson ever again. Honestly, it seemed like a relief. Like he was admitting we were truly done. It seemed a small price to pay for that freedom."

Hayden gripped his hands again. "Then came the job offer from the casting director."

"Exactly. The job was a godsend, because my relationship with Jayson changed everything, but if I wiped my life and ran, maybe that would put me back on the right track."

"Yeah, I'm calling Marco. We need to share this with him. Get a record of it. It might be the only way to fight back." Hayden flipped the box of chocolates over. "You wouldn't even eat these anyway. There's dairy in them."

"I love you." Hayden might not ever become a vegan, but Jez adored the fact that Hayden just accepted his veganism and made their lives work around it, rather than try to cajole him.

"I love you too." Hayden's voice was soft and warm, like being wrapped in a fuzzy blanket. And there were better things to do than talking with his firefighter boyfriend who'd been gone for two weeks being a hero.

"Can we just forget about this for now? For a day? I want to go upstairs and spend the rest of the day in bed with you, whether we have sex or sleep."

Hayden smiled, wide and happy. "Both would be better. But sleep first."

Jez smiled back. "Sleep first."

"Let's go. The chocolates will keep until morning."

Thank God he'd stocked up on edibles like chips and dip and veggie crudités. They'd have plenty of fuel to keep them going without any major interruptions.

Chapter 12

JEZ THOUGHT he'd be awake long before Hayden, but between the stress of Hayden being gone, the extra work he'd put into redecorating one of the rooms, and then the panic of the secret admirer gift, he'd actually slept in a little bit. Until Hayden had gone to work under the covers, reminding Jez of one of the many, many reasons living with Hayden was the best thing ever.

After they'd cleaned up, they went downstairs. While Hayden started making coffee, Jez tossed the box of chocolates in a cupboard in the mudroom where he wouldn't have to look at it every time he walked into the kitchen.

They drank coffee while Fang danced around their feet.

"When do you have to be back at the firehouse?"

Hayden shrugged. "I have another few days off. When are you due on set?"

That was the best news ever. "I have today off. We can just… stay home."

With a grin, Hayden pulled him close with one arm. "Best homecoming ever." He glanced down at Fang doing his puppy pee-pee dance. "Should we just put him out in the yard or get dressed and take him for a walk?"

As much as Jez wanted to stay holed up indoors, taking their dog for a walk wasn't a bad thing. The weather was good, and Hayden might like to enjoy some fresh air that wasn't filled with ash and soot. They could even go past the doughnut place Hayden liked—which also carried vegan doughnuts—and get a treat for breakfast. Later, he could enjoy one of his favorite activities: stripping his boyfriend out of his clothes. Always a fun time.

With Fang's increasing desperation, they got dressed lightning fast, snapped on Fang's leash, then got going.

AN HOUR later, with Fang's energy depleted, they walked hand in hand up their street, Hayden carrying a box of doughnuts and Jez carrying a sleepy pup.

They turned up their walkway and Jez yanked on Hayden's hand, pulling him to a stop.

"What's up, baby?"

Jez thrust his chin toward the door. "Were you expecting a delivery?"

Expression fierce, Hayden drew himself up, then let go of Jez's hand to inspect the cellophane-wrapped bundle.

"It's a fruit basket," Hayden called out.

Jez approached slowly, cuddling Fang close to his chest. "Read the card."

"Your secret admirer." Hayden's tone was positively glacial. "We're calling Marco."

"It's a fruit basket." Jez tried to reason with Hayden, although as far as he was concerned, it might as well have been a basket of vipers. "The cops won't take this any more seriously than they did in New York. Even if you are friends with some of them."

Hayden sighed. "Maybe you're right. This isn't exactly dangerous. But we're taking pictures of this too, just in case."

"Put it in the mudroom for now, please." It could rot there with the chocolates for all Jez cared, but he suspected Hayden would make sure the perishables went out with the next garbage pickup. Jez had no desire to be subjected to ridicule a second time, didn't want anyone implying he had some sort of mental illness beyond the anxiety that was all Jayson's fault anyway.

Hayden grasped the handle with his free hand, then peered more closely at the contents. "Mangos? You don't even like mangos. Can we be sure this was Jayson? Between the nonvegan chocolates and these mangos, how could this be an ex-boyfriend?"

Those words filled Jez with more warmth and love than a standing ovation. "I have to admit, that was a big part of why I broke up with him. He never listened when I spoke, never thought about me as a person at all beyond being his boyfriend. You know, in private, where no one from the league would find out."

The fates could not be so cruel as to give Jez another stalker. The simplest explanation was Jayson. "Maybe this is Jayson's way of apologizing? I mean, he's got a high-profile career to think about now. And no one is going to believe chocolates and mangos are a problem."

The look Hayden sent his way said he was not convinced. "Maybe. But I still think I should call Marco. Not officially, but as a friend."

Hayden led them inside and put the fruit basket in the mudroom while Jez started another pot of coffee to have with their doughnuts.

Hayden got out plates, because that was a given, and they sat at the kitchen table waiting for the coffee to brew. After pushing the fried, glazed, sprinkle-covered pastry around the plate for a few minutes, Hayden huffed. "Look. I understand why you want to avoid talking to the cops. I get it. I do. But here's the thing. He's the one who has a restraining order, so whether or not he manufactured the incidents required to get one, that piece of paper is going to color your interactions with anyone official. What if he wants to take this a step further? What if he's trying to goad you into violating the protection order?"

Shit, shit, shit. Jez had just started wondering if he should call Jayson. Tell him to back off or ask him if he was responsible for sending the gifts. But Hayden made a damn good point. Considering Hayden made a lifelong habit of avoiding conflict, the least Jez could do was take Hayden's suggestion seriously. Especially since such a diabolical plan suited his scheming, vindictive ex.

The basket's arrival had already cast a pall over the day anyway. "Fine. Call Marco. We can get his opinion."

Hayden beamed, and Jez suspected he'd be giving in to Hayden's persuasiveness more often than not.

After the phone call where they decided Marco would stop by sometime after noon, Hayden inhaled three doughnuts. "C'mon. Let's watch a movie or something. Take our mind off things."

Jez did his best to smile. "Sounds good."

AT THE dining room table he almost never used, Hayden sat between Jez and Marco. They'd been there for an hour now while Marco took notes and picked apart every bit of Jez's story. If this was "unofficial" Marco, Hayden could only imagine how much more exacting he was when interrogating an actual criminal. Aside from some uncomfortable hand-wringing, Jez's answers and comportment seemed to… thaw Marco somewhat. He hadn't gone so far as to be impressed, but Hayden was confident he'd treat the situation with gravity and fairness.

Marco tapped his notebook with his pen. "Okay, I don't want to give you false hope." Those words sent Hayden's stomach plummeting ankleward. "I have confidence that the majority of my fellow law enforcement in New York would have investigated your claim with the same impartiality they would have any other. That being said, mistakes are made. And even cops can be assholes. From what you've told me, it's possible that you slipped through the cracks. But honestly, it's also possible that you did what this Jayson Bain said you did, and you're lying right now."

Hayden scowled at his friend. Marco'd never said anything derogatory in Hayden's presence that he could recall, but could he still have some deep-seated prejudices? "What the fuck, Marco? He's not lying to you. I'm not lying to you. I see people stunned, in shock, on a weekly fucking basis, and Jez was totally taken by surprise when those things showed up."

"Relax, Hayden. I don't think you're lying, Jez. But your ex has already met the burden of proof, and that's going to tip things in his favor."

"There's nothing you can do?" Hayden wanted to nip things in the bud before anything escalated.

"I didn't say that either. I can ask some questions, see if there's enough to open an official investigation. You already told me that they think you paid for all of those gifts, both to yourself and later to Jayson. That's quite damning."

"And I also told you I didn't. I don't know who paid for them, but it wasn't me. I swear. I can give you my bank statements. My credit card statements. Can't you get his financial records?"

Marco shook his head. "Nope. It'd take an act of God to open an investigation and subpoena records with what you've given me so far. But send me your statements. I'll do some digging. See if there's anything I can use to take to a judge."

"Thanks, Marco. I appreciate anything you can do." Jez said all the right things, but he clearly didn't have faith that Marco would accomplish anything. Hayden didn't care. Documentation was important.

But Hayden wasn't going to let Jayson tear Jez's life apart a second time.

They stood and walked Marco to the door. Jez had his arms wrapped around his torso like he was cold. After Marco left, Hayden pulled him close and kissed him. "It's all going to work out fine." Hayden wouldn't stand for any other outcome, even if it meant hiring a pit bull of a lawyer.

"I hope so." Jez sighed. "I sometimes think if I hadn't tried to get a restraining order in the first place, this wouldn't be happening now."

"You don't know that. And you can't blame yourself. Your ex did some seriously shady shit. Just stealing your passwords is pretty fucking skeevy. If he wasn't already doing okay, you could be out a lot of money, because who says he'd stop at getting your banking passwords and PINs too? Or he might have physically hurt you. Second-guessing is a useless exercise."

"Yeah. I guess."

Hayden tilted his head. "How about a happier topic? Did you end up doing any decorating? Can I see?" He hadn't seen anything out of place, but he had noticed Jez had been extra careful to ensure Hayden hadn't come home to a mess, confirming he'd picked the right man to fall in love with. He was surprisingly eager to see what Jez had done.

Jez clapped his hands. "Oh, yes. Maria and I had a great time." Then he pouted. "But it's not quite ready. I had to order some stuff that hasn't arrived yet. Don't go into any of the guest rooms, okay?"

Hayden's pulse picked up just a bit. "Any? I thought we agreed one room."

"We did, but decorating can create a bit of a mess, so I kept it all in the other two rooms. When the new room is ready, the other two will get cleaned up too, I promise."

All right. He could accept that. "Then how about we settle in on the couch. Watch TV and order pizza." One day Hayden was going to have to take Jez out to a club or something, but he was glad Jez didn't seem to mind hanging out around home. Without any gay friends, clubbing had been a means to an end. But Hayden thought he might enjoy dancing with his boyfriend and knowing that man would be coming home with him and getting into their bed.

"Sounds awesome."

HAYDEN GRINNED as he parked his car outside the house. He and a completely new and nontoxic group of firefighters had hit the bar after shift for wings and beer. Without the shroud of Jordan's negativity, Hayden discovered his coworkers liked him, and he felt confident he'd be able to build a new circle of friends. The worst this group had done was dare him to order a hotter wing sauce than he normally ate. Mostly harmless fun, although he might change his mind about that next time he went to the bathroom.

After he'd eaten his fill of wings—his face was still burning—he and Kevin had gone shopping together, since they'd been heading to the same general area. Hayden had gotten Jez what he hoped was the perfect Christmas gift. He wasn't sure how he was going to resist waiting a whole week to give it to Jez. This was also the first year since his gran died that he hadn't volunteered to work Christmas Day. Miguel was going to come over, and the three of them were going to have a small family dinner with all the trimmings. And whatever vegans ate for holiday dinners. He sincerely hoped Tofurky was something comedians had made up for laughs.

Lost in his thoughts, he was on the porch before he noticed the enormous rainbow bouquet of gerbera daisies in a glass vase. Just like that, Jayson "secret admirer" Bain ruined another good mood. That dude had an impeccable sense of timing. It had been a few days since the last "gift," and Hayden had just started to hope that maybe there wouldn't be any more.

Bastard.

He brought the vase inside and set it on the kitchen counter before he called Marco.

"Dude. There's another gift."

"Is Jez there with you?"

"No, but I expect him home in an hour or so."

"Okay, I'll be by in about ninety minutes or thereabouts. It'll be better if you're both there."

Hayden disconnected the call, then dashed upstairs to hide Jez's gift, take a quick shower, and get Fang outside for a pee. He went back to the kitchen. He wanted have a diet Cuba libre ready to soothe the blow of getting another damned gift. Dinner would be delivery again—no way either of them would want to cook after Marco left, even if he said he could go and arrest Jayson.

Hayden had just finished pouring the Diet Coke over the dark rum when he heard Jez's key in the lock. Hayden snatched up the glass and dashed to the door, standing next to Fang to greet Jez.

"Hello there." Jez smiled at him. "This is a nice surprise."

Hayden kissed him, took his bag and hung it up while Jez greeted Fang, then handed Jez the glass.

"I could definitely get used to this sort of treatment," Jez teased.

Hayden grimaced and the smile fell off Jez's face.

"Wait. This is booze to cushion a blow, isn't it?" Jez wrinkled his nose, then sneezed. And sneezed again.

"Are you getting a cold?" Maybe the flu? They were smack in the middle of flu season, and firefighters saw a number of flu victims, primarily the elderly, who'd called 911 for emergency services.

Jez frowned. "I don't know. Maybe. But never mind that. What happened? No, wait." Jez waved a hand at him before taking a giant gulp of his Cuba libre.

"You missed your calling as a bartender." Jez sucked in a deep breath. "Okay, I think I'm ready."

Another sneeze prevented Hayden from speaking right away. "Another gift came today." He checked his watch. "Marco should be here in about ten minutes or so."

"Fucking hell." Jez drew in a deep breath, then handed Hayden his glass before letting out an explosive series of sneezes, scaring Fang right upstairs. When he stopped convulsing, he straightened up. "I'm so sorry." The *s* sounds had become *th* sounds, and tears streamed from reddened eyes.

"Holy shit. This cold came on fast." Scary fast. What the hell kind of virus was that?

Jez shook his head. "Let me guess. That fucker sent flowers. Daisies?"

"Oh shit. Yeah. A giant bouquet of gerbera daisies."

Jez bared his teeth in a snarl before he started sneezing again.

"Let me grab you something."

"No, I'll grab some toilet paper from the bathroom. You get rid of those fucking flowers."

Hayden sped back to the kitchen and set Jez's glass on the counter before getting out the garbage bags. Shit, he'd known certain flowers were terrible for Jez, but he'd never seen him around daisies. He should have thought of allergies first off.

The doorbell rang, and Hayden tossed the flowers in the mudroom before answering the door. "Hey, Marco."

"Where's the flowers?"

Hayden rolled his eyes. "Inside two garbage bags in the mudroom." Double-knotted too, completely bypassing the drawstrings.

"Was that necessary?" Marco asked as he followed Hayden into the dining room and sat down.

Hayden gestured at Jez, who appeared in the room carrying a roll of toilet paper, eyes red and streaming, nose shiny and pink.

"Are you crying?" Marco half stood. "Have you been hurt?"

Jez rolled his eyes, sat down, and sneezed again. Hayden answered for him. "He's allergic to the flowers that Jayson gifted."

"Allegedly gifted."

This time both he and Jez rolled their eyes. "Fine. Allegedly. But I should think this would help convince you that Jez didn't buy these flowers himself." As if the milk chocolate and mangoes hadn't been convincing enough. "Jez was in the house all of two or three minutes before the sneezing started. Hence double-bagging the flowers. I left the card out in case you want it."

"I do want it. But I've also got a bit of information for you." Marco pulled out his notebook. "A credit card in the name of Jez Bouchet was used to purchase both chocolates and fruit basket via an online transaction. I assume the card was used for the flowers."

Jez sat up straight and sputtered. "But I didn't. I didn't, I swear."

"Calm down. I'm not done yet."

"I thought you said you couldn't get a subpoena for financial records." That got Hayden an amused look, which Hayden took heart from. If Marco was amused, there was hope.

"Sometimes people will just cooperate with the police when they ask, you know. Despite what TV would have you think. And the name on a credit card slip isn't on par with state secrets. Or financial records from a bank. I also requested copies of the supporting documentation used to initiate the protection order. There were also credit card slips. Obviously the full card number wasn't visible, but the last four digits and expiry date were the same, so I think we can say the same card was used to buy all gifts, including the ones you've just received."

"But I don't understand. How is that even possible?"

Marco gave Jez a pitying look. "There are a number of ways someone could take out a credit card in your name. It remains to be seen if your alleged stalker is the one who did so, but since I can't find any record of payments made to this card from the bank statements you gave me and the card number doesn't match the credit card you have... I have enough to open up an official inquiry. If I can get a sympathetic judge, yeah, we should be able to requisition the appropriate records, but even if that happens, it's going to take a while. Without a definite threat, this is going to be considered low priority."

Jez's shoulders dropped. "I understand."

Marco gave them a few things to look out for in case the gift-giver—he would not admit it was Jayson—was watching them or following them, and then they said their goodbyes.

They sat together on the couch, taking comfort in the other's presence. Hayden had no more words for Jez. Only time would see this through, but hopefully Christmas would lift his spirits.

Partway through the evening, a brilliant if terrifying idea struck Hayden in the midst of yet another onslaught of holiday-themed commercials.

"I have an idea. Why don't we go out this weekend and get a Christmas tree, have dinner someplace nice, then come back and decorate it."

Jez snorted and pulled out of Hayden's arms to sit cross-legged on the couch, staring at the side of his face. "A Christmas tree? Really? I'm okay not having a tree. I haven't for years. I never had room in my apartment for one anyway."

"All the more reason to get one. I used to love putting up a tree with Gran, and I think I'd regret not having one for our first Christmas together."

Quickly, Jez kissed his cheek. "Won't dropping needles trigger your issues?"

Hayden laughed. "It won't be a real tree. Those things a fire hazard. We'll get a nice, fake, fire-retardant tree from Target. Better for your allergies too."

"Okay, that makes more sense. Do you have any decorations?"

In the mostly empty attic, he'd stored a single box of ornaments. But the thought of bringing them down, in all their mismatched ugliness, made him shudder. "We'll buy some of those too. Maybe just one or two colors to start with." Hayden thought about that for a moment and nodded. "Yes, that will be okay, I think."

If it turned out to not be okay, they could donate the tree or pack it away in the attic to try again another year.

"It's a plan. I'll make reservations somewhere." Jez bounced a couple of times before snuggling back against Hayden.

Just like that, the specter of Jayson Bain had been banished. Temporarily.

Chapter 13

JEZ HAD had the best day. Since it was the Saturday before Christmas, they'd had to scour four different Targets to get everything they needed—in only blue and silver—for their tree. And because it was in fact only three days before Christmas, all of the Targets were bustling. But everyone was filled with the best of the holiday spirit, and Jez hadn't needed a Xanax or had to take a break. Then they'd gone to a place that offered steaks and vegan dishes. Hayden had worked the day after the flowers had arrived, and in his absence, Jez had put the finishing touches on the guest room. He wanted to show it to Hayden so bad, but he didn't want to overwhelm him. The Christmas tree would be enough for today, and if that went well, he'd share the room with Hayden on Christmas Day.

He reached over and squeezed Hayden's knee.

"Love you, baby." Hayden shot him a quick grin before he turned onto their street.

"Love you too." Then he got a look at the parking situation. "Whoo. Busy night in the hood. Someone must be having a party."

Although they'd gone very minimalist with the decorations and fake tree, Jez suspected they'd need at least two trips to get everything in the house. Two trips would suck.

Hayden pulled into a spot three doors down, and they hopped out of the truck. "Bags first, then come back for the tree?"

Jez nodded. "Yeah. Let's do that."

Armed with their purchases, they started walking toward their place.

A grunting bark made Jez pause. "Did you hear Fang?"

Hayden stopped and listened. "I don't know. We shouldn't be able to hear him from here, should we?"

Jez couldn't see the front of their house for the shrubbery that separated the property from the Johnsons' on the east side. "I don't think so. Could we have left a window open?"

Hayden shook his head. "Not hardly. It's been too cool to open windows."

Jez shrugged, took another step, then heard Fang's silly bark before the fat puppy burst out of the bushes, tail wagging, fur covered in bits of dried grass, twigs, and leaves.

"What the hell?" He set his bags down and scooped up Fang. "What are you doing here?" Sweat broke out all over his body. Fang was so fucking eager. What if he'd bounded into the street? He could have been hit by a car and Jez might never have known what happened.

Hayden looked just as stricken and had dropped his bags so he could hold them both. "I don't like this," Hayden whispered.

"What do you mean?"

"We are both so careful. We didn't leave a door or window open that Fang could have gotten out of. How did he get out here?"

Then fear beyond Jez's concern for Fang's safety sent his heart galloping.

Hayden peeked around the bushes. Holding Fang tight to his chest, Jez did the same. Nothing appeared out of place. No packages sat on the doorstep. Light from the lamp in the den they turned on when they left the house gave the front windows a golden glow.

Everything looked perfectly normal. They must have just had a lapse when they'd left the house. Fang had slipped out with them or something. He hated the thought of his baby on his own outside for so long, but they'd just have to be more careful. Jez's breathing started to slow, and Hayden relaxed, standing up straight.

Then a shadow moved at the edge of that warming golden glow, but liquid nitrogen had frozen Jez's blood.

"What the fuck?" he whispered.

Hayden yanked him back behind the shrubs, pulled out his phone, scrolled through his contact list. "Marco. Someone's in our house," Hayden said into the phone, barely louder than a whisper.

There was a pause. "We're outside. We just parked down the street and we saw a shadow inside."

Another pause. "Thanks." He shoved his phone back in his pocket.

"They're coming. Marco said go back to the truck and wait."

Jez nodded. It wasn't a bulletproof truck or anything, but he'd feel a lot safer there than out in the open.

They kept craning their heads around, and Hayden swore and started the truck.

"What are you doing?" Jez whispered, like the intruder could hear them three doors down and inside a truck.

"Turning the fuck around." Hayden drove farther down the street, made a U-turn, then parked on the other side of the street. They could see their front door from here, and hopefully the intruder hadn't heard anything suspicious.

"Why did you do that?"

Hayden snorted. "If I see whoever it is leaving before the cops get here, I'm going to fucking follow them."

"What if the engine scared them away?"

"Someone on this street is having a party. Cars driving down this street shouldn't concern him."

Jez liked this better anyway. They'd be able to see what happened instead of trying to see out the back window.

Within moments, cop cars without sirens converged on the house. Officers got out and some went around the back. Then, suddenly, it was all over.

Two officers emerged from the house with a struggling man between them. Jez hopped down from the truck, Fang still in his arms. In the dark, and from this distance, he couldn't tell if it was Jayson, and he fucking needed to know.

Marco caught up with him as he strode onto the front lawn. "Jez, you shouldn't be here."

The flashing red and blue lights brought neighbors out onto their lawns. Then the intruder and his captors moved closer to the ring of police cruisers with their bright headlights.

Jayson. It was definitely Jayson. Who caught sight of Jez at the same time.

"No. Arrest *him*," Jayson screamed, staring at Jez. "I have a restraining order. He's in violation. He's too close. Arrest *him*."

"It doesn't work that way, dumbass. You broke into *his* house," one of the officers beside Jayson said.

As soon as Jayson was secured in the cruiser, Jez went into the house, grabbed Fang's leash, then attached leash to dog and the other end of the leash to belt. Wherever Jez went tonight, Fang was going to follow.

Marco accompanied Jayson to the station while Jez and Hayden stayed at the house and gave their statements to other officers. Hours later, Jez's eyes burned from exhaustion, and he'd just made the fourth pot of coffee. The emergency locksmith who'd changed all their locks had drunk a cup. Cops and crime-scene techs had been in and out of his kitchen getting coffee. They'd taken possession of Jayson's gifts, which Hayden—surprisingly—hadn't tossed out yet, then assessed the rest of the house. They'd soon determined Jayson had spent most of his time in their bedroom vandalizing their bed.

Jez had been afraid that piece of information would send Hayden over the edge, but he'd been a rock. Maybe he'd have a delayed reaction, or maybe the years had healed him some. Maybe Hayden's quirks were more a symptom of grief rather than full-blown OCD. Either way, Jez had already sent their therapist a message while Hayden was in the bathroom, because whether or not this set Hayden off, Jez was pretty sure they'd be nervous sleeping in their bedroom for a while.

Yet another crime-scene tech came into the kitchen. "Can I take a look at the other rooms upstairs?" Jez asked. Because if Jayson had destroyed his hard work in the guest room, he might have to break into the jail and strangle the bastard.

"Sure. Just not the master bedroom."

Good. Because they also needed a place to sleep, and he'd like to get fresh sheets on the bed in his old room so they could crash the second the house emptied. God. What would this be like if someone had been *murdered*?

"You okay?"

Hayden nodded and started pouring his own coffee.

"Okay, I'll be back in a few."

Brave going upstairs all by himself with all these cops around, but Jez suspected he'd be sticking close to Hayden and turning on a lot of lights over the next few days.

First he checked out the room he'd decorated just for Hayden. The door was still closed. Jez took a deep breath and turned the knob.

Then let out a gusty sigh of relief. Pristine. Absolutely pristine. He shut the door again, then quickly set up his old room so it would be basically habitable.

When he got downstairs, Marco had returned.

"Long night, you guys. But it's almost over. They're getting ready to head out."

"Anything we should know?" Hayden asked. Jez almost wanted to shepherd them into the dining room, since that had sort of become the "debriefing" room, but Marco merely pulled a kitchen chair away from the table and sat down.

Marco gave them a stern look. "No spreading this around, got it? Because I shouldn't be telling you this. Not until all the paperwork's been signed off on." Then he grinned at them. "It was incredible. He started talking as soon as we got him in the interrogation room. We'll have to follow up on everything to get supporting documentation, but there's no doubt in my mind he was behind all the gifts, both here and in New York."

"Really?" The relief was more euphoric than an hour-long massage.

"Really. He admitted to learning your passwords, as you'd suspected. He also used your computer and banking information to open a credit card in your name. Once we get his financial records, I'm certain we'll have proof he was paying those bills. Probably had them mailed to a PO box. He'd also opened a web-based email account, user JB1993, so he could get updates and submit online orders without it being easily traced to him. He used the new credit card to buy a burner phone in your name."

"How did he find me? I thought I'd disappeared pretty thoroughly, and even changed my phone number."

Marco held out his hand. "Give me your phone." Jez handed it over, and Marco worked with it a few moments before turning the screen. "Just as he said. He installed a phone-finding app on your phone, hid it in the utility apps folder. You know, the folder with all the junk the providers front-load on the phone that only ever annoys the fuck out of you."

Jez backed out of the app and inspected the icon. He never would have looked in that folder, and the icon looked quite innocuous.

"So he knew where I was all the time?" Had he even engineered a trade to the LA team because of Jez?

"Yes, I'm afraid so. And he's also the one who slashed your tires."

"What?"

"Yeah. Your phone and car spent all night at some guy's house. He was pissed."

Jez frowned. "But I've been living with Hayden for months."

Marco laughed, a sound Jez had never heard before, but it suited the man to occasionally leave that super serious mien behind. "That's our Hayden. He just doesn't *look* gay, you know?"

Jez bristled. "There's no look. Gay comes in all shapes and sizes and colors."

Marco laughed some more. "Yes, we all know that. But Hayden fooled Jayson. Until recently, probably right around when the first gift came, he thought you were just renting a room here. Not cozying up with the homeowner, who most people think is straight until he tells them otherwise."

Jez turned to share his indignation with Hayden, only to find him resting on his arms on the table, fast asleep.

Marco smiled gently. "It's over." He stood up and peered out of the window. "That's the last of them. I'll get out of your hair, and you can get him upstairs. But don't worry. Between breaking in and identity theft, we've got plenty to put him in prison for a while. There may also be charges filed related to the documentation he provided for the restraining order. It's over," Marco repeated. He ruffled Jez's hair and then was gone. Jez pocketed the shiny new keys from the kitchen table and tried to assimilate that thought.

It was over.

THE SCENTS of bacon and coffee tickled Hayden's nose, bringing him to wakefulness. The stairs creaked, followed by the floorboards in the hallway, heralding Jez's return. Jayson's vandalism of the master bedroom had been too close to Christmas for them to fix it up yet, so they'd moved the essentials into Jez's old room and would likely be living in there well into January.

"Merry Christmas!" Jez appeared in the doorway, carrying a tray bearing breakfast.

Hayden leaped out of bed to grab the tray and set it on the dresser.

"Hey. This is supposed to be breakfast in bed."

"It's a long way from the kitchen up here with a heavy tray."

Jez rolled his eyes. "I may not have muscles on muscles like you do, but I am strong, you know."

"I'm not allowed to help you out, just because?"

With a huff, Jez sat on the bed. "Fine. Bring that over here. It's actually for both of us. And I left the coffee and juice downstairs. I figured syrup was enough of a gamble on the tray."

Hayden laughed. "Crazy man." Nevertheless, he obeyed Jez's orders and sat down beside him. "You made bacon. That's so sweet, but you didn't have to."

"Don't get used to it. Or breakfast in bed, for that matter. And the pancakes are vegan, so we're sharing those."

"I appreciate it, don't get me wrong. But it wasn't necessary." And if it had been croissants or something crumbly, Hayden didn't think he could have handled eating that in bed.

Jez shrugged, and Hayden suddenly caught the nervous tension. "What's wrong?"

"Just worried you won't like your present."

"I'll love it, no matter what." Hayden kissed his temple.

AFTER THEY ate, Hayden got back out of bed and pulled on pajamas. Eating naked in bed had been super decadent, but he didn't think he wanted to sit around the den opening presents in the same state. "Shall we head downstairs?" Hayden was nervous about his present for Jez too.

"Not yet. I mean, there are a few things under the tree for you, but the big present is up here." Jez grabbed his hand and led him to the door of the guest room. The one that had held the boxes of his gran's stuff. Hayden swallowed heavily. This was not the room he'd expected Jez to tackle first, and he was afraid. He also wanted to know where all his gran's stuff had gone, but despite a niggle of fear, he was sure Jez hadn't just dumped it.

Jez took a deep breath, then flung the door open.

Hayden gasped. *Incredible.* He stepped inside. The primary color scheme was black and white. Black and white photography in simple black frames covered the walls. Not just any photos, but his gran's photos. Publicity stills of her in ballet costumes and with the cast of her movies. Candid photos of her with stars like Rock Hudson and Steve McQueen and Paul Newman. Faye Dunaway, Loretta Swit, and Eileen Brennan.

The lush burgundy fabric Hayden remembered packing away with his gran's sewing and craftwork had been repurposed into curtains and a bedspread. He recognized his gran's cross-stitch in the square decorative pillows. A small vanity sat in the corner, the mirror surrounded by light bulbs like the kind you'd find in a movie star's dressing room. Everything was so elegant, a beautiful tribute to the only family Hayden would ever claim.

He sniffed, determined not to cry. His gran, in better times, would have been over the moon.

"Thank you." Hayden spun around and grabbed up his boyfriend in a hug. "It's perfect. I love it."

"Are you sure?" Jez asked anxiously. "I packed up all the other stuff and put it in the attic. There was a lot more than could easily fit in here, but I made sure it was all packed up safely."

"Positive." Although Hayden could have inspected those pictures for hours, he was also eager to give Jez his present. "C'mon. Let's go downstairs."

HAYDEN PLUCKED a card from the tree and handed it to Jez, feeling shaky, like it had been too long since he'd eaten. He wasn't sure he'd ever been this nervous.

Jez opened the envelope and pulled out the business card that had been tucked inside. He turned it over in his hands, then looked quizzically at Hayden.

Hayden cleared his throat. "I know you want to do some more decorating. And we'll have to go slow. But I don't spend any time in the sunroom, and I thought you'd like to transform it into a proper practice space. Studio. Whatever you need for dancing. Those guys there, they've got experience with that sort of remodeling. I've already put down a deposit, one that should cover the majority of the remodeling, and I'll pay for the rest when we've had them in to do a full estimate."

Jez stared at him. "That's… that's too much."

"It isn't. Jez, you've given me my life. I want you to know this house is your home too. Do you… uh… do you like it?" Maybe it had been a stupid idea after all.

Suddenly he found himself with an armful of boyfriend kissing his face. "It's too damn much, but it's perfect. I love you. Thank you."

"You're welcome. I love you too."

And they combusted together, hot and fierce as always, right there on the floor under the Christmas tree.

Epilogue

JEZ LEANED back on the couch Christmas Eve, waiting for Hayden to finish cleaning up in the kitchen. The gorgeous white tree they'd bought together last year—with blue and silver ornaments—sparkled even more against the midnight blue backdrop of the accent wall in the den. Fortunately, the dark tan leather of Hayden's super comfy couches and chairs fit right in to the blue-and-white color scheme Jez had chosen for this room.

He cuddled up with a navy corduroy pillow on his lap, fat, snuffly Fang sleeping beside him, and sighed happily. They'd both come a long way in the nearly fifteen months they'd been together, and the journey had been a good one. Half of the house was no longer plain white, and Jez didn't need Xanax when surrounded by friends, although he was still working on controlling his panic when confronted with fans. After the success of the first season of his show, he had fans. More than he'd ever had for his Broadway shows, and although he appreciated their fervor, they did tend to startle him as they sprang out at the grocery store and in restaurants. He was filming the second season now, with a contract for at least two more.

"Gonna be much longer, babe?" He was ready to subject Hayden to some sickly-sweet Christmas rom-coms. After having to watch more than his fair share of baseball—LA had been in the playoffs again— Hayden owed him. And these were his guilty pleasure.

"Ready now." Hayden rounded the couch holding two flutes filled with something fizzy that looked an awful lot like champagne.

"Are we celebrating something?"

Hayden set the glasses down on the coffee table, then sank to one knee. "I hope so, baby."

Jez sucked in a breath and sat up straight. He pressed trembling hands to his mouth. Was this…? Was he…?

Hayden plucked a small box out of his pocket. "I've never been so happy as I've been since the day I laid eyes on you sleeping on my porch. I love you, and I want what we're building to be permanent and forever. Will you marry me?"

Hayden's beautiful, beloved face blurred, then cleared as tears of joy slid down Jez's face. "Oh yes. Please. I love you so much."

Jez flung his arms around Hayden's neck, sending the box skittering across the floor. Hayden kissed him, both of their cheeks now wet with tears even as they laughed.

"Don't want the ring?" Hayden teased.

"Don't ever think it," Jez scolded. He kissed Hayden, and as always, it ignited the crazy chemistry between them, but Jez pulled back. "We should maybe find that box before Fang gets into it."

Hayden eyed Fang's oblivious sleeping form. "Yeah, that looks like a real danger." His boyfriend— no, his *fiancé*—glanced around. Jez did too. That precious little box couldn't have gone far. Then Hayden flattened and peered under the couch before reaching underneath.

With a proud grin, he brandished the box at Jez. Jez opened it and pulled out the bigger ring meant for Hayden. He slipped it on Hayden's finger, and Hayden slid the other ring on Jez's.

Hayden picked up the champagne and sat to Jez's left before handing him a glass. "To my Jez, who opened my eyes to love."

"To my Hayden, my home and hearth."

They sipped at their champagne between exchanging kisses.

"Want to go upstairs?" Hayden asked.

Jez stood and held his hand out for Hayden. Jez had years of Christmases to come to torture Hayden with romantic Christmas movies. Tonight, he was going to enjoy his own happy ever after.

KEEP READING FOR AN EXCERPT FROM

KC Burn

COP OUT

www. dreamspinnerpress.com

Toronto Tales: Book One

Detective Kurt O'Donnell is used to digging up other people's secrets, but when he discovers his slain partner was married to another man, it shakes him. Determined to do the right thing, Kurt offers the mourning Davy his assistance. Helping Davy through his grief helps Kurt deal with the guilt that his partner didn't trust him enough to tell him the truth, and somewhere along the way Davy stops being an obligation and becomes a friend, the closest friend Kurt has ever had.

His growing attraction to Davy complicates matters, leaving Kurt struggling to reevaluate his sexuality. Then a sensual encounter neither man is ready for confuses them further. To be with Davy, Kurt must face the prospect of coming out, but his job and his relationship with his Catholic family are on the line. Can he risk destroying his life for the uncertain possibility of a relationship with a newly widowed man?

Now Available at
www.dreamspinnerpress.com

Chapter One

KURT HUNKERED down behind the car, waiting for Ben's signal. How bulletproof were these cars? Thirty years ago they were built like tanks. His father still had one, called it an antique land yacht. Now... well, they sure as hell weren't titanium.

The sun blazed, heating his face, making sweat drip down from his short hair and into his collar. His navy blue shirt was already drenched—Kevlar vests were hot and heavy, but they were a necessary evil. Last Tuesday in May, but the temperature rivaled the middle of July. He fucking hated midday busts on sunny, summery days. The sunshine meant they had no visibility advantages, and a sudden glare could blind someone at a critical moment.

He swiped the back of his hand across his forehead. At least if he were undercover, he could be wearing a bandana to soak up the sweat. The acrid scent of the tar heating in the asphalt battled with rotting fish and garbage from the nearby market district. He wished they'd waited for backup. But he'd only been a detective for three years—Ben had been doing this for a lot longer, and he had to bow to Ben's greater experience. His partner might be taciturn and reticent, but he was a dedicated and effective officer. Kurt trusted him with his life.

As it should be.

Ben slipped into position by the front door of the building and gave him the signal he'd been waiting for. Tugging the collar of his vest one final time, Kurt crept around to cover the rear of the building, holding himself close to the wall, out of any of the windows' sight lines.

Gustav, one of Ben's informants, had contacted Ben with a tip about a suspect. Ben said they had to follow up immediately, and Kurt trusted his partner to do what was best, even though the tip was for a case that wasn't even theirs. But Ben had contacts everywhere, and it couldn't hurt to get a few kudos from the drug squad.

Glock poised, the familiar grip kept him grounded while he waited for the inevitable dash for the back when an officer announced himself at the front. He stretched to peer through the dirty window. There were no people. No movement. Nothing to suggest the room he observed had been used in a long time. A layer of dust coated the table and chairs.

Ben demanded entrance loudly enough for Kurt to hear, bringing his attention back to the door. Almost simultaneously, Ben booted in the front door and the building exploded, throwing Kurt backward.

THE LIGHT hurt his eyes, but Kurt couldn't shut them any farther than they were. He wished he could scrunch his ears shut, too, against the infernal beeping.

"Are you awake?" a strident female voice asked.

He cringed.

"Come on now, it's time to wake up."

The beeping was regular, rhythmic... like a heart monitor. Right. The harsh smell of cleansers should have given it away. He was in a hospital. The monitors must have alerted someone of his return to consciousness.

"What happened?" God. That didn't sound like him—that sounded like someone who'd swallowed gravel for breakfast. Talking hurt like a bitch too.

"Can you open your eyes, Detective O'Donnell?"

No fucking way. "Too bright," he managed to say. A throbbing heartbeat of pain started in his temples. Other body parts threatened to chime in, which he wasn't looking forward to, but hell, it meant he wasn't dead.

The light level dropped, and Kurt cracked open his lids. A nurse with—he strained to focus—teddy bears on her scrubs stood over him, holding a clipboard and scratching out a few notes with the loudest pen ever created.

"Thirsty."

Despite her glass-cracking voice, the woman smiled down at him in sympathy. "I know. But you can't have anything until the doctor sees you."

She patted his shoulder gently and left the room, rubber soles squeaking, making him wince.

What the hell had happened?

He tried moving each limb gingerly, testing for soreness. Nothing screamed as loud as his head, but there were issues with his left arm and left leg. Glancing around the room, he couldn't see anything with the date or even the time. The last thing he remembered was getting into the car with Ben after receiving a tip. Did they have a car accident? Had he been shot? Trying to remember sent spikes of red-hot agony into his head. Heaving out a sigh, he relaxed as much as he could on the granite slab the hospital claimed was a mattress.

Although he wanted nothing more than to rip out his IV and storm into the hallway, demanding someone tell him what was going on, in truth he was afraid doing so would only make everything hurt worse. He'd never felt this horrible in his life—he didn't want to know how much shittier it could get.

The unmistakable sounds of an irate Irish couple arguing in the distance wafted into the room. He relaxed even further. If his parents couldn't convince the doctor to hurry up and see him, as soon as his brothers and sisters descended, the hospital staff would do whatever they could to get rid of the raucous brood as soon as possible.

"That's my baby in there!"

Uh. They were getting closer, and Kurt hoped they'd either calm his mother down or let them in, because his mother was working herself into a fine state, and her voice tap-danced in his brain.

"Mrs. O'Donnell. Mr. O'Donnell. The doctor's on his way, I promise. Come with me to the waiting area. It won't be long."

The firm voice belonged to his boss. What was he doing here? Did that confirm whatever happened had been related to the bust they'd been heading to? Why couldn't he remember what went down? And where the fuck was Ben?

Kurt brought his right hand to his head and rubbed gently. God almighty, he needed some narcotics, or hell, maybe a beheading wouldn't be so bad.

"Detective O'Donnell." A tiny white-coated woman entered his room. "I'm Doctor Sarwa. How's the head?"

"Hurts." There went that croaking voice again. "What happened?"

"In a minute. Any nausea?"

"No, not really." Not a lie, but he wasn't ready to eat anything either.

Dr. Sarwa gave a curt nod and made few notations on a clipboard before she set it down and flipped back the covers on his left side. Kurt peered down, despite the strain it put on his eyeballs, and saw a huge long bandage over his arm. Was it broken?

The doctor peeled back the bandage, revealing a number of black stitches along a jagged cut extending along the inside of his arm from midbicep to wrist.

"You're lucky, Detective O'Donnell," the doctor murmured as she gently probed at the... he couldn't call it an incision. No self-respecting surgeon in the world would make a cut that ragged and random. "You didn't break any bones."

That was her definition of lucky? Now that he'd seen the damage, his arm began throbbing in time with the pounding in his brain.

Kurt took a deep breath. His throat was so dry, he didn't want to say one more word than necessary. "Leg?"

She snorted. "Just a twisted knee, not serious at all."

"Thirsty."

"I'll tell the nurse when I leave. You can have a little juice." She retaped the bandage. "Looks good. Okay, quick rundown. You conked your head and shrapnel sliced open your arm."

Kurt laughed but shut it down after a second when it upgraded the tap-dancers in his head to a steel drum band. "Professional opinion?"

Dr. Sarwa smiled faintly at him. "I could get technical with you, but you'll remember this easier once the grogginess wears off. The shrapnel was dangerous—you had to get into surgery immediately or you were going to bleed out. But it could have been a lot worse. I'll be back later."

He might have drifted for a few minutes, but a nurse showed up almost immediately with a cup of juice, followed by his mom and dad.

"Baby, oh, baby!" His mom flew to the side of the bed opposite the nurse. At the moment he was more interested in the approaching bendy straw. The crisp bite of apples hit his nose, and his parchment-dry mouth salivated in response.

His mom grabbed his hand and squeezed lightly. Tears wet the back of his hand. This was the first time he'd been… certainly not hurt. With six elder siblings, he'd had his share of breaks and contusions. But this was the first time he'd been hurt on the job, because why else would he have a shrapnel wound, even if he couldn't remember how he got it.

With his thirst eased, if not slaked, he turned his head to his mom. The nurse left, to be replaced by his dad.

"Kurt, baby…."

"Mom, I'm okay."

"No you're not."

Kurt winced, and his father spoke softly. "Deirdre, not so loud. Remember what the doctor said."

"But he's not okay, Sean." She leaned over and kissed his cheek. "I'm sorry, baby."

"How are you feeling, son?" His father's hand hovered over his bandage and finally settled on his shoulder.

"Sore." But now that he was more awake, he was ready to go home. The pain was beginning to dull, settle, now that he knew what was physically wrong. "Dad, what happened?"

His parents exchanged a glance. His mother started weeping.

"What?" They were never at a loss for words.

"Baby, you could have died." His mom's voice broke.

The decibel level rose outside his room. The rest of his family must have arrived. Shit, this wasn't any worse than when Ian dared him to climb that rotting tree in their backyard. He'd broken an arm and a leg then. This was a bad cut, a knock to the head, and a twisted knee. Really not cause for all the histrionics. But they still acted like he was a baby, even though he was thirty-one. Why did he have to be his parents' last kid?

The door opened, but it wasn't one of his siblings who entered. It was his boss.

"Sir?" Nausea boiled in his gut, and the throbbing in his head accelerated.

"O'Donnell. Glad to see you're awake. I'm afraid I have some bad news." Like the somber expression hadn't given it away.

"What, sir?" His mother's grip tightened, and his father stepped away, looking out the window.

"Do you remember what you were doing when the explosion occurred?"

Explosion? Now the shrapnel made sense. Nothing else did. "I don't remember an explosion. Just getting the tip from Gustav before I got in the car with Ben. Did the car explode?" Why wasn't Ben telling him this? The nausea had transformed to a sharp, burning pain in his gut.

"The building your informant directed you to was rigged. We're almost positive that one of the guys Ben put away while he was on the drug squad—guy who goes by the name of Novi, the Russian Bear—was behind the explosion. He was released on parole a couple of months ago."

Novi. Kurt remembered stories about him—drug runner and dealer, among other things. But he could tell by Inspector Nadar's expression that there was more to come.

"I'm sorry, Kurt. Ben didn't make it."

Dead? He sucked in a breath. Shards of memories filled with heat and noise assaulted him.

"Honey, I'm so sorry," his mom whispered. His parents had met Ben a couple of times. Ben had been a loner, and even after three years, Kurt didn't know a lot about his personal life, but Ben was his partner. They'd worked well together, and he'd considered them friends. The almost fifteen-year age difference hadn't mattered in the least.

His eyes filled, and he broke the gaze with Inspector Nadar, facing his mom. She pulled a tissue from her purse and dabbed at his damp face.

Pulling in a deep breath, he directed his gaze back at his boss. "How long ago? Have you informed his family?" As far as he knew, there was only Ben's mother. He wanted to be there; it was his responsibility.

"I did that while you were in surgery. I don't have any details yet, but the funeral will likely be on Saturday. If you want to be there, you need to concentrate on getting well."

"Yes, sir." He'd be there, no matter if he had to drag an IV stand along behind him. Later he'd worry about getting the Russian Bear behind bars.

"Good day, Mr. and Mrs. O'Donnell." Inspector Nadar nodded sharply before he spun on his heel and left the room.

"That's right, baby. You need to get better. I don't know what I'd do if I lost you."

His brothers and sisters boiled into the room, all appropriately sympathetic for his loss and glad he was mostly okay. Every one of them hugged him, awkwardly to be sure, but it wouldn't be his family if there wasn't any hugging or kissing. One of them had to be responsible for intimidating the nursing staff, because he believed most hospital patients weren't allowed eight visitors at a time. He truly appreciated his family, and he hoped Ben's mother had someone to help her, if she was having a lucid day and was able to comprehend the loss she'd suffered.

"Mom, I want to go home."

"I know, baby. The doctor wants to keep you another day, then your dad and I will take you back home with us. Erin prepared the spare room for you while we rushed right here. We'll take good care of you."

He'd thank his sister later. Stupid to want his mom to take care of him at this age, but the thought of going back to his sterile apartment made him want to cry more. He didn't have a girlfriend; he didn't have anyone he even dated regularly. But he had his big, comforting family.

THE CHAPEL was small, but already his leg protested the trip from the taxi. Ben wouldn't care if he sat at the front or the back, so he slipped into an empty seat in the very last row. Drawing attention to himself, when he survived but Ben hadn't, made him uncomfortable.

He should have let his parents come, but for some reason he'd wanted to do this alone. Stupid. The cane wasn't quite enough support, not when he had to use the wrong arm. He scanned the attendees for anyone who looked like Mrs. Kaminski. He needed to pay his condolences to her, if nothing else. Most of the pews were filled with dress uniforms—very few in civilian dress.

The minister strolled out, appropriately somber, to start the ceremony. There was no casket as there had been at Granny O'Donnell's funeral—the only other person close to him to have died. Kurt hoped the lack of casket was due to choice and not necessity, but he'd been so exhausted from his injuries he hadn't thought to inquire about the details. The service began but didn't hold his attention. No minister could have anything to say to comfort Kurt. Not now.

Memories of the hours they'd spent in a department-issued car together flitted through his brain. Ben might have been reticent about his personal life, but he'd imparted years of wisdom to a green detective and Kurt had soaked it up, becoming better at his job every day because of Ben.

Two people, neither of them in uniform, were seated in the front row, but off to the far right. The entire front row was open, reserved for family that either didn't exist or wasn't going to arrive. From where he sat, only the woman's profile was visible, but she was around Ben's age. So not Mrs. Kaminski. Who was she? He could see no physical similarities between Ben and the strange woman—it didn't seem possible that she was family, despite her position in the family pew.

Under his gaze, she wiped at her eyes with a tissue and offered another one to the man beside her. He took it but clenched it in his fist instead of using it. The woman moved slightly, and the man's profile became visible. Kurt didn't recognize either one.

The congregation rose for a hymn, blocking his view. He didn't want to tax his leg any further by constantly standing and sitting, and he even had his mother's blessing not to. She'd been adamant he not do anything to reinjure himself.

When the inspector stood to deliver the eulogy, a small stab of regret pierced his heart. If it wasn't one of Ben's friends from outside the force, it should have been him giving it. Shame made him accept the inspector's offer to speak, and shame made him squirm in his seat while he listened, trying not dishonor his dress uniform by crying. But Nadar hadn't spent nearly as much time with Ben as Kurt had, and his words reflected that distance. He watched the strangers in the front row, expecting one of them to rise to speak when Nadar was done. But neither of them moved, except for the woman who again blotted tears from her eyes.

Fuck. Could he have worked with Ben this long and not known he had a girlfriend? The woman could be family—maybe—but Ben had never mentioned anyone besides his mother. The woman's hand fluttered to her face, moving a strand of dark hair behind her ear, and this time he caught sight of something he should have noticed immediately. A wedding band.

What the fuck?

Why hadn't Ben told him? Granted, Kurt probably talked more about his personal life than his partner had wanted to hear, but Ben deflected almost all personal questions. Kurt thought them friends, but he didn't even know Ben had been married, let alone recognize the woman he should have at least met in the three years they'd spent partnered. Hell, most of the married cops he knew hung out with their partners off the job, frequently with their wives as well. Sure, he and Ben had never done more than eat lunch together, but Ben had met his parents and all of his siblings at least once, when they'd stopped by the station.

A burning pain lanced up his arm. Looking down, Kurt realized he'd rested the cane across his lap and was squeezing the shit out of it with both hands. Fine for his right, but definitely too much activity for his still-stitched left arm. Taking a deep breath, he unclenched his fingers. He'd talk to the two strangers after the service. He had a duty as Ben's partner, and he needed to know. As long as he could keep his bitterness contained. Why hadn't Ben asked for a transfer if he hated Kurt so much? Because Kurt couldn't imagine any other reason for him not to mention a wife, even an estranged one, to his partner.

He couldn't talk to Ben's previous partner, find out if Ed had known. Ed had died of a coronary, after which Ben got partnered up with Kurt. The ache in his heart, knowing his partner hadn't trusted him—at all—rivaled the emptiness inside where a friend had lived. It might have been a one-sided relationship, but Kurt missed his friend. God. Why hadn't he known? Had he been too self-absorbed, or had Ben deliberately hidden the information from him? Guilt ate through him like acid, the burning pain in his gut returning. He had to have been at fault.

The service ended abruptly, or so it seemed, since Kurt hadn't paid attention at all. The two people slipped out a side door almost before the minister had finished speaking. Without thinking, Kurt was up and out of the chapel, hobbling as best he could around the side of the church, to try and catch up to them in the parking lot.

"Wait! Wait!"

Two dark heads swiveled toward him, the man murmuring something to the woman, who nodded.

"Thank you," he puffed out. God, he hoped he got his strength back soon. He stood before them and shifted his cane to his left hand so he could shake their hands at least. They were undoubtedly siblings, but the woman was several years older and had that slight puffy cast to her jawline his own sisters had displayed in early pregnancy. Ben was going to be a father? He wasn't sure if he could find words beneath the bitter guilt drowning him.

"I'm Kurt O'Donnell. Ben's partner." The man gasped slightly and turned away. His sister elbowed him in the arm.

"It's nice to meet you, Kurt. I'm Sandra. This is Davy, my brother." She would have made an excellent witness on the stand. Her words gave him only a modicum of data that he didn't have before.

"I'm very sorry for your loss." Kurt took her hand and gently squeezed it. Her eyes were red-rimmed, and her face had the yellowish pallor he associated more with illness than with grief.

"I'm sorry for yours," she replied.

He stretched his hand out to Davy, glad that Sandra at least had a brother to aid her through this, but their body language warred with his expectations. Sandra had her left arm around her brother's waist, shoulders tilting toward him in a protective gesture. It should have been the other way around.

Davy turned red-rimmed eyes, like his sister's, to him. But that was the only similarity.

Sandra was sad. Davy was devastated. Davy's chocolaty eyes were filled with all the desolation in the universe. The scleras were more than bloodshot, like he'd been crying for days, and his nose was as swollen and red as his eyelids. His face had the deathly white hue of shock that Sandra's should have had, and he didn't appear to be focusing too well.

"I'm so sorry," he whispered, Davy's hand in his, shake forgotten. He had a sudden urge to hug Davy, but he was too busy trying to keep the shock and betrayal off his face. The world spun dizzily as all his preconceptions and conclusions vaporized, to be replaced by the new information now in his possession.

Davy's mouth worked, but nothing came out. He dropped his gaze, but he left his hand in Kurt's. Sandra separated them.

"We need to go now, Kurt. Thanks for introducing yourself." She tried to smile.

They got into a car, Sandra behind the wheel.

"Wait!"

Sandra twisted around in her seat.

"What about Ben's mom?"

"Oh, well, she wasn't having a good day. Sunshine Manors advised against bringing her."

Kurt stood back and let them—there was no other word for it—escape. He steadied himself on his cane while the taillights receded. Assuming Ben hadn't lied about his mother, it was entirely possible she'd been too ill or too disoriented to attend the funeral. But Sandra had been lying. He'd been a cop too long. He knew.

KC BURN has been writing for as long as she can remember and is a sucker for happy endings (of all kinds). After moving from Toronto to Florida for her husband to take a dream job, she discovered a love of gay romance and fulfilled a dream of her own—getting published. After a few years of editing web content by day, and neglecting her supportive, understanding hubby and needy cat at night to write stories about men loving men, she was uprooted yet again and now resides in California. Writing is always fun and rewarding, but writing about her guys is the most fun she's had in a long time, and she hopes you'll enjoy them as much as she does.

Website: kcburn.com
Twitter: @authorkcburn
Facebook: www.facebook.com/kcburn

Toronto
Tales

COVER UP

KC Burn

Toronto Tales: Book Two

Detective Ivan Bekker has hit rock bottom. Not only is he recovering from a bad breakup with a cheating boyfriend, he's also involved in a drug bust gone bad. Ivan had to kill a man, and his friend was shot and is now fighting for his life. Though Ivan is under investigation for his part in the shooting, his boss sends him on an off-the-books undercover operation to close the case. The timing is critical—this could be their chance to plug a leak in the department.

Off-balance and without backup, Ivan finds himself playing a recent divorcé and becoming Parker Wakefield's roommate. He finds it hard to believe that sweet Parker could possibly be a criminal, much less have ties to a Russian mafia drug-trafficking operation, and Ivan lets down his guard. His affection is unprofessional, but Parker is irresistible.

When Ivan comes across clear evidence of Parker's criminal involvement, he has to choose: protect their relationship, regardless of the consequences, or save his career and arrest the man he loves.

www.dreamspinnerpress.com

Toronto Tales

CAST OFF

KC Burn

Toronto Tales: Book Three

Thirty-five-year-old Rick Haviland is a well-respected speech pathologist, but while his friends are all settling into relationships, he refuses to give up his no-strings-attached club boy sex life. For him, relationships are dangerous; he's got a secret to hide. When he meets Ian O'Donnell, an account manager with a local tabloid, Rick figures his personal rules for relationships should be enough to keep him safe from more than a one-night stand.

When Ian comes out of the closet, tired of anonymous hook-ups and keeping secrets from his large Catholic family, Rick is right there, and he's just the sort of man Ian might like to get to know better. Their attraction is immediate, electric and mutual. Ian convinces Rick to break more and more of his rules, and his defenses crumble. But someone watches, someone who'd like to see this new relationship fail. When Ian's job becomes a means to expose Rick's secret, it could destroy both their careers and their hearts.

www.dreamspinnerpress.com

Punk's not dead, but it's time to redefine life.

Devlin Waters thought he'd have music forever. But the tragic death of his best friend ended the twenty-year run of his punk band, Negative Impression. Unable to process the loss, Devlin distances himself from everyone and everything that reminds him of the band. But forty-one is too young to curl up and wait for the end. In a search for a second career, he finds himself at university with a bunch of kids young enough to be… his kids. His sexy archeology professor, however, makes Devlin think about life beyond his grief….

Dr. Jack Johnson does not appreciate Devlin's lack of respect, his inability to be serious, or his chronic lateness. Worse, he hates that he's attracted to a student. When he realizes Devlin is the rock star he crushed on in his youth, he drops his guard—against his better judgment.

Before they can move forward together, Jack must admit to Devlin that he's not only an admirer, but he also sings in a cover band. How will Devlin react to his ultimate fanboy when his own music has died?

www.dreamspinnerpress.com

TEA *or* CONSEQUENCES

KC Burn

Riley Parker: temp, twink, geek… sleuth?

Maybe Riley isn't living up to his full potential, but being a temp executive assistant suits him. He's never bored at work, he's got friends who let him geek out, and he's got a carefully crafted twink exterior… which might be getting constrictive now that he's on the other side of thirty. Life isn't perfect, but it's comfortable.

It all unravels when he takes a job working for a tea-obsessed cosmetics queen, the owner of Gautier Cosmetics. During the launch party for a new product, Riley finds his boss dead under suspicious circumstances, and the homicide detective is none other than Tadeo Martin, Riley's high school obsession who never knew he was alive.

Tad drafts Riley to get the scoop on the inner workings of Gautier, and for Riley, it's like a drug. His natural inquisitiveness is rewarded with more and more Tad. Unfortunately, his snooping puts him in the running for two other roles: suspect and victim. The killer doesn't care which.

www.dreamspinnerpress.com

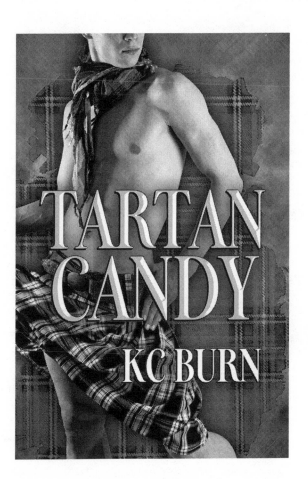

TARTAN CANDY

KC BURN

A Fabric Hearts Story

Finlay McIntyre (aka Raven) is a successful adult film star with a penchant for kilts, until an accident cuts short his stardom and leaves him with zero sexual desire, lowered self-esteem, and no job. He knew his porn career wouldn't last forever, but he wasn't prepared for retirement at twenty-eight. While trying to figure out the rest of his life, Raven agrees to attend a high school reunion. That's when a malfunctioning AC unit in his hotel room changes everything.

Caleb Sanderson, an entrepreneur with his own HVAC business, has no idea what to expect when he steps into Raven's hotel room to fix his AC unit. They're attracted to each other, but Caleb, closeted, can't afford a gay relationship, not with his mom pressuring him to produce grandchildren. If he wants to keep Raven—who no closet could hold—he'll need to tell his family the truth. But Raven has a few secrets of his own. He refuses to reveal his porn past to Caleb, a past that might be the final obstacle to Caleb and Raven having any kind of relationship.

www.dreamspinnerpress.com

PLAID
VERSUS
PAISLEY

KC BURN

A Fabric Hearts Story

Two years after his life fell apart, Will Dawson moved to Florida to start over. His job in the tech department of Idyll Fling, a gay porn studio, is ideal for him. When his boss forces him to take on a new hire, the last person he expects is Dallas Greene—the man who cost him his job and his boyfriend back in Connecticut. He doesn't know what's on Dallas's agenda, but he won't be blindsided by a wolf masquerading as a runway model. Not again.

Dallas might have thrown himself on his brother's mercy, but his skills are needed at Idyll Fling. Working with Will is a bonus, since Dallas has never forgotten the man. A good working relationship is only the beginning of what Dallas wants with Will.

But Dallas doesn't realize how deep Will's distrust runs, and Will doesn't know that the man he's torn between loving and hating is the boss's brother. When all truths are revealed, how can a relationship built on lies still stand?

www.dreamspinnerpress.com

FOR MORE

OF THE

BEST

GAY

ROMANCE

DREAMSPINNER

PRESS

dreamspinnerpress.com